PRAISE FOR JUDITH O'BRIEN'S ROMANCE NOVELS . . .

MAIDEN VOYAGE

"In *Maiden Voyage*, Judith O'Brien creates one of the most original, entertaining and mystifying reincarnation romances to come along. . . . *Maiden Voyage* is a moving romance that . . . stars two haunting souls sharing two lifetimes together. Ms. O'Brien is a superb writer who enables readers to suspend their disbelief so that they can fully immerse themselves in an entertaining tale."

—Harriet Klausner, Amazon Books

"Fine humor, a bit of Irish blarney and a ghost named Fitzwilliam Connolly are the backbone of this latest from O'Brien. . . . Perky dialogue and humor . . . keep it moving at an easy clip."

—*Publishers Weekly*

"*Maiden Voyage* is another hit for Judith O'Brien. . . . Fun and exciting. O'Brien fans, get ready to laugh, cry and enjoy!"

—Maria C. Ferrer, *Romantic Times*

"An extraordinary, enchanting tale. . . . Written with intense emotion, *Maiden Voyage* is . . . a unique and powerful story *that* is not soon forgotten."

—*Rendezvous*

"Judith O'Brien makes you cry and she makes you laugh. *Ashton's Bride* is an utterly heartwarming love story with characters who will captivate you and leave you basking in a warm, magical glow."

—Dorothy Cannel, author of *Femmes Fatal*

"This is one new writer who has a whole new light on the art of writing. I enjoyed this book, and it was with real regret that I had to stop when the story ended. Five bells, NOT TO BE MISSED!"

—Bell, Book and Candle

". . . A rare and delightful book. . . . Judith O'Brien has a wonderful sense of humor and she knows how to combine it with the kind of drama, fantasy, and romance readers cherish."

—Deborah Smith, author of *Silk & Stone*

RHAPSODY IN TIME

"Ms. O'Brien takes you on a journey into the Roaring Twenties you'll never forget. The storyline takes many exciting and dangerous twists and turns to a stunning conclusion. This one is a must-read. Excellent."

—*Rendezvous*

"*Rhapsody in Time* is an exciting time-travel romance that pays homage to the New York City of the Roaring Twenties. Judith O'Brien has gifted the audience with two dynamic lead characters and a fast-paced romance."

—Harriet Klausner, *Affaire de Coeur*

"Her characters are wonderful and so believable that readers can't help cheer them on. Time travel has a new voice, and her name is Judith O'Brien."

—Maria C. Ferrer, *Romantic Times*

Books by Judith O'Brien

Rhapsody in Time
Ashton's Bride
Once Upon a Rose
Maiden Voyage
To Marry a British Lord

Published by POCKET BOOKS

An *Original* Publication of POCKET BOOKS

A Pocket Star Book published by
POCKET BOOKS, a division of Simon & Schuster Inc.
1230 Avenue of the Americas, New York, NY 10020

ISBN 978-1-4516-7765-2

First Pocket Books printing October 1997

10 9 8 7 6 5 4 3 2 1

POCKET STAR BOOKS and colophon are registered trademarks of Simon & Schuster Inc.

Front cover illustration by Gregg Gulbronson

Printed in the U.S.A.

JUDITH O'BRIEN

TO MARRY A BRITISH LORD

POCKET **STAR** BOOKS

New York   London   Toronto   Sydney   Tokyo   Singapore

To my friend Mary Curry, who once said, "Hey, have you ever thought of writing a romance novel?" To tell you the truth, I hadn't. But ever since that day we've spent hours on the phone as our children clamor for cookies and attention, plotting and planning our books, and living them more vividly than real life.

Thank you, Mary.

PROLOGUE

RICHMOND, VIRGINIA
AUGUST 1865

The heat was almost unbearable. Constance Lloyd dabbed at her temples with a handkerchief, worn and frayed but freshly laundered and pressed. About her wrist was a small drawstring bag containing the last few Union dollars in her possession. She dared not leave it behind at the Smithers sisters' boarding house, even for the brief walk to the post office. Sweet as the elderly women were, and as respectable as the other boarders seemed to be, Constance was not foolhardy enough to leave her worldly goods unprotected. Had she been so reckless, she never would have survived the past four years.

A cart rolled by on the unpaved street, the dust rising in a dry swirl, causing her to pause and close her eyes.

Had it *ever* been so hot in Richmond?

"Good day, Miss Lloyd."

Constance opened her eyes to see Mr. Bryce, features sharp and haggard, tip his hat. Although he was of an age with her own father, he had just returned from active duty in the Confederate Army. It had taken him months to walk back to Richmond after the war had ended.

"Good day, Mr. Bryce." She smiled, remembering him years ago, a stout man who would always slip her a licorice whip when he came visiting at the Lloyd plantation.

"Is it hot enough for you?" Mr. Bryce's face was mottled in the heat, the sparse gray hair dampened against his scalp.

"Not quite, Mr. Bryce," she replied sincerely. "That's why I'm heading further south today, towards the post office. I'm hoping there will be less of a chill down there."

Mr. Bryce laughed, more of a brittle cackle, and the laugh became a cough. She politely ignored the cough, and he tipped his hat once more, saluted her with two fingers, and continued on his way.

How strange the encounters were with people she had always known. Now they seemed to be strangers, separated by the very ordeal that should have drawn them together. At first, the defeat of the Confederacy *did* unite them. As the weeks became months, blame and mistrust and simple fear of the future seemed to overtake everyone. Even the simplest of facts became distorted in the mundane discomfort of daily life. Instead of patriotic songs and speeches, the survivors engaged in finger-pointing and accusing every neighbor of harboring sympathetic thoughts toward the Yankees. Instead of going forward with their lives, most seemed to dwell in the past, playing games of what might have been if only so-and-so had done such-and-such. The only ones to escape suspicion were the fallen heroes. They alone were at peace.

Constance glanced up at two of the intact structures remaining in Richmond, the State House and the Confederate Executive Mansion. Both stood solid and proud as always, surrounded by half-walls and empty shells of spectral ruins, skeletal remains of the city that once was Richmond. Planted firmly above both roofs were large American flags, waving in the blistering August heat. How strange those flags still seemed to her eyes.

Had it *ever* been this hot in Richmond?

The post office was just ahead. Constance did not acknowledge the trio of Union soldiers who stepped aside for her to pass, all three mumbling a greeting. Her failure to recognize the men had nothing to do with the Union victory or any latent hostility. She had no more energy for that sort of thing. Instead, it was an admission of how things had changed. Not everyone in Richmond was a friend.

Not so long ago she would have been chastised for walking on the street without an escort. Had Wade Cowen seen her stroll down a public street alone, he would have been furious. But Wade, her fiancé, was dead these four months.

Although they had not seen each other for over two years, they had agreed—in a furious, impassioned exchange of letters—to marry when the war ended. She had wondered of late if Wade, whom she had known since childhood, had truly loved her as a woman. It didn't matter now, not really. The day after peace had been declared, Wade—who had never been much of a horseman—had been killed leading a charge against a group of picnicking Federal soldiers.

He was given a hero's burial, the last of the fallen Confederates, it said on his tombstone. Constance had been told the truth by one of Wade's fellow officers: poor Wade had simply lost control of his horse. When he realized he was riding towards a cluster of stunned Feds, he probably went through his choices, and decided it was better to die a hero than to live a fool. So at the last moment, struggling with the reins, he pulled out his sword and waved it, more in an effort to regain balance than as a threat.

The Feds shouted at him to stop, and when he could not, they shot him once through the forehead. Just once. The officer who shot Wade had written Constance a note about her fiancé's bravery, and everyone agreed he felt terrible about the shooting.

The line at the post office was long, as Constance knew it would be. Everyone was hoping that some distant relation up North would mail them money. Virginians who had previously declared to have no connections whatsoever with the Union were now writing frantic letters, asking for loans, reminding cousins by marriage in New York and Ohio and Vermont of the binding thickness of blood.

The line snaked forward as the single clerk shook his head at requests for free postage, inquiries concerning a parcel an individual knew, just *knew,* would be arriving any day now.

"Poor Miss Lloyd."

It had not been a greeting. Someone behind her had simply issued a statement.

"Poor Miss Lloyd indeed." Another woman echoed her companion's opinion.

Constance did not even blink. She was used to it by now, the murmurs and gentle tisking of acquaintances who pitied her. It seemed absurd that after four years of violent death and disease, of moral destruction, of tragedy such as the world had seldom seen, the plight of eighteen-year-old Constance Lloyd seemed to wring condolences from even the hardest of hearts.

True, her father had perished of the mumps shortly after enlisting in the Confederate Army. Soon after that, her mother died of what seemed to have been little more than a bad cold. By the time the main house of the plantation erupted in fire, there were too

4

few servants, or slaves as the Feds called them, to do much more than watch the conflagration.

Wade's death had been the final blow, although by then she was too numb to feel much of a loss. Everyone had suffered during the war; not a single person was left unscathed. But Constance, whose path to maturity was marked by each devastation, seemed to evoke pity in everyone.

It was absolutely intolerable. There was no place for her to escape the downturned mouths and sad eyes of sympathy.

". . . and then her beloved fiancé Wade Cowen . . ."

She clutched the drawstring bag so tightly her knuckles turned white.

". . . and her mother. Don't forget her mother. I was at her coming out, and never was there such a belle in all of Virginia. She was English, you know, from England."

The women's voices rose as they discussed Constance, the marble-columned mansion where she grew up, the paragon that was her father, the perfection that was her mother, her poverty, the mended tear in the skirt of her dress.

Constance stifled the urge to scream. How delightful it would be to turn around and face the old hens, to hit them over the head with her purse, or to tell Mrs. Witherspoon that her beloved son had sold the family silver for Union whiskey.

Instead she moved ahead with the line.

"Miss Lloyd," said the clerk when at last she reached the window. "There is a letter for you."

The clerk seemed relieved to finally have something to give to someone. He bobbed behind the shelves and emerged holding a battered envelope. "It's from England," he announced in a loud voice. A quivering hush fell over the post office as she took the letter in her bare hands—when had she last worn gloves?—and stepped away from the window.

Her hands were trembling. "Please, God," she whispered, aware that she had not prayed for a very long time.

With her thumb, she gently loosened a flap, pausing only once. "Please," she repeated.

This was it. She had written her mother's cousins, asking if they knew of a position as a governess amongst their friends in England. It had been a last resort, a final attempt to regain control of her life. Should this fail, she had no place to turn.

She stepped to a corner of the post office for privacy she knew would elude her, but she couldn't possibly wait until she reached her tiny room at the Smithers sisters' house. She held her future in her hands.

Taking a deep breath, she slid the letter from the envelope and tilted the first of what seemed to be many pages towards the light.

My dear Cousin Constance,

We are delighted to inform you that there is, indeed, a position for you here in England. Come as soon as possible. Enclosed is a one-way passage. . . .

That was all she could read before her vision misted with tears. Clamping her hand over her mouth, she was unable to stop the gasp that escaped.

She was saved.

The gasp was followed by another, and before she could leave the post office she was weeping with relief, loud, wrenching sounds, tears rolling freely from her eyes.

She had not cried in years. But it didn't matter, nothing mattered.

She was saved.

"Poor Miss Lloyd. More bad news, no doubt," said Mrs. Witherspoon as Constance ran from the building, bumping into a brass spittoon and begging its forgiveness in her haste. "Was there ever a more wretched, unfortunate girl on the face of this earth?"

1

COWES, ISLE OF WIGHT, ENGLAND
AUGUST 1874

My goodness, Miss Lloyd! You are so very, very lucky! How I envy you! Was there ever a more fortunate girl on the face of the earth?"

Constance smiled as she held the veil over her head. "I doubt it, Melody. I doubt it very much indeed. But at the age of twenty and seven, I do believe I ceased being a girl sometime during the last decade."

"Do you know how the other girls envy you? The coming out was for us, after all. And who won the glittering prize? Who danced with the Prince of Wales himself for three waltzes in a row? Who did the son of a duke ask to be his wife? My own governess! Honestly, Miss Lloyd, if I didn't love you so much, I do believe I would hate you."

Constance was about to respond when she glanced at her former charge. "Oh, Melody," she breathed. "I can scarcely believe it myself."

A luscious breeze, sharp and salty from the sea, billowed the curtains of Constance's room. It seemed impossible that, after nine years in the employ of Mrs.

Whitestone as a governess and, more importantly, as a friend, she would be leaving within the week to join her fiancé at his family's estate. And he would arrive in his father's carriage, ducal emblem encrusted on the doors, any day now, to escort her to her new home.

It would be a temporary home, of course, because she was sure that when they were married, he would want to establish a household of their own. Perhaps they would live in London. Perhaps her fiancé had a different idea, one he had not shared with her yet simply because the whole engagement had been so deliriously swift.

Her fiancé. The word seemed peculiar, a different feeling entirely from when she had been engaged during the war. Wade had seemed such a child, perhaps because she had known him all of her life and could even now recall him as a little boy with freckles and a chipped front tooth.

Now the very word fiancé was filled with mystery and surprise and romance.

"Oh, Miss Lloyd, please tell me again. Tell me the whole story."

Melody Whitestone sighed as she rested her head upon her hand. She was the prettiest of the two Whitestone girls and, unfortunately—in spite of all of Constance's attempts to counter Melody's high opinion of herself—she knew it, and used those charms mercilessly. Her beauty was of the plumpish sort, a childlike softness that reminded Constance of an idealized Cupid, all pink cheeks and golden curls.

Constance, by contrast, was tall—some said too tall—and dark. Her height, well above five-and-a-half feet, had been quite an advantage as a governess. It was only during her first moments dancing with the portly Prince that she felt a flush of embarrassment because of her stature. Instead of looking directly into

His Majesty's small, protruding eyes, she was forced to cast her gaze downward, just slightly, but noticeably.

Her coloring, dark hair, and pale blue eyes, also seemed remarkable to some of the Whitestones' neighbors, and to the curious onlookers at the ball. She had been noticed before by the cream of society, always during the brief Cowes season. The first time she had come to anyone's attention was when she came to Lady Montclair's rescue when her horse bolted from the gently trotting pack of sidesaddled ladies. Constance Lloyd, with her practical gray dress, curiously adorned with a sprig of dried laurel leaves at the throat, grabbed the reins and calmed both the horse and the whimpering Lady Montclair.

For that service Lord Montclair offered her a glass of sherry. Constance declined with grace, her peculiar American accent both soft and charming.

She declined the sherry, but she had most certainly been noted. And because of her startling good looks and surprisingly expert handling of horses, two unheard-of traits in a governess, more than one observer speculated out loud that perhaps Miss Lloyd was part savage. She was, after all, from America. Hair as dark and lustrous as hers was seldom paired with eyes the shade of fine turquoise.

The rumor was further spun that her grandfather had been an Indian warrior, of a tribe varying from Cherokee to Mohawk, and he had scalped her grandmother—a highborn English beauty—on the very day of her mother's birth. The Indian warrior, of course, had wanted a son, not a daughter, and the scalping was merely a suitable punishment for the warrior's disappointment. Such things were appallingly common in America, it was said.

Constance did nothing to clarify the idle suspicion. Again, it was quite an advantage as a governess. When the children were very young, they obeyed her simply out of fear that she would, at any moment, turn savage—a notion Constance reinforced on a regular basis by eyeing their hairlines when they misbehaved.

It would never do to reveal that both maternal grandparents were, in fact, natives of London, and that the most barbarous display she had ever seen her grandfather perform was his habit of eating green peas with the blade of his knife.

"Please, Miss Lloyd," Melody begged. "Please tell me everything that happened the night of the ball."

"You were there, Melody," Constance laughed, carefully folding the veil. It had been sent by her fiancé's mother, most likely the very same delicate veil she had worn when she married the duke. "You saw more than I did, for you were a spectator. I was in the middle of the play, so I was not able to see the entire event."

Melody slumped onto the bed and rolled over on her back, clutching a pillow of Battenberg lace against her chest. "It was such a blur, I hardly know what I saw. But, Miss Lloyd, I knew the night would be special when you came down the stairs in Mother's gown."

"That was so very kind of her, not only to allow me to attend the ball, but to lend me one of her gowns." How they had worked on the gown, both Constance and Harriet, and even Melody, lengthening the hem, elongating the waist, and adding bits and pieces of other garments. The end result had stunned not only its creators, but everyone who had seen it, a frothy confection of pale pinks and ivorys with a bold neckline that highlighted Constance's slender, surprisingly alabaster shoulders. Her thick hair had been woven with pink ribbons, the gloss of her hair rivaling the shimmer of the satin. Never had a mere governess been so bedecked, if not bejeweled.

It had been a farewell gesture, a final dash of kindness from the generous Harriet Whitestone. Since Captain Whitestone's death several years before, the family fortune had been on a decline, and upon the coming out of Melody it was understood that Constance would have to find another position. Mrs. Whitestone simply could not afford the luxury of a governess for three now-grown children, nor did Constance expect to remain.

So Mrs. Whitestone managed to have Constance added to the list of attendees at the Royal Yacht Squadron Ball. The late captain's name still carried some weight in military circles; the bulk of his legacy had been in honor rather than in tangible goods. It was an unheard-of gesture, inviting a governess—one of the most invisible members of any household—to such a regal event. But Harriet Whitestone knew Constance would rise to the occasion, and then some. After all, before Constance was reduced by the events of the American Civil War, the Lloyd fortune had been well-regarded in England, and the Lloyds themselves had been above reproach.

Melody closed her eyes, recalling the night just weeks earlier. "You came down the staircase, and Miles was the first to gasp. Did you hear him, Miss Lloyd?"

"How could I not?" She smiled. "I feared he was suffering yet another bout of the hiccups. Remember how he used to be overtaken by them when he was a child?"

"I'd almost forgot. But he has always rather fancied you, Miss Lloyd. He may have been your charge, but he is only five years younger than you."

"A fact Master Miles has always taken great delight in mentioning on a frequent basis," Constance laughed.

"Miss Lloyd, had you ever seen him before?"

"Miles? Why of course." A small dimple appeared on one side of her chin, a telltale sign to those who knew her well that she was repressing a grin.

"No, I mean *your* him. Your fiancé."

Constance paused, wondering if she should tell young Melody the whole truth. In fact, Constance had been very much aware of Philip Cyril St. John Arthur Albert Hastings, the second son of the venerable Duke of Ballsbridge. For the past seven years she had seen him ride past the Whitestone home for the two weeks of the Cowes season, always riding a superb mount, always wearing an impeccable riding suit of the latest cut.

In short, he was glorious.

Never had Constance uttered his name out loud. He was her private dream, a fantasy to weave and cherish during the long hours in the schoolroom or in her small corner of the house. Rain would beat against the window panes as the seasons passed, weeks and months lapsing into years, when once again it was time to see the splendid image of young Lord Hastings—his spine straight, his aquiline profile set, his pale hair ruffling in the breeze—ride past the house where she was employed.

Once he seemed to turn towards her, perhaps alerted by the sound of some birds in a nearby shrub, but his gaze did not rest on her. She had been wearing a dull gray gown that day, appropriate to her position as a governess, rendering her as invisible as she indeed was to society. Pinned at her collar had been her customary sprigs of bay, a habit she had fostered during the war, when jewelry had been a distant memory and the fragrant laurel had both adorned her increasingly limited wardrobe and reminded her of a distant hope of victory.

Lord Hastings, as she had learned was his name

from the local blacksmith, had been clad in magnificent shades of evergreen and black, his boots gleaming even in the sunless afternoon.

He had not even seen her. No one ever saw the reliable Constance Lloyd, tucked away in her neat quarters above the rest of the house.

And then, when she was dancing with the Prince of Wales, he did see her. Everyone saw Constance Lloyd. Everything changed in the span of two hours.

"May I, Your Majesty?"

Those were the first words she ever heard Philip speak. He was standing just beyond the prince, a stiff bow, a small smile on his lips. The prince laughed and said something, what it was she would never recall, and then she was waltzing with Philip Cyril St. John Arthur Albert Hastings, son of the Duke of Ballsbridge.

"Have we met before?"

Those were the first words he ever addressed to her. Constance smiled and shook her head, still looking up at his face. He smelled vaguely of brandy and cigars, a scent that was not at all unpleasant and seemed to suit him very well indeed.

They stepped outside for some Roman punch, and he crooked his arm for her to clasp, for her to touch. The night air was misty and cold, and they spoke of his home and his title and his hopes to be elected to Parliament, to the House of Commons, representing his ancestral seat of Ballsbridge.

As a second son, he was not entitled to a seat in the House of Lords. In time, his elder brother would claim that right, along with the entire estate. Philip was not bitter about his position, did not seem to mind that, barring a family tragedy, he was forever consigned to the role of second son, the "spare" born following the all-important "heir."

Another aspect of Philip was his lack of curiosity

about her past. He did not seem the least bit interested in anything concerning her life before that first waltz. Once he asked if she was an American, and she admitted to the fact. Once he asked what part of America she was from, and she began to describe Virginia and the plantation that had been her home a long time ago, but he had simply looked to the ocean and asked if she minded if he smoked a cigar.

When was the last time a gentleman had asked Constance permission to do anything? Of course it was against the strictest code of behavior to ever smoke in front of a lady. Yet he was a lord, and she was a governess, and his asking permission seemed the kindest, most considerate gesture of all.

After the ball she went home in the Whitestones' rented carriage. It had been a lovely interlude, a brief spell before the real world intruded. Melody Whitestone was bubbling over with news; Mrs. Whitestone smiled and stared at Constance, who imagined she could still detect the fragrance of Lord Hastings on her borrowed gloves and hidden in the folds of her employer's fan.

The next morning, she finished packing her bags and wrote a final note to her new employers in Bath, letting them know when she would be arriving. They were a young family, with four children and another on the way. As she continued her arrangements to leave, Lord Hastings called on her, this time in a spectacular ruby-colored jacket. Harriet Whitestone, just past forty herself and still every inch a romantic, asked Constance to delay her departure for just a while longer, for the house would seem desperately empty without her, at least until Melicent—her eldest daughter, now married to a Mr. Furman of Newcastle—arrived for a visit.

Of course, Harriet simply wanted the duke's young son to have a chance to forge a bond with Miss Lloyd.

And within four days, with his mother's permission, Philip had proposed marriage.

It still seemed a dream, a fairy tale come magically to life.

How much should she tell Melody, or even her future husband, of the times she had watched him from such an impossible distance? She looked over at Melody, her eyes still unfocused with her own day-dreams. Perhaps she should keep it to herself, the truth that she had been so very aware of Philip long before they met.

The door to the governess's room received a gentle tap before Harriet Whitestone entered.

"So there you are, the two of you." She smiled. Even four years after the death of Captain Whitestone, Harriet still wore half mourning, shades of gray and jet, and a simple brooch made of her husband's hair, braided and set in a gold circle.

It had been fortunate for the Whitestone finances that Queen Victoria's mourning had lasted well over a decade. That made Harriet's perpetual status as a grieving widow fashionable, although the mourning clothes were more a nod to economy than to overwhelming grief. One could wear the same mourning gown for years with nary a comment from the neighbors, something that could never be said of a more cheerful dress.

"Mrs. Whitestone." Constance rose to her feet, and Harriet began to laugh.

"My dear! Do you realize that within the month you will be Lady Philip Hastings? Please, allow me to get accustomed to rising upon *your* entry to a room!"

"Mother, isn't this the most exciting, romantic thing in the world?" Melody Whitestone again sighed.

"Indeed it is, Melody. But this just arrived, Constance. It's a letter from Hastings House. I wanted to get this into your hands as soon as possible."

Harriet passed the letter to Constance, who stared for a moment at the unfamiliar handwriting. It was small and very neat, and she assumed it was the hand of Philip's mother.

"May I?" Constance automatically asked Harriet's permission before opening her mail, not noticing her former employer's quick wink at Melody before nodding towards Constance.

When she opened the letter she realized it was from Philip himself.

"How odd," she muttered before she even began to read the contents.

"Is anything wrong?" Harriet was far too polite to peer over her shoulder, and kept a distance.

"No. It's just that I've never seen Philip's handwriting before."

"It's quite a tidy hand," commented Harriet, repressing a smile. "I imagine there is a great deal you will very soon learn of your future husband. Come, Melody. Let us allow Miss Lloyd her privacy."

But Constance held up her hand. "Oh, dear," she frowned, scanning the words.

"I do hope there is no bad news." Harriet paused.

"No. no. This is just rather odd. Philip will not be able to take me to Hastings House after all."

"Indeed?"

"No. His mother feels it would be a better use of his time to actively campaign for the election instead of wasting four full days in fetching me." She blinked, shaking her head. "I suppose she's right. After all, Philip has been in London all these years, so only his name is fully known in Ballsbridge."

"Four full days?" Harriet tilted her head in confusion. "But by the railroad a journey to Yorkshire should take much less time."

"According to this letter, the duchess does not trust the railroads." Constance shook her head. "She feels they are unnatural and perhaps ungodly. So she wishes me to travel by coach."

"Oh, how sad," Melody reached out and touched Constance's wrist. "I was rather looking forward to seeing the dashing Lord Hastings again. Have you noticed his nose, Mother? It's terribly well-formed. Regal, almost. Miss Lloyd, I'm sure you have noticed what a magnificent nose your future husband has."

"I have noticed that very fact." Constance smiled. "And it is so attractively placed, right between his eyes and above his mouth."

Harriet laughed, giving Constance an affectionate hug. "Oh, my dear, you have no idea how much I'm going to miss you. How I do envy those lucky persons at Hastings House."

"They do have a treat in store for them, Mrs. Whitestone." Constance returned the hug.

"But, Miss Lloyd." Melody lead the way towards the door. "How will you get to Hastings House if Lord Hastings is not going to accompany you? How will your safety be ensured? My goodness, the stories I have read of these roads at night, with all sorts of dangerous pirates and murderers lurking about behind trees at every turn. They are all but abandoned since the railroad. Surely you are not expected to make the journey on your own."

"No, I am not. This is the curious part; he is sending an old schoolfriend of his to collect me. Let's see." She again glanced through the letter. "Oh, here it is. He's a very dear friend from public school and then Oxford. His name is Mr. Joseph Smith."

"Joseph Smith?" Melody frowned, and then, realizing the expression might spoil her complexion with wrinkles, set her face into a line-free, neutrally pleasant cast. "What a dreadfully common name. I don't suppose he is anyone important, certainly not a peer. He can't possibly be anyone at all."

"Why, Miss Whitestone, what a monstrous snob you have become," her mother scolded. "I must speak to your governess directly."

And the three women, laughing, descended the stairs for their afternoon tea.

"The things I do for you, Hastings," Joseph Smith muttered, taking yet another liberal swallow of whiskey.

Philip raised a finger in a subtle gesture to the impeccably dressed steward, who silently placed the crystal decanter on the mahogany table between the two leather chairs. The loud noises of London, the barbarous shouts of street urchins and the grinding of carriage wheels, were muffled on the quiet Pall Mall street, and further subdued by the club's thick walls and heavy drapes. If one had to be in London, this was the most civilized place to be, apart from the Prince of Wales' Marlborough House. Of course, Marlborough House was widely known to be the best-run household in all of London, and therefore all the world.

One day soon, Philip had high hopes of being invited as a guest to HM's home. He had seen the glint in the Prince's eyes as he danced with Miss Lloyd, a most certain signal that anyone attached to Miss Lloyd would be received eagerly by the future king. Once she was his wife, he would very soon be established in the Marlborough House set. One day very soon. Perhaps he would even be invited to join the prince's exclusive Marlborough Club, the royal heir's own bastion within a stone's throw of Marlborough House.

He grinned at his friend, the hopelessly unfashionable Joseph Smith. "Come, come, Smith. It will only take you four days to fetch her, and I know for a fact that you need to look in on that new factory of yours. Where is it again?"

"Nowhere near the Isle of Wight. For God's sake, Philip, why couldn't you marry a girl from London, and save us all the travel time?"

Philip was aware that his friend was angry. At such times his accent, usually a studied Oxbridge blend, reverted to the lilting cadences of his childhood in Wales. Philip never did know exactly what town Joseph was from. All he was told by his friend was that it was a very long name with very few vowels. Philip gladly left the subject alone.

"She's to be *your* bride. You should get her yourself, not send me. You know that, don't you?" Joseph splashed more whiskey into his glass.

"Mother insists I remain behind." Philip suddenly became quite interested in his fingernails, examining them for any unsightly shreds or tears.

"Tell me more about her, Hastings. All I know is that she is an American of good stock. That's all you've revealed thus far. Where is she from in America?"

"The eastern part, I believe. Did you hear that Randolph Churchill is in town? I need to talk to him about marrying an American. I wonder if his wife knows my fiancée. Both from America, you know."

"Good old Gooseberry." Joseph grinned, referring to their young friend's schoolboy name. He had been an infamous "scug" while at Eaton, such a rascal that even those who had left the school years earlier knew him by reputation. There was not much hope for Churchill's future, rather a general feeling that he would spend the rest of his life disgracing his family's illustrious past. "So what's her name?"

"You remember, Joseph. She is the former Jennie Jerome, the daughter of Leonard Jerome of New York

21

City. Now, of course, she is Lady Randolph Churchill. She's about to pop their first child. A boy, no doubt. American women always seem to have boys, bless them. That's what Mother says, at any rate."

Joseph Smith took a deep breath and shook his head. Unlike his friend, who was pale and elegant and utterly patrician, Joseph was unfashionably tanned from being outdoors. While Philip wore an impressive set of sideburn whiskers, slightly darker than his blond hair, Joseph's face was clean-shaven, leaving the very slight—but in Philip's mind unsightly—scar on his left cheek visible for all the world to see.

His lack of facial hair was more a result of his restless nature than a comment on fashion. He simply did not have the interest nor the inclination to embark on the never-ending quest to cultivate a splendid set of whiskers. Joseph Smith—his auburn hair too long, his skin too bronzed and his body too muscular for elegance—did not have the patience to fit in with the rest of the patrons of the Carlton Club.

But he was a member. His wealth, new though it was, made him more than acceptable in most clubs and as an extra man at the finest of assemblies. And many women, more than would openly admit, found him absolutely fascinating, and his masculine edge— just slightly wild—a refreshing change from the most refined gentlemen.

"Philip, I am asking about *your* fiancée, not Gooseberry's wife. What is her name?"

"Oh. Constance. Well, er, yes. She is an orphan as far as I know, although I do believe her family at one time had some sort of wealth. Her name is Constance Lloyd."

"And she's from the eastern coast of America? Any clue as to where exactly?"

"What do you mean, 'where'? Joseph, your obsession with details can be quite tiresome."

"If I am to spend long hours in a closed carriage with this woman, I would like to know as much as possible about her. A start would be where she is from. Now can you recall if she is from Maine or New Jersey?"

Philip gave his friend a disinterested shrug.

"I will make it easy, Hastings. She's from the coast. Now, is her place of origin up or down?"

"I can't recall. You know bloody well I've never been there, Joseph. Wait. Virginia. That's it—she's from Virginia. Or was it South Carolina?"

"A Confederate, then," Joseph said. "Interesting." He grinned at his friend. "So she stole your heart at first glance?"

"Well . . . er . . ."

"It's no use hedging with me. I know you too damn well. Why on earth is the very eligible Lord Hastings marrying a penniless, orphaned, Confederate governess? Just curious, I suppose. Tell me."

"Blast. All right. Because no one else would have me."

Joseph had not been prepared for that answer. Had he anticipated the nature of the response, he never would have taken such a liberal swallow of whiskey, and therefore he never would have spit it directly into his friend's face.

"Not on my whiskers, Smith! I've just had them trimmed and powdered!" Philip dabbed carefully at his sideburns.

"Sorry, Philip. Just what do you mean, 'no one else would have me'? To the left, you missed a spot."

Philip glared at his friend, annoyed to discover the obvious amusement on the sun-darkened features.

"Because of my father. Bloody hell—now I smell like a distillery."

"You usually do anyway. What do you mean, because of your father?"

"You know as well as anyone that my father is considered rather eccentric. Is my cravat wet?"

"No. It's as impeccable as ever. Your father is considered eccentric? But he is also considered one of the wealthiest peers in England. That should count for something."

"It does, certainly. You and your investment suggestions have had more to do with our financial status than any of our land holdings. Chemical dyes, what? Who would imagine that synthetic indigo would save us from disaster. But, damn it, Smith, he spends his days digging tunnels at Hastings House. Do you know he just had a ballroom built that can hold over two hundred people?"

"Did he, now? That should be a welcome addition to the house."

"It would be, but he built the thing underground, beneath the apple orchard. One has to journey through his tunnels in handcarts to reach the place." Philip folded his handkerchief and returned it to his pocket. "I am fully aware that Father is called the Mole Man by most of polite society. I do wish you would wipe that smile off your face, Smith. It does not become you."

"Sorry. The truth is, I am enormously fond of your father. He has shown me more genuine affection than my own relations back in Wales. He's a good, kind man, Philip. If I were you, I would be proud of him."

"Proud of him? He hasn't left the estate in fifteen years! He will only travel by tunnel, and then he insists on carrying a lunch pail, convinced that nothing can go wrong if one is provided with a packed meal. I think his ultimate goal must be to tunnel his way to London, so he will never have to venture above ground again. My poor mother . . ."

"Your poor mother couldn't be more pleased with the situation," Joseph interrupted. "She likes to think she controls everything, the running of the estate, most of the business matters." Under his breath he added, "And she controls you."

Philip seemed not to hear. "The papers refuse to print her latest notice. She is most vexed, Smith. Most vexed, indeed."

"Is she still sending the *Times* those fraudulent death notices? They simply evoke more comments, Philip. No one believes your father is dead. When he does pass on, and God willing that will not be for many years, you will have a devil of a time convincing anyone, including his physician, that his time has come. What cause of death did your mother cook up this time?"

"Oh, well. She issued a notice proclaiming that he had been killed in a hunting accident."

Joseph Smith laughed. "Your father hasn't hunted in years!"

"It's not funny, Smith. She had hoped that with Father out of the way, or at least believed to be out of the way, I might have a chance at one of the better women who came out this season. I'm a second son with no means of employment, and I do have something of a reputation for being rather reckless."

"Come, come, Philip, it can't be as bad as all that."

"It is, and worse. I offered myself to no less than five women this season, and every single one of them refused me. Even Lillian Lisle."

Joseph chuckled. "How is Miss Lisle? I have yet to see her since last Christmas."

"Well, she gained another stone and her mustache is becoming quite alarming. But even Lillian Lisle had the audacity to laugh at me when I professed my love for her."

"For God's sake, Hastings, what did you expect? It was only last year that you sent her the hedge trimmer for her upper lip. Surely you can't be surprised that she did not want to spend the rest of her life receiving gardening tools for her dresser top."

Philip was silent for a moment. "Was it only last year, that hedge-trimmer incident? Good Lord, I had almost forgotten. I was terribly drunk at the time, you know."

"Of course you were. What about the others you proposed to?"

"They are all afraid that insanity runs in the family. It's because of my father, blast it all. No woman will have me because my father is the mad Mole Man."

"Your father is not insane. He's one of the sanest men I've ever met. He just wisely chooses to avoid society, which makes him very clever indeed."

"It doesn't matter. My brother seems to remain untouched by the family curse. It's because he's the eldest, you know. He'll have no trouble at all finding a wife. He's to inherit. He could be mad as a hatter, and still have his absolute pick of any season."

"Still, he's never made it to the altar."

"He's come damn close, and that's the thing. No, Mother is not worried about Dishy finding a wife. It's me she's worried about. All those rumors, Smith, all about some of my, well, escapades. Not all of us have our nose to the grindstone like you, old boy."

"Not all of us have to," Smith added grimly. "In any case, you have managed to snare a beautiful bride. From what I've heard, she is a real corker. And there must be an element of love on your part, to hasten the ceremony."

Philip shrugged. "Mother insists that I marry before the elections."

"What on earth for?"

"Well, she fears that, as a bachelor well into my thirties, my being single would seem, well, peculiar. I went to Cowes with the intention of finding a bride. And just when I was about to give up, I saw HM dancing with an extraordinary-looking young woman. Old Bertie was positively glowing, and the Princess of Wales was eyeing the woman as well. So I waited three waltzes, cutting off that Rafferty fellow with the scar on his face. Oh, sorry. No offense."

Smith smiled and nodded, and his friend continued. "So, I asked this creature for a dance. Mother did a quick check—she has her sources, you know. It seems that her family is solid, and the fact that they are dead was also quite appealing to Mother."

This time Smith swallowed the whiskey instead of spitting it out. "Why on earth would that be appealing?"

"Because with no family we do not have to worry about a shipment of loud Americans descending upon Hastings House, or any vulgar mother snapping up the jewelry and snuff boxes or influencing my sons."

"Sons?"

"American women always have sons. Other than for the elections, that is the main reason for my marriage. Mother made sure her hips are wide enough for breeding—we took her measurements for the wedding gown Mother is having made."

"This is absolutely ridiculous. Do you know anything about the woman who is to be your wife? What is she like, Philip?"

"She is lovely, dark hair, as I recall, and her accent is tolerable."

"Well, that's all we need to know, isn't it?"

A steward appeared at Joseph's left arm, bearing a silver salver with a sealed note upon it. The return address was facedown, as was always the case when a gentleman received mail at his club. Many a lady's reputation would be lost forever if her club correspondence were revealed.

"Sir?"

Joseph took the letter. "Thank you," he muttered to

the steward as he opened the envelope and scanned the contents. The lines on his forehead became more pronounced as he read, then folded the letter and replaced it.

"A reply, sir?" the steward asked, bowing slightly.

"No, Baker. No reply is necessary, but I thank you."

Philip waited for the man to withdraw before he spoke.

"So you'll do it, Smith? You'll fetch Constance to Hastings House for me?" In spite of his dampened whiskers, Lord Hastings suddenly looked like a worried adolescent.

"Of course I will. It seems I have some business in that direction after all." Joseph was silent for a moment, his gaze focused on the fire screen. Then he shook his head, his expression lightening. "One of these days, you know, I'm going to call upon *you* for a favor, and it's going to be immensely costly and inconvenient."

Finally Philip chuckled. "I expect it will. Thank you, Joseph. You are a true friend." He lifted his glass, and they toasted their friendship.

Constance glanced for the third time at the mantel clock. She was dressed in a new traveling suit, a dark maroon dress more tightly fitted than she was accustomed to as a governess. The dress, along with several others, had arrived just the day before from Hastings House. The note attached to the parcel, from Philip's mother, was brief and to the point. The clothing was to keep her from possible embarrassment that might arise should she be improperly attired.

There was no note from Philip. He added no message, nor was there even a reference to the upcoming marriage in his mother's letter. It was almost as if she did not want to dwell on the event. Constance wondered if Philip even knew of the package his mother had sent.

In the Whitestones' hallway was her single trunk and her scuffed wooden lap desk, all she required even with the addition of the new, antihumiliation disguises. The battered trunk was the same piece of luggage that had traveled with her from Richmond almost a decade earlier. Now it was once again taking her to a new life.

The writing desk, which had been her mother's, had given her joy even in the darkest moments of her life. At times she could not bear to face it, to open the hinged lid and see the corked crystal ink bottles and the quill pens with the tips still darkened from the last words her mother wrote.

Tucked into a secret compartment were some yellowing sheets of her mother's notepaper, embossed with her initials, paper that had been ordered well before the war. The desk was all that remained now of her life before becoming a governess. That was all she had taken with her from her home.

"He should be here soon, Constance," Harriet Whitestone smiled, noting the younger woman's restlessness. "He was quite precise in his note, he would arrive between ten o'clock and ten-thirty in the morning, and it is now just twenty minutes past ten. I would be very much surprised if he is late."

Constance nodded in agreement. "As would I. From his correspondence with me thus far, he seems a remarkably prompt man."

"That is not such an evil trait, my dear. You should not be cross with him simply because he is not the man you had hoped would escort you to Hastings House. Your fiancé thinks highly enough of this Joseph Smith to entrust him with his most precious possession. His only flaw at the moment is that he is not Lord Hastings. Oh, I hear a coach out front."

The two women remained seated, listening as the Whitestones' maid, Betty, answered the door.

Constance heard a man's voice, low and not at all unappealing to her ears. The parlor door opened, and Betty, her face flushed and her starched caplet just slightly tilted, bobbed into the room.

"Mr. Joseph Smith has arrived, ma'am." She held the door, and Joseph Smith entered the small room.

He was not at all what Constance had been expecting. In spite of his rather ordinary name, Constance had imagined he would be a man much like Philip, very slender and elegant and smooth and whiskered. This man was tall, perhaps even taller than Philip, but he was broad of shoulder, as if he could toss a chair across the room with little effort. His hair was thick and coppery dark, very straight, very unlike the flaxen hair of Philip. His eyes seemed to take in everything at once, and Constance could not tell their precise color, but they seemed to be of the same burnished copper as his hair. And his face itself, free of whiskers, was more than pleasing, more than handsome. She was used to men with beards to hide their every expression. Seeing so much skin, even on his face, seemed peculiar and intimate, especially when paired with his very correct attire. It was a striking and almost unsettling combination.

"Miss Lloyd?" He addressed Harriet, who reddened and shook her head.

"I'm afraid not, Mr. Smith. I am Harriet Whitestone. This is Miss Lloyd." Harriet held her hand towards Constance, who nodded and smiled with just a slight hesitation.

For some reason, this man made her feel uncomfortable.

"Excuse me, Miss Lloyd." He did not seem to look at her again; instead he shifted his gloves to the other hand, as if his single glance had been enough to fully form his opinion. And, from his expression, his opinion of Constance Lloyd was not a favorable one.

"I would like to begin our journey as quickly as possible. Shall I have the coachman fetch your trunks?" Already he was backing towards the door.

"I, well, yes. Certainly." Her eyes met those of

Harriet Whitestone, who also seemed surprised at the abruptness of Mr. Smith's manner. "I only have one trunk. And a lap desk."

"Only one trunk? And a lap desk?" His voice betrayed incredulity, and then he paused and nodded. "I see." His eyes flicked once more over her form, and she had the distinct impression that Mr. Joseph Smith disapproved not only of Constance Lloyd, but also of the fact that she only had one trunk, and above all that she had a lap desk.

Before she stopped to think, she stiffened, clasping her hands together and hoping to keep her voice even. "I have been a governess for almost a decade, Mr. Smith. There has been little need for a vast wardrobe. If you have objections to my single-trunk state, I am indeed sorry, but I cannot at the present time remedy the situation. And about my lap desk, well, I see no need whatsoever to explain my desk, sir. No reason whatsoever."

The man paused and gave her a long, slow perusal, starting at the top of her head, where her temples had suddenly begun to throb, dwelling briefly at the sprig of laurel at her throat, all the way to her shoes, which she was acutely aware were not of the highest quality. Philip's mother had neglected to ask for her shoe size.

Why on earth had she spoken? When Philip heard how she behaved, she wouldn't be surprised if he withdrew his offer and instead dismissed her to . . .

Laughter. Mr. Joseph Smith was standing in the Whitestones' parlor, laughing a rich, lilting chuckle. Harriet's face went from too pale to flushed and then she, too, began to laugh. Finally Mr. Smith was able to speak.

"Forgive me, Miss Lloyd. Philip is forever chiding me for my overly blunt ways, but never with such effective candor. You must be quite a marvelous governess, Miss Lloyd."

"Oh, Mr. Smith, she is!" Harriet stepped forward. "How I'm to do without her, I'll never know."

Constance blinked, startled by the change in Mr. Smith, who had entered the room like a rolling thundercloud and was now smiling as if he had always been the most pleasant and agreeable man on the face of the earth.

"I, well . . ." she stammered.

"I will await you outside, Miss Lloyd. I am sure you would like to have a few moments to bid farewell to Mrs. Whitestone."

He bowed to both women and left swiftly.

"Thank you, Mr. Smith," Constance said to the closing door.

"You are most welcome, Miss Lloyd," she heard his retreating voice reply from the hallway. Then the shuffling of her trunk being removed overpowered his voice. If he had said anything else, she did not hear a word.

"My, Constance," Harriet said as she embraced her former employee. "Your journey to Hastings House should be quite interesting, to say the least."

Constance returned the gentle squeeze. "How I'm going to miss you, all of you. I don't know if I can ever thank you enough. You have been so kind, so wonderfully kind, and I don't know what would have become of me had you not taken me in."

"Shush, enough of that," Harriet soothed, aware that her own eyes were dangerously close to filling with tears. "We could have never done without you, my dear, dear Constance. All is well, my eldest daughter and son are happily married, Melody is out, and you have done a splendid job of raising and educating them. It is only just that you have your turn now. And what a turn! Goodness, you are marrying the son of a duke! Soon you will be dining with the Prince of Wales, perhaps even the Queen of England herself! Oh, Constance, I couldn't be more proud of you if you were my own daughter."

Constance swallowed and nodded, not trusting her voice. She had survived for so long by not showing her emotions, not giving in to the hysteria that was so fashionable amongst well-reared ladies. Yet she feared that if she allowed herself the luxury of expression, if she gave in to her feelings—which had always been sharp enough to frighten her with their ferocity and intensity—she might never be able to rein them in. Once she lost control, she was afraid of losing it forever.

"Here, let me help you with the hat pin." Harriet guided the pin through Constance's thick hair, smiling as she recalled all of the hours her daughters had spent playing with Miss Lloyd's beautiful hair, fashioning the waist-length dark silk into all sorts of fantastic creations, each one gently undone by Miss Lloyd when the children went to bed.

"I will write to you the moment I arrive," Constance said softly, picking up her small reticule.

"And I will hold you to that promise." Harriet led Constance to the front door and down the outside steps in silence.

"Tell Melody not to pucker her face so when anything displeases her," Constance whispered, her voice rough. "And also tell her that I understand why she could not be here today. I understand."

"I know you do," Harriet replied. "You are one of the few who understands how sentimental poor Melody is, that she has never been able to tolerate good-byes."

"When I am settled, you must come to visit me. I wish you could be there for the wedding, but it is all out of my hands . . ."

"Of course it is! I would never dream of impinging, me a widow, and . . . oh, Mr. Smith."

Joseph Smith seemed to appear out of nowhere.

"I will take good care of Miss Lloyd, ma'am." He bowed, and Harriet nodded.

"I know you will. Let us not prolong this good-bye. And I have no doubt that we shall soon meet again, Constance. No doubt at all."

Constance nodded, realizing there was no reason to remain. It was time to leave. She glanced just beyond Harriet, where Betty and the gardener Ben stood, along with old Conner the former butler.

"Good-bye," she mouthed, but before she could smile, Betty sobbed and ran inside. "Goodness, you would think this was an execution."

Harriet chuckled and gave Constance a final embrace. "God's speed to you, my dear."

Joseph waited for a moment before helping Constance into the closed carriage. And as they rolled down the gravel path towards the ferry that would take them to the mainland, Constance leaned out of the window, imprinting every detail she could take in upon her memory. The gate, with its rusting hinges, the garden where she had taught the children their botany lessons, the window to her room, now shuttered tightly.

As the coach turned, Constance, caught off guard by her musings, was thrown against Mr. Smith.

"Excuse me," she mumbled, pushing her hat back into place and scooting across the leather seat to the opposite side, as far away as possible from the warmth of Mr. Smith's body.

He said nothing.

Constance took a deep breath and closed her eyes, aware that this was going to be a very long, long journey.

* * *

The roads were dry, the sea was smooth, and so they were able to land at Southampton sooner than expected.

"Would you like some refreshment?"

His voice startled her. Somehow they had managed to travel for hours without so much as a simple yes or no. If she didn't know better, Constance might have wondered if English was Mr. Smith's first language. Perhaps he was Russian or Italian, and used the almost comically plain name of Joseph Smith in an effort to appear British.

She had seen that before, in Richmond when she was a child. A family from Germany had moved into town just before the war. The children were all born in the United States, and had no accents at all. The parents went by the name of John and Mary Jones, although they pronounced their last name "Yo-hans," and often it would take one or two calls of their names to elicit a response. They had moved up North when the war began, and she wondered sometimes whatever happened to the family, to the bewildered-looking parents and the three children.

"Miss Lloyd?"

She jumped, and he seemed just slightly annoyed. "I asked if you would be well-disposed to taking refreshment."

"Oh. Thank you, Mr. Smith. That would be quite nice."

There had been a great debate earlier in the day as to whether Cook should pack up some sandwiches for Constance to eat on the journey, and if sandwiches were prepared, if extra should be packed for Mr. Smith. In the end, Harriet and Cook agreed that they had never heard of a peer pulling out sandwiches on a journey, and since Constance herself would have a title, it would never do to have her munching on sandwiches, spilling crumbs on her new dress. The entire dilemma of a beverage clinched the matter. No matter what container they could use to carry tea or water or cider, Harriet thought it would look as if Constance was nipping brandy or wine.

As she looked at her traveling companion, she concluded that brandy or wine, perhaps even whiskey, would not be such a bad idea.

He did not smile. Other than that all-too-brief moment in the parlor with Harriet Whitestone, Joseph Smith did not seem quite human. He seemed to be lost in thought, pondering something that had nothing to do with the passing scenery.

The coach, rented rather than one belonging to the duke, pulled up before an inn. Constance loved that about England, all the cozy inns and taverns. In America there did not seem to be as many places on a road to pause and rest. Of course, her America was the Confederate States, and there had been little time to build cozy taverns during the war. Still, she assumed that the entire North American continent was simply too vast and too new to ever have the taverns that England could boast.

She was about to mention that, about taverns and inns, and turned towards Mr. Smith, her mouth parted as if to speak.

He had been looking at her. The moment she turned, he looked away, out the window.

It seemed such a silly thing to mention, how very much she enjoyed English inns, not worth calling his attention away from whatever consumed him. And then he was out of the carriage, and in an instant he had her door opened, the stepping block in place, waiting for her to descend.

Without meeting his gaze, she stepped down, all of her conscious efforts focused on the task of not falling into the dirt and muck. He took her hand gently, and guided her by holding her elbow in his other palm.

"Thank you, sir," she muttered, averting her eyes as she stepped. For a brief instant their eyes were level, and then she was again shorter by at least a half foot.

His eyes were, as she had supposed, a strange shade of brown, almost copper.

Again without words, he took her into the Golden Eagle Inn. It seemed a pleasant place, and she could not help but enjoy the simple act of walking. Although they had not been traveling long, every bone in her body felt rattled and tossed, and her legs and arms were stiff from staying in one position.

She was grateful, not for the first time, that the fashion for exaggerated linen and horsehair crinolines had given way to the less-excruciating bustle, allowing the act of sitting to go from active pain to mild torment. And although the traveling suit was somewhat more embellished than she had been accustomed to—the ornamentation consisted mainly of silk frog fastenings starting at the throat and continuing to the waist—the trimmings were not as out-of-hand as some of the ridiculous styles she had seen. The collar was indeed velvet, as were the cuffs, but they were of the same deep maroon as the rest of the dress.

As a governess, fashion had made little difference to her, but the small trousseau from her future mother-in-law made it clear that clothing would soon become a matter of some importance. Constance sighed and looked down at her new kid gloves, another gift from the duchess. Melody had told her that most ladies went through at least a pair of gloves a day, and that they should fit so snugly that the outline of the fingernails should be plainly visible.

It was difficult for Constance, for whom so much of life had been a matter of survival, to take the matter of kid gloves seriously.

The inn was rather dark inside, lit with flickering brass lanterns and a sparse amount of candles. From the fragrance, slightly animal-like, she realized they were tallow candles.

The innkeeper, a man with no spare flesh except for on his nose, which seemed excessive, gladly led them to a small parlor away from the tavern room. Instead of the hard settle benches the parlor boasted several tables with more welcoming chairs. There was no door to close it off from the rest of the tavern. The rougher patrons hardly seemed to notice them as they entered, and the large woman pulling from a tap behind the bar barely glanced in their direction.

Mr. Smith held her chair as she sat, an odd sensation. His hand seemed to rest on her back for a few moments, as if he was deciding what to do next.

The menu board was just beyond their table. Suddenly, Mr. Smith brightened.

"They have fresh oysters!" He seemed genuinely pleased.

"They do?" Constance was reluctant to mention what had just come into her mind, but felt in all fairness she should. "Mr. Smith, I do hate to say this, yet I feel I must."

He stared at her for a moment, his eyes at once openly on her. "Please, Miss Lloyd. Say whatever you feel compelled to say."

"Well." She looked about to make sure the innkeeper was not within earshot. "I would advise you not to order the fresh oysters."

"Why on earth not? Because they are a common food, found in the poorest of homes? Because they are not a fashionable dish. Because . . ."

"Because there has been an outbreak of illness of late, and most believe it has to do with fresh oysters." The innkeeper walked past, and she lowered her voice until he was in the next room.

The bluster seemed to leave his face, and he sighed. "Miss Lloyd, I do appreciate your concern, but I am of a strong constitution. I grew up on oysters—whenever I was fortunate enough to have them, that is. And I am in a mood for them at present. Please, do not take this single bit of pleasure from my day."

She was about to speak, when she stopped and looked at his features. At the same precise moment, they both seemed to realize the implications of what he had said.

"Oh." She glanced away, anxious to look anyplace but at the man for whom diseased oysters were to provide the day's one bright spot.

"I did not mean that as it sounds, Miss Lloyd. Not at all."

Still she could not meet his gaze. Instead, she feigned great interest in the menu board.

"Please look at me, Miss Lloyd."

Slowly she turned towards him once more.

"I believe we should be honest with each other," he began. "I am here with you because of my friendship with Philip. In all truth, I did have some business to conduct nearby, but in general I am here to see you safely to your new home. So you see, this is neither an inconvenience nor an unpleasant chore. I am simply of a dour nature. This has nothing to do with you, Miss Lloyd, nor should my ill manners reflect in any way on Philip. I am the complete clod, the socially defective escort. And I apologize, as I'm sure I will be required to do often, for my behavior."

Constance said nothing for a few moments. Their eyes met, and a strange understanding seemed to pass across the table. Just before she smiled, a small dimple appeared just beside her lower lip, and only on her right side.

He stared at it, then realized she was smiling.

"Thank you, Mr. Smith, for your candor. And now may I be free to say something?"

"By all means."

"If I were you, I would avoid the fresh oysters like the plague."

He returned the smile. "Thank you, Miss Lloyd. And do you know what you would like?" He gestured for the innkeeper to come to their table.

"Yes, indeed. I would like the stewed chicken, please."

When the innkeeper was beside their table, Smith repeated her order, and then, in a loud voice, asked for the largest portion of fresh oysters they had.

"And how would you like them cooked, sir?"

"Not cooked," he announced. "Raw."

Constance winced, and Joseph Smith was so amused by her reaction that he failed to see the innkeeper wince just a bit as well.

"And to drink, sir?"

"I believe the lady would like a bit of sherry, and I would like a pint of ale."

"Very well." He hesitated for just an instant, as if wanting very much to say something. From behind the counter the large woman in a great, green apron called out.

"Horace! Go on with ye, man!"

The innkeeper nodded and turned to Joseph. "My wife," he hissed, as if that explained everything. And then he was gone.

"So tell me, Miss Lloyd, what part of America are you from?"

Constance was taken aback. When was the last time someone had inquired of her past?

"Oh. Well, sir, I am from Virginia, from just outside of Richmond."

"It is a beautiful land."

"You've been there?"

"Indeed I have. I was thinking of importing tobacco

41

a few years back, and spent several months there. In fact, I spent the vast majority of my time in Richmond itself."

"Since the war?"

"Ours or yours?"

"Ours. Have you been there since the war?"

"Yes. As a matter of fact I was there the year before last."

"You were?" She leaned forward in her excitement. "What does the town look like? Have they rebuilt, for when I was there last it was still in ruins! The Stars and Stripes were flying over the statehouse, which seemed so very peculiar after the Stars and Bars for so many years. Oh, and did you meet anyone in town . . ." She stopped suddenly, then blinked as if emerging from a dream. For a moment she just looked at him, her lips slightly parted, and then she drew her hand across her forehead and sank against the back of the chair.

Joseph, who had been watching her animation with enjoyment, waited for her to continue. But she did not. Instead she remained silent, an awkward smile on her face as she looked down at her hands.

Something caught in his throat, something he had not felt for a very long time, yet he did not stop to ponder the feeling. He simply watched her, as the tender light of the candles illuminated her features. Hers was a gentle face, a complexion that was almost luminous, an expression of softness.

"Go on, Miss Lloyd," he urged in a voice so low, only she could hear his words.

She shook her head. "No. It really doesn't matter. I was a different person then. I was going to ask about some people I used to know, but the truth is they would probably have nothing to do with me now. I'm just a governess."

"Not true. You are about to marry a title, Miss

Lloyd. I believe your acquaintances will be clamoring for attention then."

Rather than seeming pleased, she did not react at all. Joseph looked closely at her, the sudden sadness that seemed to overtake her. It was an odd reaction, he thought. She was soon to be raised socially above almost everyone in England, yet she did not seem to be reveling in her new status. He was disturbed somehow, and was about to ask her why she was so reticent.

"So, tell me, Mr. Smith," she said before he could speak. "What sort of factory do you have?"

"My factory? Oh, I manufacture dyes for textiles. It's a new science, really, creating artificial pigments. There is such a limited amount of plant-based dyes, they have become expensive and difficult to obtain."

"Interesting. So you must know a great deal about chemistry and science?"

"I do, indeed, Miss Lloyd. I'm working on some other projects as well, and we're hoping to expand, using a new process the French have devised. Hopefully, it will make beverages safe to drink."

"Really?"

Constance was fascinated by the change that came over him when he discussed his work. He was animated, excited, his words tumbled forth in a rush so swiftly that it was hard to hear each word clearly.

"Yes. You see, I've always wondered why it is that so many people become ill after drinking water that seems perfectly fine, or . . ."

"Or eating raw oysters?" She couldn't help interrupt him, and instead of becoming angry he smiled, a bright flash of very white teeth before he continued.

"Exactly! So I've been exploring the possibilities, along with developing some long-lasting dyes."

"So what do you think the answer is?"

"Well, clearly disease can be carried in many forms. But if we kill the disease in water, kill it so that it does not reappear, well, we can do the same with milk and other items. It would mean a great deal to most of the population to know that their diet was safer."

Somehow this surprised her. What he was doing was not simply making money, but actively researching and trying to solve a problem that had led to the death of thousands of people a year.

"But what if they boil the liquids?"

"Ah, that is only a short-term answer, and doesn't do at all for milk. In addition, boiling water requires fuel, and most of those who live in poverty, especially the city dwellers, may not have access at all to coal or wood or even a place in which to burn them. If they are lucky enough to have a stove or a chimney, they reserve the precious fuel for warmth. It's difficult to help these people, to stress the vital importance of simple sanitation. It's not terribly fashionable, but by going into these people's homes and showing them what science now knows, we could save hundreds of thousands of lives, mostly children's.

"And then we need a way to safely transport milk to populations far removed from the countryside. We need to take care of the children in cities—we must not ignore them any longer, turn our backs and hope the unpleasantness goes away. All of this talk of children and women working shorter hours and fewer days is fine and well, I heartily embrace and actively support these causes. But if they are too ill to walk, what difference does it make if they work eight hours or eight hundred? Their lives will be a misery, and a short one at that."

Constance needed to change the subject before his enthusiasm moved her too much. The complete passion with which he spoke was unlike anything she had ever seen before. As it was, there was something curious about him, something about his expressions and the way he moved his body and the way he spoke.

"How did you and Philip meet?"

He blinked, then took a deep breath, his voice more controlled now, the lilt not nearly as pronounced.

"Ah. At public school, and then we were at Oxford together." He was slightly distracted by her sudden change of mood.

"And where are you from originally?"

"I'm from Wales. An anonymous benefactor supplied me with the funds to attend school, so I was the contemptible charity child at school. Philip was kind enough to ask me to his home for the holidays after Michaelmas Term when I was but nine."

"He did?" She seemed pleased, and Joseph was glad that he had not elaborated further, that the invitation had been a direct order of the duke, who felt that his rather spoiled sons could learn modesty from the unfortunate orphan boy. It was a safer lesson than sending Philip around to the backstreets of London, and the headmaster had personally assured the duke that young Smith was unlikely to slit their throats as they slept.

The duke himself had told Joseph of the endorsement not long ago, over a bottle of fine claret. And although he had laughed along with the duke, some of the old sting of humiliation had returned upon hearing those words.

"Are your parents still in Wales?"

"They are, but they've been dead for over twenty-five years."

"I'm sorry."

He did not answer. "Your parents are deceased as well, are they not?"

"Yes."

"So here we are, two orphans directed by fate and chance." The innkeeper placed their drinks before them, and Joseph raised his glass. "Shall we have a toast to ourselves?"

"That's a lovely idea, Mr. Smith. But I believe etiquette dictates that we are not to drink to ourselves. Others may drink, but we, the honorees, should not."

"Well, then, let's be naughty and defy etiquette, shall we?" His thick mug of ale touched her slender glass of sherry, and she returned his smile.

"To us, then," she nodded. "Two orphans."

They both drank; his was a rather long swallow, while she simply touched the sherry to her lips. And then the innkeeper was beside them, and placed her chicken before her with great pride.

"I believe you'll enjoy this, ma'am," he said. "The best dish south of London, I've heard many a customer say."

Somewhat hesitantly, he slid a huge pot of oysters in front of Joseph. He paused, but before he could speak his wife's voice pierced the air.

"Horace!" It was at once a command and a threat, and he plopped the bread and cheese on the table before ducking away, again muttering to himself, "My wife."

"How are your oysters, sir?" Constance asked after Joseph had taken a first bite.

"Absolutely delicious." He grinned, so very satisfied that she only nodded. "Would you like some?"

"No, thank you."

"Well, Miss Lloyd, that is your loss, I'm afraid."

"Thank you for your concern, Mr. Smith, but I am quite satisfied with my own meal."

He motioned for another ale for himself, gesturing to her still-full sherry, and she shook her head.

It was a very large portion of oysters, she thought, and then tried to put the matter out of her mind.

"Here, Mr. Smith," she soothed as the carriage rolled over what felt like a large tree trunk. "I have some medicine in my reticule that is always effective for dyspepsia."

Joseph Smith, his face a peculiar shade of green, shook his head. "I am fine, Miss Lloyd," he rasped. His need to take a deep breath in the middle of the sentence somewhat weakened his proclamation.

His head was leaning heavily against the squab, and he was swallowing at an alarming rate.

"Please, at least allow me to loosen your cravat and collar." He said nothing, but held a hand in the air. Constance, not certain if the hand in the air was a yes or a no, decided to take it as a yes, and began to unknot the silk cravat at his throat.

He did not meet her gaze, and she knew all too well from her experience as a governess that he was about to be very sick indeed.

As she worked, she watched his face, extraordinarily handsome even when tinted green. The silk cravat came away easily, as did the starched collar attached to the fine linen shirt.

He took another deep breath, then closed his eyes.

"Mr. Smith, I do not recommend you close your eyes . . ."

She did not have the chance to complete the thought. At once he leapt to his feet and pounded on the roof of the coach. "Stop!"

The coachman somehow heard, and the vehicle halted just as Joseph flung himself from the carriage.

They remained there for well over ten minutes, the horses scratching the gravel road with their hooves, the coachman speaking gently, soothing the beasts. Finally Joseph Smith reentered the carriage.

"Forgive me," he said softly. A little bit of the color had returned to his face, but he still appeared rather shaky.

"Are you feeling better, Mr. Smith?"

With a tight smile that was utterly disarming because it was so very unexpected, he slipped back into his place beside her. "And whatever gave you the idea that I was ill, Miss Lloyd?"

She bit her lower lip to keep from laughing out loud. "I just assumed that was the reason for hurling yourself from the moving coach."

"It was not a hurl, Miss Lloyd. It was a calculated descent." He tapped the roof, and they began to move again.

"Well, in that case, Mr. Smith, it's a good thing we were not on the Cornwall cliffs."

He chuckled weakly. "It is indeed." He shifted several times in the leather seat in an attempt to get comfortable. Although the interior of the coach was well-appointed, the single seat was just large enough for two adults to sit upright.

Constance watched him in his efforts, again trying not to laugh aloud. "Mr. Smith, may I make a suggestion?"

He paused. "In all honesty, Miss Lloyd, this is the second suggestion you have made in our brief acquaintance. I failed to accept the first, over luncheon. Believe me, ma'am, I would be a complete imbecile not to seriously consider the second."

"Well, at the risk of sounding overly bold," she began hesitantly, then looked at his expression, one of absolute misery. "Oh, hang it all. There is not much room, and you need to be comfortable. Why don't you just rest your head upon my lap?"

She had expected an argument, and was ready to list the reasons it would not be improper, from the many layers of petticoats to the simple truth that she had been a governess. But he said nothing in protest. He smiled sheepishly. "Thank you." And he placed his head on her lap. After a few moments his eyes closed, and his breathing became deep and regular.

How peculiar, she thought, very aware of the heavy

weight of his head upon her thighs. No man had ever rested his head in her lap. Never. It felt warm, rather pleasant. And for the first time in her life, she felt protective of a grown man.

As he slept, and the thoughts swirled in her mind, she stroked his hair from his forehead. Odd, how such thick hair could still be so soft. It needed to be trimmed in the front. When they were at the inn, and he had been discussing his work, a lock of hair kept falling into his eyes, and he would toss it back into place with a jerk of his head or a flick of his hand.

Strange, how a man's hair could be so very soft.

Before long, her own eyes began to flutter shut, but even in light sleep she caressed his hair with the same soothing strokes.

"Mr. Smith," she repeated into his ear.

Joseph had been having a wonderful dream. The details were vague, but the overall feeling had been of warmth and safety and love. In reality, he could not remember feeling any of those things. Yet, as he had slept, they flooded his senses, filling him with a completeness he had never imagined possible.

There was a woman's voice, gentle and welcoming.

"Mr. Smith," the voice repeated more firmly. "Sir, I believe you had better wake up now."

Reluctantly he opened his eyes. And then he remembered he had been riding on a coach, had been ill on oysters—the very thought made his stomach roil—and he had been sleeping on Miss Lloyd's lap. He sat up slowly, still disoriented and still feeling the effects of his illness.

"Why are we stopped?"

Miss Lloyd helped him into a sitting position, and before he could repeat the question, the answer was apparent.

He was staring directly into the barrel of a pistol.

3

Joseph did not move at first.

"Are you hurt, Miss Lloyd?" His voice was steady, and his hand grazed her palm.

The man holding the pistol opened the door wider, the leather hinges creaking. "Step out now, both of ye. Mind I can see your hands."

Slowly, Joseph slid from the coach, then he reached up to assist Constance. Her face was drained of all color, and their eyes met as he eased her to the ground. Almost imperceptibly, he winked. And in return, the dimple that appeared before she smiled deepened for just a moment.

"Hurry up. You can move faster than that." The man waved the pistol.

There were two men that Joseph could count without making his assessment obvious. From the corner of his eye he saw two others working to loosen the horses from the coach yoke and tether them to their own scruffy mounts.

It was four against two, never ideal odds, but even

less desirable when one of the outnumbered party happened to be a recently retired nanny.

The coachman was slumped forward on his seat, and Joseph could only hope he was not seriously hurt, although from the rough clothing, outer filth, and demeanor of the men pulling apart Constance's trunk, they were most certainly capable of anything.

All traces of his illness were forgotten. He had only one thing on his mind now, and that was protecting Constance. Very calmly, he reached towards his coat pocket.

"Won't do you any good, gov'ner." Joseph noticed the man with the pistol seemed to have only one tooth remaining in his head, and it was yellowed and chipped. He did not answer the man.

"If that pistol looks familiar, Mr. Smith, it is because it was removed from your pocket." Constance spoke softly, although the man with the pistol seemed to take great delight in her information.

Joseph glared. It was indeed his pistol, one he had carried with him in the unlikely event they were faced with any danger on the journey.

A thump from the coach caused them to glance up. "Blast it all, Eustice! The lady has no jewels, none whatsoever!" The short man atop the coach pushed the trunk off the roof in disgust. The trunk slammed into the ground and splintered into pieces, her possessions—the new dresses and her undergarments—scattering over the grass and dirt and knotty tree roots like so much refuse. He yanked apart the carefully wrapped wedding veil, taking apparent delight with the way the fabric came apart in wispy shreds in his rough hands. A corset was the last item to tumble to the ground.

Then he saw the writing desk. He ripped open the hinges, the sound of splintering wood carrying through the air. With a single blow he kicked in the bottom of the desk, sending the last few sheets of her mother's stationery into a mud puddle. And then he broke the ink bottles, which glittered even as they shattered into pieces, and crushed the remaining quills into the same puddle with the paper.

Constance did not flinch.

The toothless pistol man joined in the laughter before he spoke. "All right. Enough of this. Hand me yer money—all of it. My fingers are getting twitchy to try out this fine piece of iron."

Constance gave him her battered reticule, which he tore open, pawing through her apothecary bottles, dumping them onto the ground where all but the corks exploded into glimmering slivers.

"I have no money," she stated.

He said nothing, but turned to Joseph, who began to reach into his coat. The man stopped him. "None of yer funny business. Let the lady search for your wallet."

Two of the other men cackled in agreement.

Constance did not react.

"I said, get his money for us. And I want you to do it now."

She took a deep breath and turned to face Joseph. His features were bland and composed, which made her feel better, as if they were not surrounded by a pack of thieves in possession of too few teeth and too many arms. The only evidence that he was experiencing any emotions at all was a vein that seemed to throb fiercely at his temple.

Gingerly, she touched his shoulder, then turned to the pistol-bearer, lifting her chin.

"Sir, this is most improper. I will not touch this man. I am engaged to another." She straightened, and Joseph tried to keep his expression blank.

But what the hell was she doing? Did she realize what these men were capable of? From the stench of the three standing nearest to them, they had been imbibing a beverage a great deal stronger than tea. And they had not been stingy in their portions.

The man with the pistol raised a straggly eyebrow. "Gentlemen! Come 'round, we're about to have a regular show here!"

The other three men gathered in a half circle surrounding the leader, all grinning. One man nudged his neighbor, then wiped his mouth on the back of his hand.

Constance remained indignant. "Please, sir, allow me to return to the coach."

"Touch him." He waved the pistol. "We want to see you find his money, and let's hope it's good and hidden."

A couple of them chuckled in anticipation.

"No," she replied calmly, as if refusing a cucumber sandwich at high tea.

"Miss Lloyd, I suggest you do as the man says, no matter how distasteful you find the chore," Joseph mumbled from between clenched teeth.

She shot him a venomous look. "Very well," she hissed without looking directly into his eyes. More chuckling and snickering escaped from the men, who were now fully entertained.

Hesitantly, she patted his shoulder again, then his upper arm.

"Lady, it ain't likely he has a money belt on his shoulder. Look further down."

Joseph saw her eyelashes lower, and for a moment he was surprised. She had seemed stronger before, less timid. Then again, she didn't have a gun pointed towards her back at the time.

Her hand touched his sides, his inner pocket where he kept his wallet, but she kept on going, not pausing to remove the billfold.

Certainly she must have felt it?

Then she patted down his leg, and one of the men whistled in appreciation. Further she went, then she stopped for just an instant.

She had felt it. The matching pistol. Again, he remained motionless, neither his stance nor his features betraying any of the questions that were racing through his mind.

Before he could decide what to do next, she rose to her feet.

"Sir, I feel faint," she whispered. Her accent, which had been mildly American before, was suddenly thickly Southern.

The men stepped forward. Joseph made a motion as if to catch her, when her arms flew out before her with swift assurance.

"Don't you move, any of you," she ordered coolly. Between her two palms was the pistol she had just removed from inside his trouser leg.

How had she done that?

"Throw the pistol to the ground." She pointed towards the leader, who paused for a moment, uncertain as to what he should do next. The weapon in his own hand pointed downward, forgotten in his surprise.

"Throw it down now," she repeated. Her voice did not waver.

He did as he was told.

"I know more of you must have weapons. Please place them on the ground next to Mr. Smith's pistol."

There was no movement. The men remained still, although the air was heavy with tension.

"I suggest you place any remaining weapons on the ground, gentlemen." Instead of weakening, her words seemed to gather strength. "Now."

Again, no one moved.

With barely a blink, she raised the pistol and fired, shooting the hat off the man who had only seconds before held her within his aim.

The men gasped, including Joseph.

How had she done that? For the second time he marveled at how she had pulled out the pistol he had hidden. And that was either the luckiest shot he'd ever seen, or the governess was an expert marksman. Joseph's mouth was open in astonishment. He raised his own hands along with the gang.

Constance cast a sideways glance. "Oh, for goodness sake, Mr. Smith. Not you."

The coachman, who had been jolted out of his stupor by the gunshot, also raised his hands in submission. His expression was one of pure fear as he watched her.

Constance gestured towards the coachman with her pistol. "You may lower your hands as well," she sighed in exasperation.

His eyes met those of the gang leader, and a silent exchange of mutual confusion passed between them before he lowered his hands.

"I believe it is safe, James," Joseph said to the perplexed coachman, whose face was one of tormented bewilderment.

On the end of the semicircle of villains was the man with the red scarf about his neck.

"Here, lady. Take it." The pistol on the ground was joined by another, then another.

"Anything else?" Her tone was calm, yet full of authority.

Clubs, chains, and some items she was unable to identify were added to the pile.

"Mr. Smith, is there anything here in this collection that appeals to you?"

As if jolted out of his bleary bafflement, Smith

quickly grabbed his other pistol from the stack, then removed three others, tucking them into his pockets and the waistband of his trousers.

His mind worked to come up with the next step, with how to proceed.

Perhaps if he felt better, if he had not eaten the damned oysters, he could think more clearly. Without warning, another wave of nausea gripped his stomach.

He couldn't let the thieves see his weakness. They would overtake them immediately, weapons or no weapons. He swallowed and kept his hand steady. That's all he had to do. All that was required of him until he could think of something else, or until another coach passed by to aid them. It was one of the better, well-traveled roads. They shouldn't have too long to wait until . . .

"Excuse me," he muttered, and ducked behind the nearest tree.

Four sets of eyes, in various stages of bloodshot fury, were now focused on Constance.

Joseph took a deep breath after becoming ill.

Hopefully Constance had been able to hold the four men at bay. Since he hadn't heard anything to lead him to believe otherwise, he assumed that all had been well. They were just beyond the tree; he could see her maroon dress.

Then he heard the other noise.

Very slowly, he stepped back behind a thick bush. To his left were two other men, even larger and less appealing than the four Constance was holding. By some miracle of foliage, they had not seen him.

"What the hell are we going to do?" the larger man asked.

The second man held his arm up for his companion to be silent.

"I don't know. But I just remembered something."

"What is that?" the first man asked.

"It's been a good long while since I've had myself a lady."

The other one gave a short bark of a laugh. Constance almost turned her head, but she did not, and the two men crouched lower.

"You grab her legs, I'll get the gun," the second man croaked.

As they formed their plan, Joseph crept behind them. They were so intent on their discussion, they did not hear the rustle of leaves.

But the coachman, his eyes widening with horror, saw the two men, with Joseph behind them.

Before the coachman could speak, Joseph grabbed a handful of the thieves' hair in each fist and slammed the two men's heads together. There was a sickening crack, and the shorter one crumpled to the ground.

The taller one, groggy from the blow, took a powerful swing at Joseph, who ducked. Using his forearm, Joseph thrust the man's neck against the thick tree trunk.

"Sorry," he muttered absent-mindedly to the motionless forms before rushing back to Constance.

Where had he run off to?

Constance straightened her back, hoping her hand would not start trembling.

The coachman made a peculiar sound, and for just a moment she wavered.

The leader of the four saw her hesitation, and a slow grin spread across his face as he stepped forward.

It came back to her then, just as it had earlier, before Mr. Smith stepped into the woods.

Cornered by the Union stragglers. They had tried to take her. They had tried to kill her, or worse, but she would not allow them the chance. It came back to her, the terror of that moment.

But she had triumphed back then, ten years before on a dusty Virginia road. She would triumph now.

"Mr. Smith," she called, her mind churning to come up with something. Nothing else mattered. Then an idea came to her, forming itself even as she spoke. "Please come back here at once."

Two of the men exchanged glances.

"Oh, dear," she sighed in feigned exasperation. This had to work. There was no other choice. She lightened her voice. "He's gone off again."

"What do you mean?" The leader asked the question in a wary tone.

"It's just that he always does this before a kill."

The words took a moment to sink in.

"A kill?" She wasn't sure who spoke, but the voice cracked just a bit.

Shaking her head, she looked at their faces one by one. "I am so very sorry," she whispered sympathetically.

"What do you mean by 'a kill'?" Someone from the end asked the question, and two others nodded.

"He's not quite right in the head," she confided. "Every once in a while, well, he goes off. The doctor in Switzerland called them 'episodes,' although after he witnessed the carnage—well. He is now a patient in the very same sanitarium, poor man. We can't do anything about it, nothing at all. They say it's because Mr. Smith was bitten by a rabid tiger in Bengal. It always happens the same way—first, the illness returns. He becomes sick in the stomach, then sick in the head, if you understand my meaning."

The silence lasted a few moments, punctuated by the sound of Joseph becoming ill just beyond the trees. "Lady, we don't believe you." The leader stepped forward. The men were restless; clearly they would make a move. "If he's so dangerous, why were you with him?"

Constance did not miss a beat. "I am his nurse. There would be some hope that I could control him, but you, sir, destroyed his medication. Do you not recall the bottles in my reticule? The ones you smashed?"

The leader cast an anxious glance to his left and right. The men were glaring at him now. He looked at the coachman.

"Is he crazy?"

The coachman, who seemed every bit as frightened as the others, bit his lower lip. "I don't rightly know," he replied nervously. "Only hired me for the day, you see. But he did appear a mite angered by the journey. Tense, I would say. And for a while he was riding with a big man in a kilt and sporran, a giant from the Highlands of Scotland, it seemed. The giant left just before we got her. He was all riled up by the time we was to pick up the lady."

"Oh, the man with a kilt. Yes." Constance had no idea what the coachman was talking about, but played along. "That was another of his keepers, you see. A big tall man?" The coachman nodded in agreement, "He's the only one who can control him. He left when I took over; he needs a rest, and with the medication I can usually sedate Mr. Smith. But without it, well."

The leader swallowed.

"What will happen next?" The voice with the distinct crack was almost a plea now.

"His episodes are always the same," she replied in a matter-of-fact way. "He will emerge in a moment, claiming not to have been ill. That is when he is at his most dangerous, when he denies anything is wrong. That's when he's most likely to spring."

"To spring?"

"Like a tiger. It seems his physical composition was forever altered by the tiger-bite. He actually becomes part animal, with the strength of a dozen men. It's a fearful sight."

The coachman made an odd sound, and pointed just beyond Constance, his face ashen. The four men glanced at the coachman, and Constance—uncertain of what had caused the coachman to react as he did—repeated, with meaning, "Oh, the poor man's seen Mr. Smith in a temper. It's a fearful sight, indeed."

Just as she shuddered, Joseph emerged from behind the tree trunk, walking with forced assurance. They all noted the blood on his shirt.

"Are you feeling better?" she asked him without taking her eyes from the men.

"What do you mean?" He barked the answer. What the hell was she doing? All but telling the thieves he was as likely to be ill on their shoes as he was to shoot them? Why didn't she just tell them all about the blasted oysters? "I am fine, Miss Lloyd. I've never felt better. I just took care of two others beyond the hedges."

She noted the red stains on his shirt, grateful that he had managed to disable the two additional men.

Another thought came into her mind. She was not alone. For once she was facing a crisis with someone else.

With a deep breath she returned her full attention to the other men. Again she shook her head slightly. "Two more men, and still not satisfied? Very well, sir. I don't know if I can bear to watch this time."

"Please, let us go!"

"Lady, we'll run now! Please, for pity's sake . . ."

Constance turned to Joseph. "I can't bear it anymore, sir! Let these men run free, and feed upon my flesh if you must!"

She aimed the pistol towards him.

"What the bloody hell are you doing?" he roared.

Before he could ask anything else, all four of the thieves had taken off into the woods. And after just the slightest hesitation, the coachman followed the thieves, glancing back with wild eyes as he stumbled.

"Miss Lloyd, I demand to know what—"

"Please, Mr. Smith. One moment." She then threw back her head and emitted the most bloodcurdling shriek he had ever heard, ever thought possible. Pausing once, she smiled politely at him, and produced another banshee shriek, the second, if possible, far worse than the first.

By now he was unable to speak. Turning towards where the men had stood but a moment earlier, he heard the distant cries of very frightened men, growing more frightened and ever more distant by the moment.

"I think we'd better get moving, Mr. Smith." Then she saw the red stains on his shirt and paused. "Mr. Smith, were you injured?"

Following her gaze, he glanced down at his clothing. "Oh," he remarked. Holding up his knuckles, he saw they were scraped raw from the fight with the second man in the woods. "No. Not really."

"Mr. Smith," she replied, then, with her voice lowered and her eyes averted, "Thank you."

A strange silence stretched between them, yet it was not really a silence at all. There was communication, pure and wordless and so powerful she took a small step backwards, as if that would lessen the tension of the moment. It did not.

"You're welcome," he said.

"Well," She straightened, her tone crisp and businesslike.

He smiled slowly as she stepped towards the pile of weapons, examining them for a moment. "Interesting. I did not realize chains were still popular amongst cutthroats."

"Miss Lloyd . . ."

"I do hope you did not pay the coachman in advance. He did not earn a full day's wages, and seems to be something of a coward."

"Miss Lloyd, please tell me what has just happened."

The blush crept from her chest to her neck, scorching its traitorous path, revealing emotions she herself had not yet dared to examine. How could he know?

"I mean, Miss Lloyd, why did they run?"

Glancing down at the hem of her skirt, she brushed off a clump of dirt before answering.

How could a single moment be meshed with such relief and stinging disappointment? "I told them you were a crazed murderer, sir. I do hope you don't mind. All four of the gentlemen believe they have just escaped death by the narrowest of margins, and that you are at present devouring me. Unfortunately, the coachman seemed to feel more comfortable with such unsavory company than with us."

The disbelief on his face became a grin. Constance was about to look away, but his countenance was so completely transformed by his expression that she was unable to stop staring. His mouth, which she had noticed before as remarkably appealing, became even more so when she could see his teeth.

Her breath caught as she realized what an extraordinarily handsome man he was. Not in a conventional sense, of course. Not in the elegant, polished way Philip was handsome. Instead, there was a blunt strength to Mr. Smith that made him quite splendid, the way a magnificent animal is splendid. It wasn't his clothing she noticed, or his hair. With Philip she always noticed how well-groomed he was. With Mr.

Smith, there was a natural, incidental grace that could never be combed or cut from a pattern.

She swallowed, looking at his eyes. They were very brown, even in the afternoon light. And the rest of his face—the squarely defined chin, the cheekbones that seemed more prominent when he smiled, the light scar there, the way his hair swept back from his forehead . . .

"You are brilliant, Miss Lloyd. Wait until I tell Philip."

As if splashed with cold water, she came out of her reverie with a jolt. "No! Please, I beg of you, don't tell him about this!"

"Why on earth not?"

"Because . . . well." Why didn't she want Philip to know? Then she realized the reason, and lowered her voice. "Because it was not very ladylike. The last thing I wish to do is attract undue attention. Please."

The smile fell from Joseph's face. "Whether or not it was ladylike I don't suppose I could say, but I'd rather be alive than pay strict adherence to protocol."

"Please don't tell Philip."

Before he answered he looked closely at her, the furious blush that seemed to spread across her features, and he realized she was ashamed. He would not add to her discomfort, although the realization that she felt her quick thinking was in any way something to be embarrassed about bothered him more than a little. Finally, all traces of his smile gone, he replied, "As you wish."

For a few moments they simply stood in silence. She waited a few moments before speaking. "What should we do now, Mr. Smith? I wonder how far the next town is?"

Up close, she realized that Mr. Smith had freckles. You could only see them by looking very carefully, but they were there nonetheless. The discovery that he had freckles surprised her—such a boyish trait on such a very masculine face.

"I'm afraid I do not know, Miss Lloyd. I have never been on this road."

"Your hand needs tending," she said softly.

He swallowed, peering down into her face. Her eyes were exquisite, he thought. They were clear and blue and completely without guile, and he realized with a start that he trusted her.

As far as he could remember, he had never trusted a woman before. Until now.

She stepped back, and stumbled on her skirt. Without hesitation, he reached out and steadied her, both hands circling her waist.

Clearing his throat, he took a deep breath and allowed his hands to drop from her waist. The moment his hands were free of the warmth of her body, he wanted to touch her again, to feel her.

No. She was Hastings's fiancée. Although he trusted her, it was himself he did not entirely trust. When he spoke, his voice was slightly strained. "I suppose we could wait here. Another coach should be by soon."

"They may return, though," she said calmly. "I believe they will get safely away, and realize they have been duped. I don't think it will set particularly well with any of them."

"I believe you're right, Miss Lloyd." His voice was sounding stronger, and when he stepped away, he felt stronger still. "The spirit of sportsmanship does not seem to be a big issue with those men."

Joseph glanced over at the trunk and her clothing scattered on the ground.

"I am sorry about your trunk and the lap desk, Miss Lloyd," he said, nodding towards the splintered wood and muddied dresses and petticoats.

She looked at the mess, the shreds of her life now

gathered in the mud, the old and the new both destroyed.

He stepped over to the pile of clothing, ripped books, broken shoes. Leaning down, he gingerly picked up a slashed blue skirt, then lowered it back to the ground. "I'm sorry."

The clothes did not bother her. It was the desk, her mother's desk. How she had cared for it, polishing it with wax, making sure the papers—precious papers her mother had once touched—remained intact. In one single instant, the years of caring and holding the desk had been destroyed.

It was just a thing, she tried to remind herself. "I really don't care," she said softly.

"Excuse me?" Joseph stepped towards her, then halted.

"I said, I really don't care." The words failed to convince her. "I have to say that, you see."

"Why is that?"

"Because if I do tell you how very much I care, it still won't change a thing. Oh, not about the clothes, although I confess they were more than nice. It's that one can't invest too much emotion in a thing. It's a mistake, because things can break or get stolen."

"A heart's a thing, I suppose," Joseph mused, watching her face.

"Well, yes. I suppose it is. But the desk, my mother's desk, well." She stared at the wood, not seeing, just staring, recalling one last image of her mother, one last memory to go with the broken wood.

"You'll always have her memory with you," he said. "Your mother is not in that desk, she is in you, a part of you."

A frown creased her brow, and she looked at Joseph as if seeing him for the first time. He continued.

"We have both suffered misfortunes in the past. This is but another." He gestured towards the trunk and the useless coach. "I believe we both are due for a patch of splendid good fortune, don't you?"

"Yes," she stammered. "Of course, but . . ."

"But what?"

"Nothing."

"Very well. I believe we should leave this place as swiftly as possible. We have no other choice, Miss Lloyd. As you yourself mentioned, they may soon return. Now, are your shoes suitably comfortable for a brisk walk?"

"Yes, I suppose so."

"Very well. Shall we proceed on to the next town?"

"The weapons," she offered, pointing to the pile of abandoned chains and knives.

"Of course. We can't possibly carry all of them. Perhaps we should bury them, in case the thieves return?"

He waited for her nod, and together they found a pile of leaves and hastily covered them up.

"That will have to do for now," he said, taking her arm. "Is there anything you might wish to take with you from the trunk?"

Constance thought for a moment. She almost reached for a piece of her mother's paper, but withdrew her hand. He was about to speak when she straightened. "Perhaps I should take a warm wrap."

"I don't believe there will be any need." He smiled, wishing to touch her, to comfort her somehow, but unable to find the words. "The day seemed to be getting only warmer, and we are sure to be settled at an inn by nightfall. Thanks to you, the thieves did not make off with any of my money."

"Still, I think a cloak would be helpful should it become chilly . . ."

"Miss Lloyd, please trust me on this. Carrying a heavy cloak will be cumbersome at best. I wager we will find a town within an hour, and then we'll have someone come back and fetch all of these belongings."

"How much are you willing to wager?"

"Excuse me?"

"You said you are willing to wager. I have agreed to take you up on that wager. How about five pounds, Mr. Smith?"

He laughed, running a hand through his hair. "Very well. Five pounds it is, Miss Lloyd. Shall we?"

And he crooked his arm, which she accepted. With one last glance at the coach, the two started down the unknown road, hoping the next town was but a short distance away.

4

The first clap of thunder was only mildly surprising to Constance and Joseph. Perhaps it would have been more of a jolt had the gale-force winds and pelting rain not already blown them off the road and drenched them with ice water.

With the ominous rumble, Joseph was quick to remove his light overcoat and place it over her shoulders. But as the intensity of the rain grew, it was apparent that the overcoat was little more than an additional soggy layer of clothing, and that further travel was impossible.

Her hair was hanging in thick, black ropes down her back, all pins long since gone, her carefully placed hat abandoned when the rim became a catch basin for rain, depositing it in trickles onto her shoulders. The new traveling suit, once maroon, was now losing its color, the dye washing away with the rain. Even darkened by the wet, it was clear the garment was fading.

He squinted against the rain, glancing at her as they

trudged through the mud. Slowly he reached up, about to brush a droplet from her cheek, and he halted before she could see what he intended.

But she had seen the gesture, and turned towards him. A small line appeared between her eyes, silently questioning him. There was no rebuke or censure in her expression, only curiosity.

"Your dress is losing its color," he shouted over the din of the storm, uncertain of what else to say.

Blinking, she looked down and smiled. "I suppose it is," she responded.

"I am developing a synthetic dye made from chemicals that won't wash away." The moment he spoke those words, he felt like a complete idiot. They had just been robbed at gunpoint, now they were hopelessly lost on a remote road during one of England's rare thunderstorms. And he was discussing synthetic dyes.

Mentally, he not only kicked himself but bound his mouth to prevent any further stupidity.

"Really?" Her voice was loud enough for him to hear, but not shrill. He hated shrill, high-pitched voices on females, but hers remained mellow and rich, even as she raised her voice. "I do wish you would hurry up," she laughed, shaking the hem. "I'm afraid this one could use your help."

Around the slight bend in the road was a small building, and he gestured towards it. Together they ran as quickly as possible, heads ducking against the rain.

The building was abandoned, but from the broken sign swinging in the wind, it had clearly served as a tavern. There was a musty, damp odor, and a vaguely pungent scent of something very old and unseen and rotting. Great holes in the roof allowed the rain to enter almost without any barrier, although a corner of the room seemed relatively dry.

In spite of the gaping roof, the place was dark, as if night had already fallen.

"Over here, Miss Lloyd." He stumbled into a broken chair as he spoke.

"This is rather odd, isn't it?" Constance murmured, joining Joseph. "Here is a building right on the side of the road, with no other stop nearby, and it is completely abandoned."

He shrugged, rubbing his shin from the table he had just knocked into. "Not really. Ever since the coming of the railroads, the roads are all but empty. They are in utter disrepair, as you can see."

"I still don't understand why we aren't making this journey by train instead of coach."

He gave a sigh of resignation. "Your fiancé's mother feels the railroads are unnatural and possibly sinful. I'm not sure what exactly she objects to, the cars themselves, the rails, or the speed."

"I suppose she didn't want anyone to accuse her future daughter-in-law of being fast." She smiled.

Joseph laughed. "I'm sure it comes down to something very much along those lines. Here, I believe I've found a comfortable corner, or at least not as uncomfortable as the rest of the place."

He took her hand to guide her to the area he had cleared.

"It just seems odd that the duchess had you fetch me. If she is so concerned with propriety and decorum, she could have simply sent a ladies' maid."

"I thought that myself." They settled together on the floor. "Perhaps she wanted to get you to Hastings House as quickly as possible, and she knows that I have business and thus cannot be delayed."

"Oh, I am sorry, Mr. Smith. I haven't apologized for what an inconvenience this has been for you."

"I shouldn't have said that." His voice was so soft

she could barely hear it. "I apologize, Miss Lloyd. Again, I have proven myself to be a buffoon."

"Of course you aren't!" Her tone was so emphatic he jumped, and she controlled her urge to laugh at his reaction before continuing. "No, Mr. Smith, you are not at all a buffoon. I believe someone must have once told you that you were, and unfortunately you believed that person. Well, whoever they were, they were most certainly wrong."

He said nothing, and she examined her skirt. "Perhaps this will start a new fashion rage—the seeping gown. Tell me, Mr. Smith, when will your new synthetic dyes be available?"

"Soon, I hope."

"How on earth did you get into the dye business?"

"Well, I was always rather keen on chemistry. I read theology at university, but always experimented in my rooms." As he spoke, his energy seemed to return. "You see, on the Continent they are doing amazing things in science. In Germany and France, even in your country, universities are turning out men of science who are making life better for everyone, not just the privileged few."

In the dim light he saw her nod. "So I gather you were to become a cleric rather than a manufacturer?"

"Yes. And many were disappointed that I did not simply find an isolated parish, preferably in a remote part of Wales, and reform the countryside. I knew all along that was not the path I would follow, but played the part of the grateful student until my education was completed. At times I feel that was dishonest."

"Not at all." She paused before continuing. "We do what we must to survive, Mr. Smith. This is not an easy world in which we live. And there can be little argument that you are presently doing far more good by employing so many people, and creating such useful items, than you would by preaching to a church full of people who have no desire to change. No, Mr. Smith. What you are doing now is very good for everyone."

He leaned against the rough wall. What had Abigail said of his interest in science? Middle-class. That was it. She had laughed at first, telling him that it was hopelessly middle-class to dabble in science. He still recalled her hair, the way it caught the light. He had once called it spun gold. Not very original, but that is exactly what it had seemed to him.

It had been so very swift, the change in Abigail. Looking back he had seen indications, hints of what was to come. She stopped finding his interest in science amusing.

"Father says science is middle-class," she had repeated. "He says if one must enjoy music, hire someone to play the fiddle, do not do it yourself. To play music with one's own hands debases the entire aristocracy."

"Ah," Joseph recalled replying. "But I am not a member of the aristocracy, not even of the middle class, so I should be allowed to play the fiddle."

Abigail had been horrified. "You play the fiddle?"

When he had confessed that once he did, indeed, play the fiddle, she had recoiled. Not just that day, but forever.

Abigail, Lady Merrymeade now. He had not seen her since . . .

"Excuse me, Mr. Smith."

Constance had been speaking to him. He hadn't heard a word, not a single word.

"Forgive me, Miss Lloyd. My thoughts were elsewhere, and I did not hear what you were saying."

"If your thoughts were elsewhere, I do hope they were warm and dry." Even in the darkness he heard the smile in her voice. "I was just wondering what sort of family are the Hastings?"

"Philip's family?"

"Why, yes. I've only met Philip, but have heard a few strange rumors about his father. Please don't repeat what I just said, it's just that, well . . ."

"I will tell you this, Miss Lloyd: the Duke of Ballsbridge has shown me nothing but kindness since I was a boy. He has warmth and humor, and loves his family very much."

"Is he at all eccentric?"

"No, not to me nor to anyone who really knows and understands him. He has a rather sensible aversion to society, and the means with which to avoid it altogether. And to keep society at bay, he has used his reputation of eccentricity. I believe he gets a great deal of enjoyment out of pretending to be slightly mad. He is all ease and kindness once he feels comfortable with someone."

"And what of the duchess?"

Joseph was silent for a few moments, trying to decide what to say. Should he tell her that her future mother-in-law cared for nothing but climbing the social ladder? That to her appearances were everything, and that, in fact, he had been rather surprised that she had allowed Philip to become betrothed to a penniless governess until he found out that Philip had already been made a laughingstock by proposing to every available female in the country, and one or two in India?

"Mr. Smith, your silence speaks volumes."

"No, not at all." He was too quick to deny, he realized. "No. You see, the duchess was not born to such an elevated rank. I believe that when she met the duke there was little likelihood of his bearing the title. It wasn't until relatively late that the duke's father and two older brothers perished, and the title was passed to the most unlikely third son."

"But that makes her acceptance of me all the more extraordinary," she puzzled. "She is very much aware that Philip could become duke. And if she wasn't born a peer . . . well, again that makes it all the more extraordinary."

"How do you mean?"

"It is simply that those who have not always been so privileged tend to cling more tightly to the rules."

"You are more than astute, Miss Lloyd."

Although he smiled as he spoke, Constance felt an odd pang at his words, a deep sadness. He had been hurt in life, and whether he realized the depth of his pain or not, she most certainly recognized his ache. She knew him, she realized. Perhaps not the details of his life, the names and events that led him to where he was now. But still she knew him, intimately, and she felt she would always know him.

They were both outsiders, not fitting into any one world. She had been born to privilege and was now little more than a glorified servant. He had started life in humble circumstances, and had elevated himself through sheer work and ability. As a result, they could move comfortably in no single realm, always aware of where they had once been.

Suddenly it was hard for her to breathe; her corset was too tight. Probably because of the damp and the rain the fabric was shrinking. That was it.

"Miss Lloyd?"

It was ridiculous, really. She felt like a small child caught doing something she very well knew was naughty. But every breath was painful and ragged, and she very much feared she would cry if she did not gather her emotions at once. It would just not do to weep in front of a perfect stranger.

"Miss Lloyd? Constance? Are you ill?"

She shook her head. "I just," she began, and then halted.

Before she could attempt another sentence, his arms were about her, pulling her close. He was so very warm, so very comfortable. He felt so very right. She should, of course, stiffen, and tell him politely but firmly that his actions were most incorrect.

When was the last time she had been soothed? She could not recall. Perhaps not since she was a child herself, a very small child.

Instead of reminding him of their proper places, she relaxed against his shoulder. It was a strong shoulder; somehow she wasn't surprised.

"Shush," he whispered, stroking her hair. "You have had a miserable day. Just relax. There." She settled further against his body, and his knuckles brushed against her cheeks, now dampened by tears.

She felt safe and protected, and her eyes began to close.

He began to speak, but she could not understand the words, hear the soothing cadences of his rich voice. He wasn't speaking English, she realized in her drowsy solace. It was Welsh, and from the rhythm he seemed to be speaking poetry, long-ago learned words from his past.

It didn't matter that she didn't understand his words. She understood the meaning exquisitely.

His hold on her tightened as one of her hands, curled into a fist, opened slowly against his chest. And they both fell into a sound slumber.

Now quite awake, Constance stirred, stretching her arms and opening her eyes. Yet could see nothing. Had she gone blind? Never had she been enveloped in such utter, consuming black. Her eyes were wide open, yet nothing was there.

"Constance." The man's arms clamped her. She

was unable to move. Those men with the pistols. The thief with the red scarf.

"Constance!" The voice was firm. "It is me, Joseph." With an explosive sigh, he grasped her hand. "Joseph. Mr. Smith. We are at the inn, the one without the roof. Please don't try to move around—there is no moon, and it's pitch dark. Please—you can hurt yourself if you're not careful . . ."

Then it all came back to her, and in the blackness she felt her face flush with hot embarrassment.

"Oh." Her own voice seemed exceedingly small. "Mr. Smith."

"Yes, Miss Lloyd," he said with resignation. "Do you think that perhaps, since we are very much alone, you could address me as Joseph?"

"Where are you?"

"Right over here . . . ouch! That was my eye."

"Forgive me, I'm just a bit disoriented."

"Perhaps if you . . . my hand, Miss Lloyd. The heel of your boot is on my hand." His voice was strained.

"Sorry."

"As I was saying, perhaps if you simply remain still, you will get your bearings."

"Is there a lantern?"

"Not that I can recall. And in any case, should there be a hundred lanterns, I don't believe it would make any difference. Everything at this inn, including us, is either wet, soaking wet, or in liquid form. Nothing will light."

"I see." She settled beside him once again, grateful for the warmth of his body. "Do you recall the name of this place?"

"I believe the sign said 'The Drainpipe Inn.'"

"No, I'm afraid you're mistaken. It's 'The Watering Hole.' I've heard so very much about this place."

He chuckled. "The drinks flow like water."

She rubbed her arms, and he felt her motion in the dark.

"Are you chilled?"

"Just a bit, Mr. Smith."

"Joseph."

"Joseph, then." His first name gave her an entirely different feeling from saying his last. Joseph. It was a soft, friendly name. The name of a gentle man, someone she could always trust.

"Bloody hell, it's cold," he mumbled to himself.

Then she felt him slump against her shoulder, then his shoulders move as he laughed. "What a dashing hero you have as an escort, shivering in the cold."

"As long as you don't swoon, I'll be content," she replied.

His arm again encircled her, but this time she did not give even a fleeting thought to how she should respond. Instead she settled against him as if she had done so a hundred times, and would do so for a thousand more.

"The least I can do is try to keep you warm. Hopefully I can manage that," he murmured against her hair.

She did not reply. But in a corner of her mind, she wondered what it would be like to go to sleep like this every night, for the rest of her life. And that thought made her smile just a little.

His hand smoothed over her arm, the warmth spreading throughout her entire body with the gentle motion.

"Is that better?" His voice was ragged.

She intended to reply yes, that she was much warmer now, that he needn't bother with her comfort anymore. But instead, all she said was "Mmmmm."

He chuckled, a light laugh deep in his throat, and she moved closer, her hand snaking against the muscles in his arms and shoulders. Then he stopped laughing.

They both seemed to hold their breath, each waiting for what would come next.

"You should go back to sleep," he said at last. And she nodded, knowing that was the very best thing they could do.

Anything else was absolutely unthinkable.

As she closed her eyes, she tried to keep her wayward thoughts from drifting back to the absolutely unthinkable.

"Hallo! Is anyone there?"

Brilliant sunlight slanted into the musty room from the openings in the roof, and bits of dust and dirt swirled through the air. Night had ended, and neither Joseph nor Constance had noticed. They had been awake for some time, but each still pretended to be asleep. The intimate encounter from the night before had left them both feeling shy and uncomfortable.

"Try over here, Mike," another voice joined the commotion, the sounds of boots crunching on damp twigs and debris, of hasty hands pulling back the inn's rotting boards.

Constance opened her eyes and looked up at Joseph, to see his eyes staring intently into hers.

And then he smiled.

Perplexed, she watched him brush off his trousers as he reached over to her and gently swept a twig from her hair.

The sound of the men pulled her back to reality, and she realized something else: The thieves had found them.

Very slowly, his arm tightened about her shoulder, as if that act could somehow protect her. There was nowhere to go, no place to hide.

"They might be over here." The voices were growing closer.

Joseph shifted, and for a moment she thought he would rise to his feet. Then she saw his free hand slide within the folds of his coat, and the flashing glint of one of his pistols. Wordlessly, he leaned toward her, his own brows lifting in a question. She nodded, understanding his meaning, and he placed the pistol into her hand before reaching back into his garment for the other weapon.

"He might be back there, Mike."

The sounds of more boot-crunching, a few garbled curses as the men approached, seemed to suspend in the air with crackling foreboding.

Both Joseph and Constance cocked the pistols, his arm slipping away from her shoulders, leaving the chill of the damp air noticeable even as she steadied her right hand.

"Naw. I don't believe Mr. Smith and Miss Lloyd are back any further. They would have made themselves known to us by now." The man's voice seemed to be retreating.

Constance glanced up at Joseph, and he returned the gaze, a frown on his features that mirrored her own.

"Did Brown have any other ideas where they might be?"

Before the other man could respond, Joseph stood up. "Gentlemen?"

The men entered the back portion of the inn with startling swiftness. At once Constance realized these were not the thieves. Both men were well-dressed, in what appeared to be hunting tweeds and high boots, with shotguns at their sides.

"Mr. Smith, there you are! You gave us quite a start, you did."

Joseph tucked his pistol back into his coat as he lifted Constance to her feet. The first man reached out and shook Joseph's hand vigorously, then tipped his cap with a large thumb towards Constance. His face was very round, with bristly sideburns and a broad smile, his small eyes glimmering from beneath bushy eyebrows.

"Mr. Crimmins, Mr. Walker." Joseph nodded towards the other man. "This is Miss Lloyd. I was accompanying her to her fiancé's estate when we were set upon by thieves."

"Yes, yes, we know. They were caught by the local constabulary, and were most grateful for the safety. Only the hired coachman was able to shed any sensible light on the subject. The other men blithered like children. One even kissed the floor of the jail cell when we realized who they were. They found the other two by a tree with—"

"Thank you, gentlemen." Joseph cut off the man in midsentence.

The man nodded once in understanding before he continued. "You were lucky, Mr. Smith. Apparently the team that had you has been responsible for a half-dozen other robberies, and more than one death."

Both men eyed Constance warily, and the other finally spoke.

"Mr. Smith, we have here a missive for you from Mr. Brown. Urgent, he says it is, and requires your assistance immediately."

Mr. Walker, the older of the two, with a great quantity of white hair and a nose covered with tiny red veins, passed a thick yellow envelope to Joseph. He opened the red wax seal, and began to read. As he did so, Crimmins and Walker smiled uneasily at Constance.

Finally Joseph was finished reading. "Miss Lloyd,"

he said, his tone suddenly formal. "These two gentlemen will escort you to a nearby inn, one with a roof, I might add. There you will find the contents of your trunk. You can rest there in dry comfort, and tomorrow morning Mr. Walker and Mr. Crimmins will take you on to Hastings House."

Stunned, she looked at all three men. "What do you mean? Where are you going?"

His voice softened, as did his expression. "Forgive me, Miss Lloyd. I have business to attend to in Scotland."

"Scotland!" That was hundreds of miles away. A different country, a different world.

"Scotland," he confirmed. "A coach is presently waiting to take me to the nearest train station."

"Oh." She couldn't think of anything else to say. "Oh, I see."

"Yes." Joseph stared at her, his eyes unwavering. "Miss Lloyd, I wish you the safest of journeys, and I daresay I will see you next on your wedding day."

"Oh. Yes." The room seemed to be spinning; everything was happening so quickly, she couldn't even identify her own emotions in the urgent rush.

"We'd best get on, Miss Lloyd," stated Crimmins. Walker nodded in agreement.

Joseph began to walk away, his broad back retreating. She had one startling thought: that she would never see him again. And when she did, it wouldn't matter. She would be married.

"Mr. Smith!"

He halted and turned, his expression now unreadable. In two steps she was at his side. She put her hand out slowly, between the two of them. They both stared at her hand.

"Thank you for everything," she whispered.

For a moment he did nothing. Then his hand

reached for hers, not as a simple greeting, but as something more, much more. His fingers enfolded her entire hand, covering them in warmth, holding her in his fierce grip. And after a brief, few seconds—too brief, far too brief—he let go.

Without another word, without another glance, he left.

"Well, Miss Lloyd." Mr. Crimmins clapped his hands once as if to gain her attention. Slowly, numbly, she turned towards him. "Shall we get you a nice, hot cup of tea?"

Later, she tried to recall if she nodded, or thanked the gentleman, or responded at all. In truth, she could never remember quite how she got from the cold, roofless shamble of a ruin to the comfort and down coverlet and hot tea of the next inn.

As she tucked the blankets under her chin that night, she could not help but think of the night before, when she had slept in the arms of a wonderful man.

There was not a single cloud in the sky on the afternoon the coach rolled up the gravel driveway to Hastings House.

So many impressions gathered in her mind, of the beautifully tended grounds, of the immense tracts of trimmed lawn, of a pierced-iron gazebo that glistened in the sun like a sparkling jewel.

Above all, she was impressed with the man in the tree.

She saw him just before her first glimpse of the actual house. He was an elderly man, impeccably dressed in what appeared to be a Napoleonic uniform of blue and black. He was quite alone on a single, bare branch, as if he had spent so much time in the tree that no leaves bothered to spring up on that particular branch.

There was no ladder in sight, and she couldn't

imagine how on earth he had managed to hoist himself twenty feet above the gravel path.

Constance leaned out of the window, craning her neck to get a better view of the gentleman. As they passed beneath him, he waved somberly. She returned the wave, and caught the shadow of a smile flickering across his lips.

She turned to Mr. Crimmins and Mr. Walker, who were sitting on the opposite seats of the large coach.

"There was a man in that tree!"

The two men exchanged puzzled glances with each other, as they had done all too frequently during the journey, and then went back to reading their newspapers and gazettes.

"The man was wearing a uniform!"

At that additional bit of information, only Mr. Crimmins peered over the top of his paper, then returned to his reading.

They had spoken few words to her, and seemed to be almost frightened of whatever she had to say. It was a most perplexing situation, one she was glad was nearly over.

For, in spite of her anticipation at being reunited with Philip, she could not keep her thoughts from returning, and dwelling, on Joseph Smith. The more she thought of it, the more she was sure that Joseph had simply been trying to keep her warm. Surely she had imagined that anything else had happened.

As she gazed out of the window, seeing nothing of the passing scenery, she was almost convinced that Mr. Crimmins and Mr. Walker knew the exact nature of her thoughts. For had they not arrived when they did, Constance would have all but begged Joseph for a kiss. Her face flushed, and she saw the two men out of the corner of her eye, impassive but observing her every move.

She had been unable to get the barest of information from the men, from how they knew Joseph Smith to who they were. Only one detail seemed to have slipped from the mouth of the less-cautious Mr. Walker.

"So we will be back then in time for the Gillie's Ball?"

Crimmins had then cast his friend such a murderous glare nothing further was said. She longed to ask, "Who are the Gillies? Are they acquaintances of Philip's?" But she did not.

The coach rolled on, and Constance was again struck by the beauty of the lands at Hastings House. And then she saw the house itself.

It wasn't a house. It was a colossal mansion, larger than any single structure she had ever seen, larger than the most sprawling plantation in Virginia. It didn't seem possible that so much marble and glass could exist in the world, much less that it was all used in the creation of Hastings House.

The setting sun bathed the mansion in a warm amber glow, as if the house itself was a living creature. Reflected from the scores of large windows was a gentle pond just behind the house, for they were apparently entering the home from the rear.

Constance could barely breathe. This was where Philip was raised, where he had spent his childhood years, where he had grown to be a man? The very notion of living within those austere walls was alien, and even more distant was the idea of thinking of it as home.

"Well, Miss?" Mr. Walker winked at Constance. "Think you can make yourself comfortable here?"

"I . . . I don't know."

It was more than overwhelming. It was positively terrifying.

The coach followed a circular path around to the

front. She was relieved they had entered from the rear, for the front was so ornate and overwrought that she had a peculiar notion that she would be entering the side of an elaborate wedding cake. Every inch of the facade was either scrolled or carved or embellished with marble busts of humorless men with unfortunate haircuts.

And then they stopped. After so many hours of being rocked back and forth in the coach, sitting across from the ever-silent Crimmins and Walker, at last she was to meet her new family.

Taking a deep breath, she straightened her shoulders and smoothed her palm over her hair. She wasn't clothed as she had hoped to be, not after the trunk and its contents had been thrown about on the ground. The only dress that had remained almost miraculously intact was the hateful gray governess attire, drab enough to allow the wearer to sink into the woodwork on virtually any occasion. Even the laurel at her throat, and the addition of new gloves, did nothing to brighten the overall impression of general gloom.

"I can't do anything about it now," she muttered to herself.

An enormous triple-width front door opened, its frame embellished with frolicking wood nymphs. And from the door emerged an older woman, her carriage erect, her shoulders set with regal confidence.

Her new mother-in-law. This was Philip's mother.

As the woman descended the small marble steps, Crimmins and Walker helped her from the carriage.

The closer the duchess got, the more Constance felt her confidence grow. There was an unmistakable softness to her face, a gentle smile of welcome growing as their eyes met. She was not a handsome woman, yet her expression made her lovely.

Constance swallowed. This woman would be her new mother. This woman would guide her, introduce her to the delicate balance of the aristocratic world.

This kindly woman would be her mentor.

"Miss Lloyd?" Her voice was as regal as her bearing, all confidence and elegance and . . . "I'm the housekeeper, Mrs. Garrity."

Before Constance could sink into the deep curtsy she had been practicing, she stopped.

The housekeeper?

Her expression must have betrayed her confusion. "The duchess has a headache, and is resting at present. However, she instructed me to get you settled into your quarters, and she will join you for tea."

Two young men skipped down the stairs, and the housekeeper glanced about for the luggage. At that the coachman lowered her trunk, now tied with rope to keep it together, a frilly undergarment poking from the sides. The young stewards looked at each other, then removed the trunk. One of them seemed to be on the verge of laughter.

"Oh, thank you," she uttered, baffled and ill at ease.

"Well, this is farewell, then," said Crimmins. Walker smiled and nodded.

"Oh, yes." They shook hands, and Constance very much wanted to ask them in for tea, to do something. But that wasn't her place. "Thank you so very much for escorting me," she added lamely.

"Not to worry." Mr. Walker shoved one of his hands into his trousers. "It was all Brown's doing, on behalf of Mr. Smith. Mr. Brown thinks the world of Mr. Smith, isn't that so?"

Walker turned to Crimmins, whose face had gone blotchy with obvious fury.

Walker flushed and looked down, scratching a line in the gravel with the toe of his boot, and Crimmins gave Constance one last nod.

"Good luck, Miss Lloyd."

The two men clambered back into the coach, and within moments they were gone. She never did know who exactly they were, where they came from, and who the mysterious Mr. Brown was.

That didn't really matter. As she followed Mrs. Garrity up the front steps, she took a deep breath and prepared herself to meet the duchess.

Her room was surprisingly simple.

It was a relief when Mrs. Garrity walked past the sumptuous, overwrought suites and led her to a third-floor room with no gold-flocking or marble tables in sight. Instead, her room consisted of a single bed, two chests of drawers, a small washstand, and a writing desk. There was one window covered with drapes of blue damask.

"Tea is served at four-thirty," said Mrs. Garrity. "Downstairs, in the red parlor. If you need anything, Miss Lloyd, please let me know. There's a pull beside the bed, and someone will come. Why don't you have a nice lie-down, then, until tea."

With a smile, the housekeeper left Constance alone. An undermaid knocked lightly, asking if she needed assistance in unpacking her trunk. It was a pitiful sight, her old battered trunk wrapped with knotted rope. Constance assured the maid that she could do it on her own, and the young woman bobbed a polite curtsy and left.

All alone, Constance sat on the bed.

She had less than forty-five minutes before tea, but she was absolutely ravenous. When had they last stopped for a meal? Mr. Walker, she recalled, had been eager to pause at a tavern for a drop of ale just after noon, but Mr. Crimmins had been insistent on traveling to Hastings House as swiftly as possible. She was left with the distinct impression that Crimmins was more than anxious to complete the mission of escorting her to Ballsbridge in out-of-the-way Yorkshire.

Was Philip in the house? There had been no mention of Philip or his older brother. Was she alone with the duke and duchess?

There had also been no mention of the duke. In fact, in her brief sweep through the west wing of the house, she had seen no evidence of his existence at all, no masculine touches whatsoever.

Sighing, she began the task of unpacking her possessions, most covered with dried mud and dust, all but a very few torn and frayed. The lap desk was so far beyond repair she had left the remains behind, too disheartened to carry the bits of wood with her to her new home.

Another thought crossed her mind. She would have to explain to the duchess that her precious wedding veil had been ruined. What an awful task that would be, for no amount of money could replace the beautiful veil.

As she placed her clothes in the drawers, her mind once again focused on Joseph Smith. What an extraordinary man he was, full of such ideals and passion and drive.

Where was he now, her Mr. Smith? Where was Joseph?

Joseph Smith rubbed a distracted hand over his mouth.

Before him were a half-dozen glass vials, corked and arranged in a wooden stand. At the base of each vial was a label marked with his neat printing.

"Balmoral. 3 September 1874. Kitchen." Another read "Balmoral. 28 April 1874. HM's Chamber." Other wooden stands were labeled "Osborne," "Windsor," "Buckingham," "Sandringham," and

"Marlborough House." All had dates and more precise locations for each sample.

In his London lab, where he developed his chemical dyes, a corner was devoted to this one vital project. Only one other person knew the precise details of this work, and of course he trusted Brown completely. Others despised the Highlander, his high-handed ways and his thick brogue and even thicker kilt, worn all year round, with heavy wool socks and a sporran covered with fur.

But Joseph Smith and John Brown had recognized a mutual kinship the moment the two men met. Smith, the wealthy Welsh outsider, and Brown, the private Scottish servant of Queen Victoria herself. There had been rumors of late, ugly pamphlets calling the widowed queen Mrs. Brown, or implying a relationship far more than that of servant and mistress.

Joseph knew better. John Brown, with his blunt, unvarnished ways and wry humor, was devoted to his queen. He had been at her side since before the death of the Prince Consort, Albert, more than a dozen years earlier. John Brown would give his life for his queen.

And yet Joseph Smith and John Brown were both outsiders, and therefore held in contempt and suspicion by most members of the so-called aristocracy. It was an open secret that the Prince of Wales despised Brown. On the other hand, the Prince had shown Smith nothing but courteous—if distant—interest, and even genuine curiosity when it came to some of his scientific writings.

Perhaps the Prince of Wales was not prejudiced against Brown because of his Celtic birth or humble beginnings. Perhaps the prince was simply jealous that a mere manservant had the constant ear of his mother the queen.

And the Prince could remember the sting of

Brown's hands when he boxed the Prince's ears. No one could remember what transgression had prompted the punishment—no doubt it had been justified. But the Prince still felt the flush of humiliation and anger whenever he saw Brown, or even heard his name mentioned in passing.

It was generally known that Victoria held no high opinion of her eldest son, and refused to allow him to even look at vital state papers. Yet she routinely asked her Highland servant his opinion on everything from members of court and Parliament to the best place for her to pass a holiday, and occasionally Brown was even trusted with state affairs.

No wonder the Prince of Wales hated him so.

Joseph paused, carefully removing one of the delicate vials from its stand, tilting the contents back and forth, watching the liquid swirl with sediment. A dozen years ago, Constance Lloyd had been a young girl in Virginia, about to endure one of the bloodiest, most horrific wars mankind had ever known.

What had she been like back then? Beautiful, to be sure, for beauty such as hers does not come about overnight, but grows and flowers like a rare bloom. Resolute, perhaps, yet twelve years earlier she had not yet been tested, was still very much a child living in cloistered safety with her parents, both of whom would be dead by the close of the war. Also dead would be her sense of security, whatever shreds were left after the conflict robbed her of the most basic of needs and expectations and dreams.

So young Constance Lloyd had the wits to contact a distant relative and secure a position as a governess. Not terribly exciting, not even compelling, but as a woman in her position, her move across the ocean was a desperate grasp at survival.

How she must have dreaded the voyage, every wave carrying her further from all she knew, from a world that had regarded her as a person of position and substance. And then in England, she was banished to the governess' room, to a distant corner of the household with only children and occasionally servants for companionship.

Yet somehow she had triumphed over even that stroke of fate. Not only had she gained the obvious affection and sincere friendship of her employer, but she was now engaged to be married to the second son of a wealthy duke.

"Damn it all," he muttered, securing the sample once again on its stand.

He was exhausted. Sleep had evaded him for days, ever since he left Constance in the capable yet hardly friendly guardianship of Crimmins and Walker. It was not the two men that had been bothering him.

Whenever he closed his eyes, he saw Constance, bright and warm and lovely Constance, in the arms of his best friend, Philip.

Philip, whom he had known since childhood. Philip, a man with a good heart, but little chance to show the world the goodness there. Through the years Joseph had learned to rely on the rakish Lord Hastings to get him out of minor, reputation-threatening scrapes. And Philip had more than once used his position as a solid member of the aristocracy to further Joseph's career. He knew very well that he was tolerated, even welcomed in most places because of the unique combination of hard-earned wealth and secondhand elegance. Philip was nothing if not elegant, which was all society really demanded of him.

There had been rumblings lately, murmurs Joseph heard that others perhaps did not hear, or did not take seriously.

There were millions of Britons who wanted to see the monarchy dead. There were pamphlets being circulated about the benefits of republicanism, of the need for a cleansing along the lines of the French Revolution the century before.

Some were openly calling for the removal, even the death, of the queen herself and of her entire family.

There had already been attempts made on her life. All that was required was a clever anarchist, an outsider with an ax to grind and the means with which to start the wheel.

What was Constance doing now?

She hadn't looked down on him because he was an orphan from a Welsh coal-mining village. She didn't bat an eye when she heard he had been a charity boy at school, or that he was in trade, that he manufactured goods for sale and profit. In truth, she seemed most excited about his work with developing safe, disease-free beverages for the underclasses.

Did she realize that, until very recently, he was counted amongst the underclasses?

"Work, damn it, work." He clenched his teeth and straightened his spine against the uncomfortable back of the chair.

This was the most important task he had ever attempted. Represented by a handful of samples, no more than a few pints in total, was not only his future, but the future of the entire nation.

Hopefully, when this new project was completed, England would be a much better place in which to live. Not for just a few, but for everyone.

5

Constance did not dare to be late for her first meeting with the duchess.

Although there was not much she could do about her gown, she brushed and repinned her hair. The vision before her in the oval mirror was that of a sensible governess wearing a hopelessly unfashionable dress.

"There's not much I can do about it," she sighed at her reflection. Then she went in search of the red room.

The problem was, just about every room seemed to have a great deal of red in it. There was a red and purple room, a red and green room, a red and blue room—every color scheme imaginable was represented. Every decorating style was also, unfortunately, evident.

The more she walked the vast, high-ceilinged halls of Hastings House, the more she realized how truly atrocious the furnishings were. They weren't just unattractive, or overwrought. Every room was aggressively odious. The emphasis seemed to be on size and color—every chair, every table, every carpet was oversized and garishly colored, with no apparent thought given to whether one piece of furniture would match the rest of the room. As a result, the house had no sense of being a home. Instead it was just a collection of rooms filled up with expensive, ornately disagreeable bric-a-brac.

The artwork was equally odd, including several full-length portraits of a very large man wearing women's clothing. There was something touching about this, Constance thought. She had heard of a personality disorder that caused a gentleman to desire nothing more than to be a member of the opposite sex, therefore to dress as a woman. Once, during the season at Cowes, she heard of a man disguising himself as a woman to gain entry to the ladies' dressing rooms, although that was for a different purpose altogether than the burly man in the paintings seemed to have in mind.

How refreshing that they did not hide the poor man's portraits. Instead they embraced him for all of his faults. Perhaps this was a good sign. If she could learn to ignore the rest of the place and concentrate on the people, maybe she would cease to be horrified at the lack of taste so brilliantly displayed.

In short, Hastings House was absolutely appalling. The only thing she could imagine benefiting the place would be to burn it down and start all over again.

Stunned as she was by the grand scale, she did manage to find a maid—busy dusting a hideous statue of the man from the portrait in what appeared to be a ball gown—and ask where the red room was for tea. With a shy smile, the maid bobbed a curtsy and showed her to a room she hadn't passed before.

When Constance entered the room, she saw a large

man standing in the center of the carpet. He was wearing a heavily decorated gown, a nightmare of purples and greens, and atop his head was a tiara. It was the man from the artwork, the man depicted by the gargantuan statue.

"Miss Lloyd?"

The shock must have been apparent on her face. For at that moment she realized that the man in the dress was, in fact, the duchess.

"Forgive me, your grace." She sank into a deep curtsy.

"This house must be quite a stunning discovery for you, Miss Lloyd," the duchess said with obvious pride.

"You have no idea," she murmured, attempting to compose her features.

Satisfied, the duchess gestured to a chair covered with a pattern of cabbages and acorns. "Please be seated, Miss Lloyd. I wish to look at you more closely."

Feeling like a specimen under a magnifying glass, Constance did as she was told. Yet she was grateful for the chance to gather her thoughts. Between the house and her future mother-in-law, she felt as if she had just been tossed into a hallucination, something from which she hoped very soon to emerge.

"Well, well," the older woman clicked. "I can certainly see what my son found so appealing. Why, I would hardly take you for an American."

Constance smiled sweetly. "What a lovely compliment." She had heard that before from Englishmen, as if the highest praise possible was to be mistaken for one of them.

"Well, well. But your hips, Miss Lloyd. They are a bit of a disappointment."

"Your grace?"

"Yes, well. I don't suppose that can be helped. Now, have you ever had children before?"

"Your grace, I've never been married!"

"Yes, but we both know that marriage often has very little to do with bearing children. So I take it that you have not ever been with child?"

"Of course not!"

"Pity. Then we would know for certain whether you are barren or not."

At that Constance said nothing. What could she possibly add? She watched as the duchess pivoted in the center of the room and walked in exaggerated steps to a large settee. With her left arm she flipped the train of her gown out of the way, then descended onto the settee. For several long moments she adjusted the yards of fabric of her gown, and then she looked once again at Constance.

Her face was a study in folds. Her small eyes were folded between her cheeks and brows. Her mouth, large and wide, was set above her chin, bracketed by more folded skin. But it was her hair that fascinated Constance. There was not only an excessive amount of it, but it was bright red, far too red for any human being to have grown on their own. Clearly the red had been carefully assisted.

"Ah, I see you are admiring my coronet." The duchess smiled. "It is the ducal coronet, well over fifty years old. As you can see, it is made of gold and diamond strawberry leaves. I routinely wear the crown in case of an upcoming coronation. I alone will be accustomed to the weight of the coronet when it comes time for the Prince of Wales to become king."

It had happened again. The duchess had managed to render Constance all but speechless. The duchess waited expectantly for a reply, and finally Constance rallied. "I'm afraid I do not have a crown, your grace."

"Don't be ridiculous. Only a duke or a duchess is allowed to wear one, Miss Lloyd. It would be most incorrect for you to wear one. And even a tiara should never be worn by an unmarried lady. It is both bold and improper."

"I will keep that in mind."

"See that you do. Now, why are you not wearing one of the gowns I sent you?"

"Because we were robbed at gunpoint on the road here."

" 'We'? Who is 'we'?"

"I was traveling with Mr. Smith, Philip's friend. Where is he, by the way?"

"How should I know? Poking about the Welsh countryside, I should imagine, or washing the coal dust out of his hair."

"Philip, with coal dust in his hair?"

"Good heaven's, no!" With that, the duchess laughed, a husky roll of a chuckle. Constance noticed the older woman's hands, large hands—like those of a farmer or a butcher. She had never seen such large hands on a woman, and involuntarily she glanced down at the duchess's feet.

They were a matched set.

"Your grace, I might as well tell you now—the veil you so kindly sent to me was destroyed during the robbery."

The duchess looked at her as if she had just sprouted a feather duster on top of her head.

"Whatever are you talking about?"

"The lace veil, your grace. It was in with the clothing you sent to me, a beautiful cream lace veil."

"I remember no such thing. Oh. Oh, my." She began to laugh, an alarming sound, almost ominous, as if a force of nature was about to be unleashed. "The lace? Miss Lloyd, that was a tablecloth. A machine-made tablecloth, at that. I ran short of tissue, and used it to pack the clothes. Why on earth would I have sent you a fine lace veil? Oh, my, this is amusing."

Constance simply sat and watched the duchess as her face turned red with the enjoyment of it all.

"Well, would you like some tea, Miss Lloyd?"

"Yes. Thank you."

"It's over there on the silver tray. I take mine with two spoons of sugar and a bit of cream."

Still smiling, Constance rose and poured the duchess a cup of tea, preparing it precisely as the duchess had requested, yet longing to add six spoonfuls of sugar and a large splash of cream.

"And I would like a sweet as well," the duchess added.

Returning to the tray, Constance put a few of the tiny cakes on a small plate and brought it over to the duchess.

"And a sandwich. Cress."

Once again at the tray, she carefully selected a cress sandwich, adding a tomato sandwich for good measure, and brought it over to the duchess. Quickly, she ate the other cress sandwich out of pure hunger. If she was not offered anything, that would be her only meal until dinner.

"You may pour yourself some, if you wish."

"Thank you, your grace," she said with relief.

The duchess nodded, and took a sip of the tea, holding the small cup in her massive, chapped hand. Although she said nothing, she smiled in contentment when she tasted the tea, prepared to her exact specifications.

"So, Philip should be returning by the end of the week."

"The end of the week?" Constance asked. "Where is he?"

"I sent him on a campaign tour of Ballsbridge."

Constance did not mention that they were within a few miles of the village of Ballsbridge. "Why doesn't he come back here at the end of each day?"

"Because, my dear, he needs to pay attention to his politics. He needs to work on his speeches, to come up with clever ideas that will entice the rabble to vote for him, to practice standing still for long periods of time, shaking hands with common people, that sort of thing. And I did want you and I to have some time alone to get to know each other. Before I forget, come over here."

Constance did as she was told. The duchess opened a drawer and handed her a small box.

"This is for you, Miss Lloyd."

"Why, thank you."

"It's your engagement ring."

"My engagement ring? Perhaps I should wait for Philip to give it to me."

"Nonsense. You might as well get used to it. Try it on."

Constance opened the black velvet box. Inside was one of the strangest things she had ever beheld. The center was a yellow stone the size of a small doorknob, and the setting seemed to be of serpents, or perhaps lizards.

"Oh. How lovely," she said.

"Of course it's lovely. I picked it out myself—Philip has no time for such things. It's in the new style, very Italian."

"I suppose this means that you and I are engaged, your grace," Constance said with a smile.

"Nonsense! I am already married. In addition, I am a woman, therefore we could never become engaged. And I do believe I am too old for you, Miss Lloyd. No, you and Philip are engaged. We will set a date soon, perhaps before the elections."

"That will be wonderful." Slowly she slipped the ring on her left ring finger. It fit perfectly, she realized with a sinking heart. She returned to the tea tray.

"Yes, well. Was there not another cress sandwich on the tray?"

"I'm sorry," Constance confessed. "I ate the other cress sandwich."

"You ate my cress sandwich?"

"Well, I . . ." She realized the futility of arguing. "Yes, your grace."

"Well, we will have to smooth out some of your rough spots before you can greet society. Come back over here, so that I can see you."

Constance returned to the chair, her own cup of tea in her hand. She swallowed, hoping that she could control the trembling so that the cup and saucer wouldn't clank together.

All in all, she realized she had felt more comfortable with the armed thieves than alone with the duchess.

"Well," the duchess said, with no apparent prompting. "This has been a treat. You may go now. We dine at seven thirty, and please be prompt."

Rising, Constance curtsied and left the salon. Whatever happened next, the worst was surely over. Dinner was bound to be a vast improvement.

By the time the dinner hour arrived, Constance was so hungry she recalled with longing the single watercress sandwich she had eaten at tea. At least the physical discomfort kept her mind off other more disturbing topics, such as her less-than-glorious first encounter with Philip's mother. Such as her inability to forget Joseph Smith.

Just as she was about to make herself as presentable as possible, there was a light knock on her door. At her answer, one of the seemingly endless supply of silent housemaids entered the room.

"The duchess sends you this gown for dinner, Miss. There are guests tonight, and she felt you would be more suited in evening attire."

"How very kind of her." She smiled to the maid, who hesitated before returning the smile. The gown was laid upon the bed, and although it was far more elaborate than anything Constance would have selected, it was most certainly the height of fashion, and obviously embarrassingly expensive. The deep-blue velvet bodice, almost daringly off the shoulder, was trimmed with rich ivory lace; the lush skirt was hemmed with satin of the same color as the ivory lace. The maid also displayed all the necessary undergarments, silk stockings, delicate slippers, and even more impossibly delicate kid gloves with tiny mother-of-pearl buttons.

"Where on earth did this come from?" Constance gasped when she had recovered her voice.

"I don't rightly know, Miss. Do you need assistance with your dress or hair?"

For a moment Constance just stared at the young housemaid. It was such a very peculiar feeling after all these years to actually have a servant ask what was required. She was so used to being in the maid's position, she simply smiled.

"Thank you. I believe I can manage."

After the maid left she was glad for the privacy. It allowed her to savor the sensation of touching new clothes, of feeling the silk stockings against her leg— so very different from the thick black cotton or wool stockings she was accustomed to. And although the gown was, indeed, ornate, it was also beautiful.

To match the glory of the gown she took extra care with her hair, brushing it to a dark, high gloss and arranging a few curls in artful disarray. Now she was ready to face whatever was waiting below, to meet whatever the evening held.

Following the sound of voices, she was able to locate the dining room. Stepping over the threshold, sidestepping a massive palm potted in a ceramic walrus head, she was greeted by at least two dozen pairs of eyes focused on her.

This wasn't a simple dinner gathering. This was a banquet. And at once she realized she was there as either the guest of honor, or the main course.

Straightening her spine, she decided that she would not, under any circumstance, allow herself to be consumed with even the most superior quality of claret.

"Good evening," she said clearly, adjusting her vision to the flickering candlelight. The men were wearing subdued dinner jackets, and the women were bedecked in evening gowns and jewels, including an impressive assortment of diamond dog-collars and glinting earbobs.

"Why, Miss Lloyd, how very lovely you are this evening," said the duchess. There was no false sincerity in her voice.

Constance was then introduced to the entire gathering, the men standing by their chairs, the women inclining their heads. Everyone seemed to be a Lord or a Lady or a Sir, and their last names sounded very much like the secondary characters from a fashionable country-house play.

The duchess, her gigantic self corseted into an approximate hourglass shape, had traded her coronet for a more simple tiara that resembled nothing so much as a fireplace fender. She then turned to the guests after the introductions were complete, and with a sweeping gesture of her large hand, said with an indulgent smile, "She's an American, you know."

There was a smattering of agreement, polite murmurs of understanding, as if the simple fact of her being an American would excuse any outlandish behavior, explain any eccentric mannerism or lapses of good taste.

It was then that she noticed Philip was there.

He rose to his feet, a vague smile on his face. Yet he seemed hesitant, and he kept glancing over at his mother as if for some signal of approval, for some cue as to what he should do next. As usual, he was splendidly dressed in a black dinner jacket, his whiskers freshly powdered and brushed, his silk cravat tied to perfection and fastened with a single pearl.

"Constance," he said at last. "Please sit by me." He walked over to her, all eyes following his every move, and placed a kiss upon her cheek.

Constance took Philip's arm, trying to ignore the stares and whispers of the other guests as he led her to her place and she attempted to gather her thoughts and emotions. Philip's presence was not only unexpected, it failed to reassure her in any way.

"Lovely weather," she said to the crowd as Philip held her chair. There was no response other than one or two automatic smiles.

It was intolerable, this silence. Anything was better than the wordless stares, so she forced herself to continue in a tone so light and airy, she very nearly fooled herself. "Where I grew up, it is still too warm for comfort at this time of year."

No one picked up the thread of her conversation, so she unfolded her napkin and hoped very much that someone, anyone, would speak.

Why wasn't Philip, who clearly saw her discomfort, making any effort to help her out? But he was too intent on watching the duchess.

There was a heavy silence before a bald man at the end of the table spoke. "This is September."

Well, that was something to work with at any rate. "Yes," Constance nodded. "Indeed, it is."

The bald man beamed. "Yes," he announced with more authority. "This is most certainly September. And just about the middle of the month, if I'm not mistaken."

A few of the guests agreed that yes, it was indeed the second Thursday in September. After the flurry of excitement concerning the confirmation of the date, the table again lapsed into silence.

"Miss Lloyd," said a gentleman at the far end of the table. "I myself have visited the United States."

"Have you? I do hope your visit was most enjoyable, sir."

"Oh, yes! Indeed it was, although I do not believe I have ever been in a place where everything is so, well. How should I phrase it?"

"Rough?" offered one woman.

"Unrefined?" suggested another.

"Brutally savage?" the first woman volunteered with expectant glee.

"No, no! Not at all! Miss Lloyd," the man grinned, "what I mean is that everything is vast. The lakes are so large, one cannot see from shore to shore. The rivers are so wide it takes hours to cross by boat, the farms contain such massive tracts of land that it would take a man days to ride from boundary to boundary. Why, some of the homes are so large, one can literally get lost."

"I understand, sir," Constance admitted. "But you see, I am from Virginia. As Confederates, we prided ourselves in keeping everything to a more manageable scale. Unfortunately, that seemed to have extended itself to our army as well—quite small enough to be manageable. Not large enough to win."

A few diners smiled, and one man made a sound that seemed very much like a chuckle.

"Pity your side lost the war," muttered a man with an enormous walrus mustache. "I always felt the Confederate States had more of an English ideal behind them. You know, the homes, the manners. Much less appalling than the North."

Some of the other men nodded in agreement, and the women parroted the men's gestures. One graying man at the end of the table added a lusty "Here, here," as if they were in the center of a Parliamentary debate.

"You must have been very young, Miss Lloyd, when the war concluded. That must have been a very lucky thing for you, to have been young enough to have escaped most of the brutality," the man with the mustache said.

"I thank you for the compliment on my youth." Constance leaned back as a servant poured wine in her goblet. "I was quite old enough to be aware of the war, and unfortunately my father's lands often served as the battlefield."

"How frightful," breathed a lady with feathers in her hair. "I do hope, Miss Lloyd, that no one in your family suffered too dreadfully."

"Well," she said quietly. "That was a long time ago, a long, long time ago."

There was again silence as a manservant offered her the soup tureen. She made a great show of watching the creamy soup splash into her bowl, hoping that at any time someone at the vast table would speak up and change the subject.

"You poor dear," said the woman with the feathers.

Philip was staring at her with an expression of surprise, as if he hadn't known about her experiences in the war. It was as if he hadn't seen her before, the oddly intense set of his well-arranged features.

"Philip," said the duchess. "You are slouching. Please sit straight."

At that, most of other guests straightened themselves as well, poking at their food or sipping the wine.

She had to say something, anything to relieve the heavy silence.

"Well, I must admit that being in England at the dawn of her glorious empire is a far sight more enjoyable than Virginia at the close of the war," she said crisply.

"I should think so," agreed the duchess.

"Tell us, Miss Lloyd, what do you like the best about our nation?" The bald gentleman smiled encouragingly.

"I must confess, I do love the notion of nobility and royalty."

"I am astonished," replied the bald gentleman. "I thought all Americans cherished their democracy. I've been in more than one row at my club with visiting Yanks, and they all profess to scorn our titles."

"Oh, but that is not true, not at all. We envy the order they give society. There is something comforting in knowing exactly how many degrees of supremacy any given individual may claim. In reality, Americans are every bit as class-conscious as the English, but since we have no one to head up the establishment, no king or queen, no prince or duke, the social seasons can get quite messy and confusing."

"I say," chimed in a woman who had previously been silent. "Do you remember the fuss made over the Prince of Wales when he visited America in sixty? Why, I understand that the women all but threw themselves at HRH."

"And didn't a floor collapse with the weight of the crush?" the woman with the feathers added cheerfully.

"Indeed, it did." Constance raised her eyebrows.

"And the crush was most certainly composed of society women and their eligible daughters. So now you know our sullied secret at last—what the grandchildren of the revolution really desire."

The man with the mustache gave a perplexed grunt. "And, my dear Miss Lloyd, what would that be?"

"Why, we all want nothing more than the chance to become the Queen of England." She took a drink of her water. "And as Americans, tainted by democracy, we still believe that we should all have a fair crack at the title."

At first no one responded. Then the bald man began to chuckle, his face turning an alarming shade of crimson. At that the other diners began to join in, the men with their low, cigar-graveled tones, the women in tittery giggles.

Philip, assured that his mother seemed pleased, grinned at last. "And what about the Confederacy? Did you all wish to become sovereign in the Southern states as well?"

"Well," she began thoughtfully, "I do believe that was our main problem."

"What was that?" Philip could barely restrain his smile, and the other guests, spoons and forks poised in midair, awaited her answer.

"Because we all firmly believed that, as Southerners, we already *were* royalty. It led to frightful confusion, as one can imagine."

The distinctive sounds of general amusement and approval clucked about the table.

Good God, she thought to herself. This is an absurdly easy group to entertain.

And Philip. In other gatherings he had seemed so in command. Now he looked to his mother for everything, even in how to respond to her, his own fiancée.

"Tell me, Miss Lloyd," boomed a round man with an absurdly drooping set of whiskers, his hair parted in the middle and combed flat with a thick layer of macassar oil. "Did you ever hear the famous 'rebel yell'?"

"In all honesty, sir, I believe the same yelp was offered at that New York ball where the Prince of Wales was introduced. So the yell was, in fact, developed by society mamas with eligible daughters, not fighting men, although the purpose of the sound—to terrify the enemy—remained the same."

And so the meal passed, and Constance remained the center of attention, Philip smiling and prodding his fiancée to perform. And she did; she put on quite a show, she thought, with more meaningless chatter than she had ever been forced to employ in the nursery. Philip seemed delighted with her.

The old duke was nowhere in sight, search as she did through the other faces basking in the dull orange glow of the candlelight, wondering if she had somehow missed her future father-in-law's name in the rush of the introductions. By the close of the evening she had discovered that the bloated young man at the end of the table was Philip's older brother, the Viscount Cavendish. Everyone at the table, however, just called him Dishy.

And she also discovered, by the thin-lipped expression on the face of the duchess, that she had gone too far, that she had made too much of a spectacle of herself and drawn too much attention away from the duchess. She had no doubt that, by the next day, the duchess would inform her of her errors.

They had a brief interlude together, Constance and Philip. The guests had left, and the duchess had already retired.

Viscount Cavendish had also gone to his room, but in truth he had retreated earlier, if not physically then in spirit. As far as she could tell, he had not uttered a single word, pleasant or unpleasant, throughout dinner, nor made a single comment either for or against any topic.

The duchess and her eldest son seemed disappointed in the way the evening had progressed. If Philip hadn't noticed, Constance most certainly had.

"I'm not sure I have won admirers in either your mother or your brother," she admitted as the servants began their silent bustling and cleaning up.

"Nonsense, Constance. You have conquered them all." He lit a cigar from the fireplace and puffed heartily, settling down into a wing chair across from hers.

Was this a glimpse of what their life together would entail? She banished the thought from her mind. It was useless to dwell on what the future might hold. Absolutely useless. She of all people knew that what one expected and what was likely to transpire were rarely the same thing.

"By Jove, Constance, I don't believe I've ever seen Lord Trendome cackle so! Well done, my girl, well done, indeed." Philip closed his eyes, savoring the fragrance of his smoke. At his other hand was a large snifter of brandy—his third.

"Where was your father, Philip? I was so hoping to meet him."

"Oh. Father." His voice fell, although he didn't bother to open his eyes. She noticed his lashes were very pale, almost transparent, like the lashes of a rabbit. "He dines alone in his own, well, quarters. By the way, that yarn about the women in Charleston was priceless, absolutely priceless! Mortimer, well, he was pleased as I've ever seen him. You know, that fellow at the end with the brown tooth?"

"I don't know, Philip. They all blended together. And more than one gentleman had a brown tooth."

He laughed. "In any case, Mortimer with the brown tooth has a friend who writes for *Punch*. Mortimer himself writes for that publication as well. As he left he asked if he could run some of your amusing tales, with complete attribution, of course. I gave him permission."

"You did? Why didn't you mention that to me, Philip?"

"I scarcely thought you'd mind, my dear. " With his eyes still closed, he managed to bring the snifter to his lips with languid contentment. After a long swallow he continued. "This is marvelous, simply marvelous."

"The brandy?"

"No, no. Well, I suppose brandy *is* marvelous, in its own way. What I mean, my dear, is that *you* are marvelous, getting all of that attention that way. This will be splendid for my career."

"For your career?"

"Of course. You won everyone over. They were here to see you, naturally, the wild American and all that. Most of those people have never been here, wouldn't deign to come without some sort of inducement."

When she said nothing, he continued, his eyes still closed in blissful reflection. Although she had gone quite pale, he did not see the alteration in her complexion.

"This has been positively splendid. I wouldn't be surprised if we get an invitation to the Prince of Wales's home. He's frightfully fond of Americans, you know. Loves all sorts of exotica. Once that happens, well, we're in."

"We'll be in what, exactly?"

"Why, the smart set, of course. The Marlborough House Set, the cream of society. Splendid. Absolutely splendid."

"I think I will go up to bed now, Philip."

Finally he opened his eyes and smiled. "You deserve a nice rest, my dear." He stood up, but released neither the cigar nor the brandy.

As they stood, her eye caught the reflection of the two of them in the gold-framed mirror over the fireplace. Their images were visible to her from her shoulders up. Even with that limited view, her bright gown stood out in sharp contrast to her blank expression. He was staring at his brandy, clearly the elegant man-about-town.

It was all wrong. Not just the clothes, inharmonious as they were. No, there was more to it than that. He leaned over to kiss her cheek, and the two faces were close enough to be seen together.

There was nothing. No spark that said, "These two belong together." No intangible link between the two. His eyes did not meet hers, there was no sense of connection even when his lips brushed against her cheek.

"Good night, my dear." He sank back into the wing chair before she left the room. Glancing back once, she saw him refill the brandy snifter and close his eyes once more, contemplating his future glory, no doubt.

Why was it, she thought as she climbed the stairs, that she could not, or more importantly, would not contemplate the future at all?

"Damn it," Joseph spat between clenched teeth.

He had done it again, lost track of the experiment.

It had been her image in his mind, not thoughts of his work, that had caused him to spill the last sample from Balmoral. Without that, the whole series of tests would be worthless.

Wearily, he rubbed his hand over his eyes. Sleep had eluded him lately, he, Joseph Smith, who had always maintained a remarkable ability to fall asleep standing up if necessary. Once or twice that had been the case. No, sleep had never been a problem with him.

Until Constance Lloyd.

"No," he said to himself. "This must not happen."

Not even Abigail had beguiled him so. No, Abigail had been a dream, a vision he had created much in his own imagination. Time and again he had been surprised when the reality of Abigail had clashed so violently with the image he had forged during their long separations.

But no one, no matter how gifted with the powers of imagination, could ever create someone like Constance Lloyd. Even her name was both a contradiction and an apt tribute, for in reality the only thing constant about the woman was her ability to surprise and delight.

And those were two things she had done to Joseph in their brief acquaintance. When he closed his eyes he saw her still, snatches of their time together, flickering images of her smile, of her face looking off into the distance, of her blue eyes—startling, clear—as she blinked up at him in response to something he said.

Her voice came to him as well, her wry comments, her pragmatic, good-natured banter. There was nothing forced or studied about Constance Lloyd, nothing that pointed to long hours of practiced conversation. She meant what she said and, unfortunately at times, said what was on her mind before thinking the dialogue through.

In short, she was delightful.

She was also Philip's intended bride, something he was finding all too easy to push aside.

Marriage to Philip would ruin her.

Not in the melodramatic, gothic sense, but in terms of her freshness and spontaneity. A year living at Hastings House would destroy all of that, the long dull evenings with the duchess holding court over no one but herself and Constance. He could see it now, Dishy in his chair, Philip reading an out-of-date

London newspaper, and Constance doing her best to keep her sanity.

Another scenario was even more appalling—entry into the Prince of Wales's vapid set. They were aristocratic dullards, trained to avoid thinking at all costs, taught to stay away from books and art and anything that might threaten their insular way of life.

Constance was a woman of real wit, not a practical joker. How would she react to the soda siphon fights, or tobogganing down the stairs of Marlborough House on a silver tray out of simple boredom? But what really alarmed him was the notion of Constance in that vicious set. Unless she herself became as malicious as the most sharp-tongued gossip, she would be destroyed for the very reasons she should be worshipped.

Philip had no idea what treasure had been handed to him by fate.

A small smile curved on Joseph's lips when he again envisioned her face. Then, with more deliberate concentration than he usually required, he returned to his work.

6

The days passed for Constance in a numbing sort of sameness. From the silent first meal of the day until the obligatory bedtime of eleven o'clock, the grinding routine became *more* difficult for her to bear rather than easier. She had even taken to moving the hands forward on the mantel clock in the red salon after dinner, to speed the end of the day by however many minutes she could manage without being obvious. Philip had seen her, under pretense of looking for a book to read, but said nothing when the chimes rang. The viscount had also watched as she quietly opened the glass and pushed the hands, but he, too, said nothing. Their mother alone was ignorant of how entire blocks of time would be lost in Constance's haste to go to her own room, where she could be comfortably alone with her thoughts.

The duchess never did make a reference to that first night, although the very fact that the initial party was the last time guests were asked to dine at Hastings House was significant. The older woman treated her with a dignified sort of aloofness, never really friendly, just as she was never truly unfriendly. Constance had been accepted in a lukewarm fashion, which was perhaps not ideal, but it was tolerable.

Philip was in and out of the house, always on the run to a rally or meeting, always going over speeches he bought from his friend Mortimer. From what Constance could tell, the campaign was going quite well, although Philip himself did not give her many details. Instead, he asked her for amusing stories, ones he could weave somehow into his speeches. Whenever she made a remark that seemed witty or the least bit clever, he jotted it down to pass on to Mortimer.

And when it came to the Viscount Cavendish, she seemed to be all but invisible. Dishy, as she could never bring herself to call him—the name indicated a dash of fun and humor she had thus far been unable to detect in the man himself—would look at her across the table at breakfast, at lunch, at dinner, from across the salon at tea. He never spoke directly to her. He never made any indication she existed at all. Even when he did appear to be watching her, he gave the impression of staring right through her, the way someone deep in thought gazes on a fixed object, yet is uncomprehending as to what it meets in the line of the gaze.

When the duchess spoke to her, it was to give instruction or impart information. There was no longer a pretense of dialogue. Constance was expected to heed everything the duchess said, but heed it silently.

"A member of the peerage always holds the small finger of the teacup hand out thusly while sipping tea. It is vulgar to do otherwise."

"One can always tell a lady by her carriage. A true aristocrat never slumps."

"Never condescend to speak to the servants as

individuals. Speak to them as their rank indicates. They do not expect to be addressed by their names and, indeed, will not respect you if you bother to learn their names."

Constance listened with polite interest, mentally contradicting the duchess on virtually every point. The pinkie finger out at teatime? She herself thought it was an absurd affectation, sure to indicate to one and all that the tea sipper was far more interested in creating an illusion of breeding rather than actually being well-bred. The aristocracy never slumps? Then what of the lords and ladies at Cowes season, not to mention the crowned princes and princesses, who did nothing *but* slump their way through the yachting and dancing and strolling? And never, but never address the servants by name.

"Stella, have you seen the left blue shoe?" Constance called as she yanked up her dress and got down on her hands and knees to look under the bed.

The young woman came immediately, a smile on her round, bright-cheeked face. Stella was an almost comically perfect country-girl-turned-domestic, from her cheerful disposition and her eagerness to please to her increasingly frank assessment of the domestic situation at Hastings House.

"The blue slipper, miss?" She placed her hands on her hips. "Now what are you about doing, and you on all fours with your new blue gown?"

Constance glanced up, knocking her head on the leg of the bed. Both women winced.

"I can't seem to find the other shoe," Constance admitted, rubbing the spot on her head.

Without hesitation Stella marched across the room and retrieved the missing slipper from under the dressing table. Wordlessly, she held it up.

"Thank you, Stella." Constance smiled as she took the shoe. "How does this dress look? It's another one of the new ones the duchess ordered. I believe she is operating under the misapprehension that a flurry of invitations are about to be tossed this way."

"Now, miss, I heard Lord Hastings himself say that his friend, Mr. Mortimer, the one that has a chum working over at that horrid magazine *Punch,* says all of London is atwitter over you. They all want to meet you, they do."

"Why in heaven's name they all want to meet a governess, I'll never know. Most of them have their own governess, and I'll bet you a Union dollar that they pay absolutely no attention to them whatsoever. They could stay at home and ignore her rather than make the effort to meet a new governess to ignore."

"You don't understand, do you, miss?"

"As a matter of fact, Stella, I don't."

"You see, these lords and ladies, well, they are all used to each other. They may look like grown-ups, but in truth they are just children what have married each other. Everyone you're bound to meet in these circles, why, they likely played together as babes, as did their mothers and fathers."

"And like children, they enjoy something new every now and then?"

"Exactly, miss!" Stella lowered her voice. "Really, though, they are more like children what's not right in the head. Have you ever seen dogs from the same litter have their own puppies?"

Constance shook her head slowly. "No. I'm afraid I have not."

"It's a fearful sight, it is. Sometimes the puppies have but one eye, sometimes they have too many legs or not enough legs. One poor puppy I saw just sat and stared, wouldn't eat none, so he withered away in no time. And I've seen my share of the muckety-mucks what do the same."

"In other words, the aristocracy is inbred," Constance whispered.

"Exactly, miss!"

"And I'm the mixed-breed outsider to offer them hope?"

"Now you've got it." Stella stepped back, as if seeing Constance for the first time, her voice hushed and almost reverent. "Why, miss, you're lovely, you are. A real beauty."

"Oh, Stella, thank you. You know, the duchess has indeed been kind, offering the clothes and all of the advice she thinks I need."

"I don't know if kindness has anything to do with it, miss."

"Excuse me?"

"What I mean is the duchess is doing it for herself and for her son, that's all. She's afraid of you, miss. She knows her son needs you on account of their father and herself not being real prime stock, if you know what I mean. As long as she needs you, she'll be kind; she'll not harm the goose what lays the golden egg, if you get my meaning."

"I see." Constance faced the large oval mirror, and for a moment she herself was stunned. The blue satin day dress—its skirt gathered in exquisite pleats, the bodice simple other than for the high-notched neckline—made her look like the furthest thing from a governess.

A thought ran through her mind like lightning: If only Joseph could see her.

Where had that stray thought come from? What deluded corner of her mind was conjuring further daydreams in the mists of her real-life fairy tale?

"Will you be down to tea soon, miss?"

"I'll be right down. Thank you, Stella."

The maid lowered her face and curtsied before she left.

Joseph. He was probably still in Scotland. Not that it mattered. Not really.

She left her room and began to walk in the general direction of the red room, where the afternoon tea was served.

What an extraordinary man he was, Joseph Smith. Such an ordinary name for such an extraordinary man.

An involuntary giggle escaped her mouth as she walked through the halls, thinking about Joseph. In her mind she played back scenes of their time together, about when he became ill on oysters, when he seemed so pleased at her ideas or comments. Never had a man expressed such admiration of her mind and ideas. That had been a first, an absolute first.

Yet he had also been there to calm her fears, to get her through what could have been a terrifying experience. But because of his kindness, his general compassion, his understanding, she could only recall the entire robbery incident with something dangerously close to fondness.

Fondness, and humiliation on her part. She behaved so boldly, and at times she would recall his touch, or the way he had looked at her, and she knew she would blush furiously.

Did he think of her at all, she wondered. And if he did, was it a favorable thought? Did he smile, too, at images of their adventure? Above all, did his memory hold the way it felt to be so close all night in that abandoned inn, to feel the warmth of each other's flesh, to . . .

"Excuse me!" She slammed into a body with a force that knocked her backwards. She was fortunate. The other person was sprawled on the carpet. "Oh, do forgive me, sir!"

He was a frail-looking elderly man with sprouts of very white hair and a face gleaming with a clean-shaven shine. As she reached her hand out, and he took it, she realized who it was.

"Your grace." She sank into a deep curtsy. "Please, I don't know how to apologize. It was my fault, entirely my fault."

"Nonsense, my girl! I shouldn't have ventured to this part of the house in the first place. It's against my general principles, you see. Now let me get a proper look at you. You're to be Philip's bride, are you not?"

The old gentleman conveyed an air of overwhelming warmth and charm, and she couldn't help but smile in return. His eyes were a stunningly dark shade of brown, all the more remarkable for the contrast with his snowy hair. The eyebrows, haphazard tufts that dipped and rose as he spoke, reminded her of a matched set of rabbits' tails.

His gray uniform seemed to be influenced greatly by Prussian military dress, although closer inspection of his badges and medals revealed that they were nothing more than fanciful depictions of unicorns, farm implements, and kitchen utensils.

"Ah, my medals. They have been bestowed upon me by my faithful army—the gardening staff, the kitchen staff, and, of course, the jolly men who tend the animals. I am most proud of each and every one, Miss Lloyd."

"You know my name?"

"Indeed I do. I have been told all about you. Where are you going, my girl? You seem to be off at a brisk pace."

"To tea with the duchess," she said, trying to keep her voice cheerful. The dread must have been apparent to the duke. He gave an exaggerated cringe, as if struck a blow on his slender shoulders. Then he straightened.

"If I may be so bold, how would you like to accompany me to tea in my own quarters?"

She hesitated just for a moment. How furious the duchess would be. How terribly annoyed Philip would be. And the young viscount, he would be displeased as well.

"I have lovely butter and cheese sandwiches," the duke urged. "They don't get butter and cheese sandwiches. I'm the only one. And Cook makes me a special cake with raisins and rum. It's delightful. And they don't get a single slice of that either."

"Your grace." She tilted her head in his direction. "I would love to have tea with you."

"Jolly good! Let us go to my own part of this dreadful monument to bad taste."

She paused, and he laughed. "You don't think I know it, my dear? Why, I've spent the better part of thirty-five years trying to avoid this place."

"Then what were you doing just now? Up here in the corridor. I do not mean to be in any way impertinent, your grace."

"Not in the least! It was a most logical question, the closest thing I've had to two words of sense together from a member of this household in years. I was examining the books, you see."

"In the library?"

"No, no, my dear, although I do often wander up to borrow a book or two. Nobody misses them. My sons and their mother are not great readers, as you have probably noticed."

She smiled and took the arm he offered.

"Well, I was just making sure the financial situation upstairs is what it should be. I run most of the economics from below, of course. But sometimes the duchess will go overbudget, or one of the boys will invest a great deal too much in horse flesh, and then I have to step in and straighten things out. Here, we turn left at this door."

It was a door she had passed frequently, but since it was always closed—and the ornate molding ran across the entire door as if to disguise it—she had assumed it was a closet for mops and brooms. Instead it was a passageway, well-lighted, of marble steps and a lovely brass handrail.

"Mind your step. There's a good girl. This way."

After two flights, they opened another door. And through that door was the most magnificent corridor she had ever beheld.

It was simply appointed, from the beautiful dark green walls, hung with exquisite works of art, some modern, others centuries old, to the carpet, an endless glory of Persian design, rich with reds and blues and greens, all existing and balancing each other in perfect concert. There were brass wall sconces, plain yet classically curved, like those of a plantation she had once visited in Petersburg, Virginia.

The hallway smelled of beeswax, and she recalled that fragrance from when she was a child. Her mother always had the furniture and the walls buffed with beeswax.

There was something odd, however. It took her a moment to realize what was missing.

As if he read her mind, the duke answered her silent question. "There is no daylight below, unfortunately. We are underground, my dear, and the only thing I lack is the light. But hopefully, you will become a regular guest, and therefore allow your sunshine downstairs. Ah, here we are."

It was a salon, a man's salon clearly, yet it was the most pleasant room she had ever entered. Instead of covering every inch of space with useless objects, there were photographs and paintings of people and places. One particularly lovely oil was of a dog, the noble head of a retriever.

"I find old Sampson's features a great deal more reassuring than those portraits upstairs. In his face I see honesty and courage and friendship."

"And upstairs, sir?"

He smiled, an expression that seemed to kindle an inner light, causing his entire face to beam. "Better left unsaid."

Then she caught sight of the portrait of an extraordinarily beautiful young woman. The painter had caught the woman's very essence in her eyes; they seemed to both glow and accuse, an intriguing blend that Constance found fascinating.

"Ah, that's Viola."

"Viola? Is she a relation? She's absolutely lovely."

"So, you haven't heard of Viola, eh? Strange. She is to marry my eldest son."

"Dishy?"

"Dishy," the duke confirmed with a nod. "It's most peculiar, if you ask me. I always thought Philip and Viola would make a match of it. They were always such rascals together as children, and always at each other's throats."

A sudden thought came to Constance's mind, of what Stella said about the peers playing together as children. Somehow, she couldn't imagine the pale blonde beauty being a rascal, although the knowing glint in her expression seemed to indicate more spirit than was strictly fashionable. And if she was indeed at anyone's throat, she couldn't imagine any single man who would mind being the focus of her attention.

There was a gentle knock, and the door opened. A maid she had not seen yet wheeled in a tea cart. "Here we go, your grace. This will put some meat on those bones."

"Thank you, Mrs. Hutchinson. And may we please have another cup? My future daughter-in-law is joining me for tea."

"I'm one step ahead of you, your grace. There's an extra setup, from tea to sandwiches to an extra few slices of that cake you're so fond of. Hope you like it as well, Miss Lloyd."

"Thank you, Mrs. Hutchinson. You are nothing short of wondrous."

"That's exactly what the late Mr. Hutchinson used to say, your grace." She curtsied and left them alone.

The duke, with surprising dexterity, poured her tea and filled her plate, not allowing Constance to rise from her seat.

As the tea progressed, they engaged in a delightful discussion of books and ideas, from Ruskin's views on education to Dickens and his characters to Mark Twain's America. The duke asked her thoughtful, well-phrased questions about the Civil War, and offered condolences on the loss of her family and position.

"How very hard it must have been for you, my dear. How very brave you are to have reinvented yourself as a magnificent governess. I can only hope my son will give you the happiness you deserve." As he spoke he watched her over the rim of his teacup, and took exaggerated care with a piece of buttered brown bread.

She swallowed and thanked him, realizing that he was the first individual in the household to speak to her plainly, to treat her as something more than a potential adornment.

Philip must have told him. How else could he have known?

Finally it was time for tea to end.

"This has been so wonderful, sir," she said truthfully.

"For me as well, my dear." He clasped her hands in his dry, parched grasp. "Please come down to visit me often."

"I will. This has been the nicest part of my stay at Hastings House."

The duke smiled and led her to the door.

"She was not always the way she is now," he said, staring just beyond where she stood.

"The duchess?"

"Yes. When I met her she was lovely, a kind and gentle girl. My parents were furious when we married, of course. But I was just the third son, and no one could possibly imagine that I would ever become duke. That's when she changed, as if all the titles and lands took away her joy in life. We stay away from each other as much as possible."

"How very sad," Constance said.

"Yes. I would hate to see that happen to anyone else, especially in the same family. Oh, and Miss Lloyd," he added as an afterthought, "jolly good thinking with those thieves on the road."

"Pardon?"

"I know all about your brilliant thinking, how you saved not only your own life, but most likely future robbery victims as well. I am heartily impressed, my dear. I don't think old Wellington himself could have come up with a better plan under the circumstances. Jolly well done."

She was startled, her mind reeling. "How . . . who . . . when . . ."

"Oh, from Joseph Smith. He wrote me a long missive all about you, Miss Lloyd. I'll say this: any person—male or female—who can make such an impression on Smith deserves to be knighted. Good night, Miss Lloyd."

In a daze, she returned from the duke's underground lair to the garish glare of the upper floors.

Constance was in her room, dressing for dinner— aware that the meal would be all but intolerable after passing such a pleasant afternoon with the duke—when there was a knock on the door.

"Come in, Stella. Do you suppose . . ."

The door opened, and in marched the duchess. As imposing a figure as she had seemed below, in rooms more suited to her in scale and decor, she seemed to dwarf every corner of Constance's modest quarters.

"Your grace." Was the duchess angry that Constance had taken tea with the duke? Was she furious because she had the audacity and vulgarity to call a servant by her name? In short, was the duchess going to order the rack for her?

Anything seemed possible. Anything at all—except for what actually happened.

"My dear, dear girl," the duchess cried. It was then Constance realized with mounting alarm that the woman had tears in her eyes, great oversized drops of tears. "My dear, sweet girl!"

And then the duchess embraced Constance.

Once she had heard of a man being mauled to death by a grizzly bear, and in her shock she wondered if this is what it would feel like. Of course, the grizzly would not have been wearing diamonds the size of pears and the texture of knives. For an alarming moment she thought she would pass out. Just when the world began to tilt, the duchess released her.

"You've done it, my girl!" It was then that Constance realized the duchess was waving a cream-colored card, a piece of paper of some sort. "The wedding plans aren't even fixed yet, and you've done it!"

"Done what?" Should she apologize? Disavow any knowledge of whatever she had done to deserve such treatment?

"The Prince! You and Philip have just been invited to spend a weekend at Sandringham! You will be the guests of the Prince and Princess of Wales! You have arrived, my dear. We have all arrived! I must send a messenger to Lady Trendome. She will be furious!"

"But what about Philip and his campaign? Isn't it important for him to stay here and work on the elections? The polling begins in a matter of days."

"Heavens, no! An invitation to Sandringham will do more good than a year of speech-making and spotty baby-kissing! An invitation to Sandringham! The Prince may not be a king yet, but he is most certainly the king of the social world. An invitation!"

And with that the duchess turned on her heel to leave. First, however, she gave another smile—an appalling expression on her face, as incongruous and unexpected as watching a ploughhorse break into song. "You must have a better room, my dear! Tonight, after our celebration, you will be moved to the gold room!"

Constance did her best to smile back. But somehow, in the pit of her stomach, she had a sinking feeling that it was far, far better to be ignored by the duchess than it was to be the center of her universe.

7

Sandringham was large and impressive, a structure of brick and stone with peaked roofs and expansive windows. Like so many great country homes, it was a mixture of styles; in this case, Tudor and Georgian seemed to have won out over Gothic and neoclassical. Yet, as Philip helpfully pointed out, it was not nearly as large, nor composed of as many architectural examples, as Hastings House. That fact seemed to please him an enormous amount.

The house had been given to the Prince of Wales on his twenty-first birthday. Instead of being a fortress of virtue for the young prince, and later his wife, as his father Prince Albert had intended, a place for them to retreat to the healthful pursuits of the country, it had become yet another place for the Marlborough House set to conduct their amusements. Not only were the more wholesome pursuits generally frowned upon at Sandringham, its location provided the added advantage of being geographically removed from London. Any incidents that could be seen as the least bit ignoble or questionable would take that much longer to reach his mother the Queen's disapproving ears.

In short, Sandringham was much like London's Marlborough House, but with more guns, shrubbery, stocked game and wild life to shoot.

Constance and Stella, now promoted to lady's maid, sat together on one side of the coach, across from Philip and his valet, Owen. She wasn't sure if Owen was the young man's first name or last, but for Philip's purposes, it served as his only name.

"This is it, Constance," Philip said with a curiously flat voice. "This weekend we will make our official entry into the smart set. From now on, we will be on the ins." He then smiled, almost as an afterthought.

Constance tried to catch even a tiny dash of Philip's enthusiasm, but she was simply too fatigued. The duchess had used the week before their journey to Sandringham to indulge in a whirlwind of dressmaking, with three seamstresses ordered up from London, and seven others to assist in the actual sewing. The head seamstress, a Madame Vendome, had displayed a most disconcerting habit of slipping in and out of her broad French accent, occasionally asking for "le bloody needle" or a swatch of that "rotting Brussels lace."

As Constance was being fitted and pinned with breakfast gowns, evening gowns, ball gowns, morning frocks, tweed walking suits, riding habits—the duchess had inquired warily, "You *do* ride, of course?" before ordering the habit—she was simultaneously bombarded with the pedigrees and peccadilloes of the peers most likely to be fellow guests at Sandringham. More than once she had wanted to cry out "Who cares!" at the slanderous tidbits the duchess had obtained secondhand at best, most likely third or fourthhand. Did it really matter that Lord So-and-so was now conducting an open affair with the former paramour of the Prince of Wales, an erstwhile bowling alley employee known as "Skittles"? Or that Lady Whatever-her-name had once packed her bags and waited under a decorative Hyde Park footbridge to elope with an Austrian count, only to discover that his proposal had been his club penalty as a result of losing a rubber of bridge?

All in all, Constance could find no reason she needed to know these rather pathetic scraps of human frailty.

As the day of their departure finally arrived, an underhouse maid appeared at her room carrying a small tin bucket containing what appeared to be lunch, all wrapped neatly in brown paper.

"It's from his grace, miss," the maid had bobbed. "He wishes you the best of luck, and sends this to you. The duke feels one can never be unprepared when carrying a nice meal, miss. Especially while on a journey. And he tucked in the cheese and butter sandwiches and raisin tea cakes himself, miss."

Constance laughed for the first time in days. She laughed from sheer exhaustion, from the absurdity of the gift, and finally because the old duke had once again shown her genuine kindness and friendship.

It was with an arched eyebrow that the duchess saw Constance leave for Sandringham with four carefully packed trunks, one ladies' maid, a velvet reticule, a veiled hat, an elegant green traveling suit, and an unadorned tin bucket.

The journey to Sandringham itself, by rail and then coach, was surprisingly swift. And in a matter of hours it seemed, they were on the threshold of royalty.

At the front entrance, where a scalloped awning covered the steps, there stood a brace of Highland gillies, men with legs like tree trunks protruding from under their heavy wool kilts, positioned to greet them, to unload the luggage, and to direct each guest inside.

If the need should arise, she felt sure they could toss a pianoforte or heft a ram over their shoulders.

Since Philip and Constance were not married, only engaged, it was understood that they would be issued rooms in separate wings. The thought, vague as it was, of seeing Philip in various stages of undress was more than unsettling, simply because she could not possibly imagine him less than polished and brushed.

Other carriages were rolling up the drive at the same time, jostling for position, the guests stubbornly refusing to descend from their coaches until they had the full attention of at least one of the gillies, preferably both. The ladies nodded at each other, the long feathers on their hats dipping in an aviary ritual greeting. Some smiled, holding eye contact for only a moment or two. Later, when the maid had unpacked their trunks and they had slipped on the newest of their tea gowns over their tightest-laced corsets, only then would the real acknowledgments begin.

The men greeted each other with hearty handshakes and bluff chuckles about their latest fishing jaunts or the best place to bag pheasant or duck. For the men as well, the real weekend would not begin until the evening, over billiards and brandy and tobacco smoke.

On the reverse side, that was also where the social shoving, the elbowing for the prince and princess's attention, and the opportunity to studiously ignore another guest would begin in earnest. The coach descent was merely the brief prologue to the adventures that would unfold later.

Constance knew she was being watched. It was like the waltz at Cowes, when the Prince had asked her to dance and suddenly everyone knew who Constance Lloyd was. This was the same sensation, and some of the same faces that had been in ball gowns and white ties were now in traveling tweeds, all appraising her with the same narrow-eyed curiosity.

Philip and Owen went in one direction, led by a footman in white stockings and, she suspected, padded calves. It was common to add a bit of horsehair muscle to outline the legs of the more slender, less strapping footmen, as well as to pay higher wages to footmen clever enough to be both well-calved and over six feet tall.

It was something of a marvel to her that the royal homes still insisted on being served by men in satin knee breeches and white powdered wigs. She wondered that the members of the royal household weren't struck by the unpleasant associations with attire from the last century, such as the American Revolution or, more to the point, the French Revolution.

Constance and Stella were led to their rooms by a charming young woman in a blue dress with a white lace cap. The house itself seemed very much a family hunting lodge, filled with stuffed game birds and photographs of friends and family members on every wall and on every surface.

Constance was well pleased with her room, a smallish bedroom that was more homey than regal. Then she caught a fragrance of something familiar and almost forgotten, so light and airy it would be missed by anyone else, and tears came to her eyes before her mind had a chance to identify the source.

Dogwood. On the large mahogany dresser covered with a delicate lace runner, held in a plain white vase, was a large armful of dogwood. With a small cry she dropped her reticule and bucket and stepped towards the bouquet, inhaling the scent she had only experienced in memory since she left Virginia almost ten years earlier.

There was a tap at the door, and Constance, her

eyes still closed and her face still buried in the flowers, was barely able to utter "Come in."

Dogwood. Images poured into her mind, of her mother trimming the dogwood trees in front of the house, her father with a sprig of dogwood in his lapel.

"Miss Lloyd? How do you like your room?"

"It's beautiful," she whispered. Then she turned to face the person she assumed would be a maid.

In her room stood Alexandra, the Princess of Wales. Constance sank into a deep curtsy. "Your Majesty."

But the princess waved an impatient hand. "Please rise, Miss Lloyd. Is your room satisfactory?"

The princess was exquisite, her eyes a blue like pale, sapphire ice, her skin fragile yet flawless, her golden hair arranged on top of her head in small curls, a few tumbling in careful tendrils over her forehead. Her voice, even with the marked Danish accent, was as eager to please as a small child.

"The room is perfect, Your Majesty. And the flowers. I haven't had the good fortune to enjoy dogwood since I was a child."

"I am so very pleased!" The Princess clasped her hands and smiled, revealing beautifully even white teeth. "I know you are from Virginia, and so I found a hothouse in London that had some dogwood trees growing. I feared they would not arrive on time for you, but they came this very morning."

"Your Majesty, thank you. Your thoughtfulness is overwhelming."

"Your happy expression is all I need to see! You may know that I am not from England, but from Denmark. Many times I have a sickness and longing for my home and all I knew as a girl. When I heard that you came here to England also as a young woman, with no family, I knew exactly how you must sometimes feel. I just hope the flowers make you happy, not sad with your memories."

"Happy, Your Majesty. Very happy indeed."

The princess smiled and stepped closer towards Constance. "Now, a few things I must tell you on this your first visit. We have tea at five o'clock. Some of the guests will still be arriving, and others will wish to rest after their journey, so tea will be quite informal. The men may wish to just poke about for harmless animals to shoot tomorrow morning. And we dine in the evening at exactly eight-thirty. The Prince is very punctual, I am not, which is why you may notice some of the clocks downstairs are fifteen minutes fast. Dear Bertie is always hoping the fast clocks will speed me up, but that hasn't happened thus far, I fear to say. Your clock in here is correct, though."

"Tea is at five, dinner is at eight-thirty," Constance repeated. "Thank you again, Your Majesty."

"Oh, and Miss Lloyd?"

"Your Majesty?"

"If you have a desire to eat," she lowered her voice, "do so quickly. We have no long five-hour meals here. Dinner is over with very quickly, and the Prince will have his plate clean in the time it takes the rest of us to pick up a fork. If you're hungry, don't bother to speak to the gentleman on your right, or the lady across the table. Just eat! Please rest, and if you wish to come, we will see you in an hour at tea, Miss Lloyd."

"Thank you, Your Majesty," was all Constance could say as the princess left her room. She walked with a very slight, but quite noticeable limp, a side effect of the rheumatic fever that had very nearly claimed her life several years before, and had left her partially deaf. Yet she refused to let her physical limitations interfere with her social duties. She heard the Princess stop at a room down the hall. "Lady Collins? Is your room quite comfortable?"

How very astonishing, Constance thought as she

again looked over at the dogwoods. How very astonishing indeed.

Tea was quite a casual affair, in spite of Constance being all but sewn into a tight cream and brown silk gown, with a square-cut neckline and earbobs borrowed from the duchess. And also in spite of, or perhaps because of, the presence of the Princess of Wales, it seemed a wonderfully amiable gathering. She held sway over the group in a quiet, gentle manner, so pleasant that any natural rivalry between any of the women was charmed into benign submission.

There was Lady Collins, whose room was just beyond Constance's—a natural storyteller with a vivacious sense of humor. Then there was an older woman, Lady Trent, who seemed so absolutely thrilled just to be there, she did nothing but smile and act pleased with every aspect of the tea, from the marmalade to the napkin ring. The lobster salad, served with every tea because the Prince requested it, sent her into a delirious state of ecstasy. Other women were there, although Constance did not quite catch their names.

And then a young woman entered the room, a slender blonde with hair so pale it seemed an ethereal halo about her head, and a walk so lissome she seemed to glide rather than take actual steps. Her curtsy to the Princess was a study in grace, and then she turned to Constance. At once she realized it was the woman from the portrait at Hastings House.

"Viola, my dear cousin!" chirped Abigail Merrymeade, an elegant young woman married to, as Constance deduced from the conversation, an elderly marquis. Lady Merrymeade was the very image of a classical English beauty, from her pale blond hair to her rich brown eyes. Her nose, slender and rather longish, was perfectly straight. Her teeth, unfortunately, were also classically English, slightly protruding and a vexing shade of yellow. But that didn't matter. She had obviously learned to avoid smiling whenever possible and seldom spoke more than five words in a row. Whether her manner was an attempt to deflect attention from her teeth, or simply her natural demeanor, it did not really matter, for it suited her very well.

But it was Viola who fascinated Constance. She remembered the comment the duke had made about Viola and Philip being so suited to each other, and had to agree. She was lovely and elegant.

As she was contemplating the issue, Viola stepped over to Constance.

"Miss Lloyd?" She extended her hand. "Hello. I do believe we are to become related. I am Viola Rathbottom, and, at the moment, I am engaged to Dishy."

"At the moment, Miss Rathbottom?" Constance asked the other woman as she sat down next to her.

"Yes. I believe this is the fourth time we've been engaged to each other."

"The fifth time," corrected Abigail Merrymeade. "Don't forget the Christmas ball."

"Good heavens, I always forget about that one. I stand corrected. Dishy and I have been engaged five times. And I do have every hope that we will actually make it down the aisle on this go-round." Viola then leaned toward Constance. "So tell me, how do you like our soon-to-be mum-in-law?"

"Well," Constance began carefully. "She is really rather formidable."

Viola smiled, and Constance wondered why the portrait artist had painted her with such a serious expression, for she had such an engaging smile. Her entire face seemed to glow.

"Formidable. That sums it up quite nicely," she agreed. "I've known her all of my life, since my family's land borders the Hastings estate. And I've known Philip all of my life, too."

"And will Dishy be joining this party? I don't recall the duchess mentioning that he would be here as well."

"No. You see, Dishy is rather odd when it comes to society. I believe he would find a visit such as this something akin to torture. In that he is much like his father, which is why the duchess places such hopes on Philip. And our engagement is not official yet, so there was really no need."

Constance found the situation rather peculiar, an engaged woman at a house party without her fiancé. There was a distinct hint that Viola was not at all eager to have her future husband at her side, neither at the present time, nor at any other time in the future. Viola seemed about to say something else when Lady Trent sat on the nearest chair, happily touching the edge of a pillow as if it were a holy relic.

"This fringe," she whispered. "It is absolutely magnificent. Unlike any other fringe, of course. Just think. This is royal fringe! Would you like to touch it, my dear?" Lady Trent offered the pillow to Constance, who politely declined. By then Viola was already in a discussion with her cousin about a wayward mutual acquaintance.

All of the rest of the women were impeccably polite to Constance, taking their cue from the Princess. There were no comments about drunken governesses, no mention of vulgar Americans. She had no other chance to speak to Viola.

After tea, when most of the other women went to their rooms to rest and contemplate the task of dressing for dinner, Constance asked, and was granted, permission to visit the library. She was given the directions and, without changing from her tea gown, went to find a book.

The heavy door opened slowly at her prodding, and at once she caught the wonderful leather and paper smell of a library. Not just any library, but an old one filled with books that had been read and reread in that very room.

It was dark inside, the sun just setting over the trees beyond the lawn. With a sigh she stepped inside the room.

"Miss Lloyd."

The masculine voice was so soft that at first she thought she had imagined it.

"Constance."

She gasped, startled for just the briefest of moments, for she knew exactly whose voice she had heard.

"Joseph," she said before she could see him. And he rose from a table to the right of the door. Before him were spread a half dozen books.

His tweeds seemed to need a pressing, and his cravat was loose, perhaps unknotted with his fingers without his realization as he read. A thatch of hair, reddish-brown in the fading sunlight, fell over his forehead, and he tossed his head in a brisk gesture to remove it from his vision.

He seemed to regain his composure before she did. "How very good it is to see you," he said warmly.

She crossed the room with a purposeful stride, her hand extended as if they had been business associates. He hesitated a moment, then smiled and shook her hand.

"I hope your business went well in Scotland." Her voice was unsteady, and she watched his eyes, the play of light reflecting in the rich color. How often in the past two weeks she had thought of him. How very often she had imagined his face, or an expression. And he would never know, must never know, that she had been thinking of him so frequently.

"It did go well, thank you."

"Good. I'm glad." She took a deep breath. "What are you reading?"

For a moment he just watched her, not reacting to her words. Then he straightened. "Excuse me? I'm afraid I didn't catch what you said."

"I just asked what you are reading."

"Reading? Ah, you mean the books. Well, chemistry, I suppose. Yes. Forgive me, I am reading some of the Prince's chemistry books."

"And are you absolutely sure?"

His laugh filled the room. "Reasonably so."

"I don't wish to look at those pages and find pictures of female French circus performers."

"Unfortunately, someone else procured it before me—nothing but an empty space where it usually is. So I settled for a book by Lister."

"Ah, and what does the good Professor Lister have to say?"

"He says, and this of course is an indirect quote, 'it is a good thing to wash one's hands.'"

"He is a learned man."

"Yes."

Again there was a lull in their conversation, although it did not feel uncomfortable or awkward. Rather, they both felt at ease, savoring the moments together.

He shook his head as if to toss back the wayward lock of hair, yet it had not fallen into his eyes. His voice was strained as he spoke. "And how are you adjusting to your new life? You must be well pleased. After all, you have managed to obtain an invitation from the Prince of Wales."

"As have you, Joseph. You never mentioned that you traveled in such exalted circles." Her hands dropped to her waist, and she clasped them tightly.

And then their eyes met, truly met, for the first

time. They remained motionless, suspended in time. She watched his gaze, his eyes as his expression softened. The small dimple at the corner of her mouth caught his attention, and as he had guessed, she then broke out in a full smile.

"Ah, well," he stammered, unable to look away. His mind raced with reasons to glance up, or to return his focus to the chemistry books he had been studying. Tapping his fingertips on the table, he willed himself to pick up one of the books, to continue reading as he had before she had entered the library.

But he couldn't. It was as if an invisible force rendered him incapable of voluntary movement. She was captivating, he thought, staring down at her face in the dusty library. She was utterly captivating, all the more so because she had no idea of her power.

"The Princess put dogwood in my room," she blurted out.

He stopped tapping his fingers. "Pardon?"

"The Princess of Wales filled my dresser with dogwood."

"Dogwood?" And then he remembered the flower from his travels to the United States. "Dogwood, from Virginia. How very much like her, to find something special for a guest."

"Is she always this kind?"

"She has been to me. She always places books she thinks will be of interest to me on my bedside table. Last time I was here it was *The Dyemaker's Companion,* an out-of-print manual from about a hundred years ago, all about how to make pigment from berries and insects. Another time it was a book of Celtic folk tales."

They both stood in silence, not quite certain of what else to say, but very much aware of each other's presence.

"Are you happy, Constance?"

His voice was a mere undertone.

"I . . . I do not know," she answered. "But right now, at this very moment, I am happy."

It was as if the world had stopped turning, as if the entire universe existed only in that room, with these two people.

His breath feathered against her cheek as he leaned over her, and she took a step towards him. And then, both suddenly and inevitably, their lips were together.

Never had she kissed, or been kissed, in such a way. The night at the inn they had shared a moment of sweet intimacy, but now it was as if the two weeks apart had intensified their emotions, firing them into an explosive roar.

It was an alien feeling, as if the floor had dropped out from beneath her feet, yet still she stood suspended and supported. There was no self-consciousness, as there had been on the few occasions when Philip had kissed her. Then she had been aware of extraneous sounds, a distant bird chirp, the clip-clop of horses' hooves.

Now all she could think of was Joseph, how he permeated her every sense. She inhaled his fragrance, a clean scent of masculine skin and the outdoors, and felt her lips against his, so soft and very warm, surprisingly soft for a man. Above all, she could taste him, her mouth pressed against his, the very air he breathed now caressing her cheek.

He made a movement, and for an awful instant she thought he was going to push her away. Instead, he drew her closer to him, against his body, their mouths still locked together.

Then his tongue plunged into her mouth, and she jumped just slightly, but his gentle movement lulled her back to his embrace. It wasn't strange at all, it was perfect, as if it was something they had always done.

And then he did pull away.

"No," he rasped. "No."

She was in a dream state, as if she had been given a narcotic and her limbs were deliciously heavy.

"Constance, we must not." His voice tore through her consciousness, shattering every comfortable fiber she had only just learned she possessed.

"Please, Joseph." Was that her voice, that husky plea?

"No." The tone was firm and gave no room for argument. Before she could speak further, he had slammed shut the leaves of the oversized book he had been reading and left the room.

His footsteps still echoed in her mind minutes later, when the light in the room finally faded, and Constance was once again alone.

Joseph walked briskly across the lawn, attempting to clear his head.

"Smith! Smith, you rascal!"

He stopped and took a deep breath. "Philip," he said at last, turning towards his friend.

"I had no idea you would be here." Philip was so pleased to see him, it was impossible not to return the smile.

"It was a rather last-minute arrangement."

"I see." Philip shoved his hands into his pockets. "Grand day, is it not?"

"Yes. I've been indoors most of the day, but it is indeed pleasant. Now if you'll excuse me, I have to be off now."

"Urgent business? I do hope nothing is amiss. You look rather shaken."

"No, no. Of course not. Everything is fine."

"Good." Philip nodded, looking down at the grass. "Mother is pleased that I was invited."

Joseph smiled. "I can imagine. And you must be pleased as well."

Philip did not answer. Instead he kicked a clump of sod over with the toe of his boot. Then, in a peculiar gesture, he wiped his mouth with the back of his hand, as if deciding how to respond. When he did, his words came out in a rush. "So far there is nothing spectacular about being here, is there?"

Joseph was not sure he had heard correctly. "Excuse me?"

"I mean, it's really just the same old crowd from London, or anyplace else for that matter."

"I'm astonished, Philip. I thought you'd be all smiles and delight to be here."

"Not really. It seems rather pointless."

Joseph blinked. "Philip, I cannot believe what I just heard."

"I suppose you are here on some business rather than pleasure."

"In a sense, yes. Why?"

"You really enjoy your work, don't you?"

"Yes. I enjoy it a great deal."

"I've never said this before, but I envy you. I always have, I suppose. You have always had a purpose, a sense of knowing exactly what direction you should take. Even as children, you seemed to know, although God knows how."

"My sense of direction is not so well-developed," Joseph admitted, surprised by the simple truth. "In many ways, I don't know what the hell I am doing."

"No, you don't understand what I mean." He looked up from the grass, and Joseph noticed for the first time that there were dark circles under his friend's eyes. "You are able to do what you want, see whomever you please, make your own way in this world."

Joseph said nothing, still startled by Philip's sudden tone.

"You know, Smith, I like Constance a great deal. I

want you to know that. Whatever happens, I like her a great deal."

Joseph swallowed. "She's a wonderful woman. You're lucky."

"I mean I like her, damn it. She deserves more than someone like me. She's intelligent and quick."

"She is," Joseph said simply.

"Did you know that Viola is here?"

"No. Is she? I didn't see her."

"Well, Viola is here. So is that wretched cousin of hers."

"Abigail." He said the name under his breath.

"Sorry, Joseph. I forgot. Anyway, Viola and Dishy are on again."

"Again? Do you suppose it will stick this time?"

Philip shrugged. "Who knows? Well, I'll let you go now."

"Wait a minute." Joseph placed his hand on his friend's arm. "What's really bothering you? You're at Sandringham, you have a beautiful fiancée, and you're all but in as an MP. Yet you're about as far from content as I've ever seen you. There's no use pretending with me—I know you far too well. I haven't seen you like this since Scuffy Williams broke your cricket bat."

Philip did not smile at the recollection.

"Tell me," Joseph prodded.

"Damn it," Philip rasped. "I don't want to be here. I don't want to live my life for my mother. I want to be free to make my own mistakes."

"Then do it."

Philip laughed, but it was with bitterness. "It's not that easy."

"Of course it's not that easy. But is the way you feel now easy?"

Philip shook his head.

"For God's sake, Philip. Listen to me. You must do

whatever it is that will secure your own happiness. And there's still time for you to follow your own dreams; I know you have them. Before they dry up, before you become just an empty shell. Follow whatever path you must."

"But my mother . . ."

"Your mother will be fine."

"But I have an obligation . . ."

"To yourself. You owe no one else a single thing. Philip, you're a good man. But if you keep on ignoring your real talents and desires, you will lose your essence. And once lost, you'll be lost forever."

Finally Philip looked directly into Joseph's eyes. He did not speak, just nodded slightly before he walked back to the house.

And Joseph stood on the lawn by himself, wondering who he had just given the lecture to . . . his friend, or himself.

If tea had been a casual affair, dinner was as choreographed as a ballet. It began with the nearly ceremonial gathering in the wood-paneled room, where sherry was delicately consumed from etched crystal glasses. One glass only; any more would be frowned upon, even in the Prince's licentious set. When the royals themselves entered, one and all curtsied and bowed, and more mingling ensued.

Constance was very much aware of Joseph. Of all the men gathered, to her he was by far the most exciting, including the Prince himself. While the others preened for the Wales's, Philip was notably quiet, almost withdrawn. She wondered if he could be ill, he seemed so distracted. But she noticed that he glanced over at Viola Rathbottom frequently, often while he was engaged in conversation with others.

"Miss Lloyd." Joseph smiled when he was at her side.

He was spectacular, she realized, in his simple black swallowtail jacket and black tie. His hair was brushed back, the first time she had seen him so carefully groomed. The result was exactly what she had expected. He was handsome, almost beyond belief.

"Mr. Smith," she replied, unable to stop smiling at the mere sight of him.

"You look beautiful tonight, Constance." His voice was serious, and so low that she alone could hear his words.

For a moment she closed her eyes. "Thank you," she whispered.

Her gown, of shimmering silk shot through with silver thread, was easily the equal of any gown present. For that she silently thanked the overbearing duchess, who had forced Constance to stand still for the tortuous hours each fitting seemed to require.

It was all worth it. He thought she looked beautiful.

"Miss Lloyd?" The voice was different, and she opened her eyes to find the round face of the Prince of Wales.

"Your Majesty." She curtsied, careful not to spill her drink all over his shoes.

"I do hope I did not wake you, Miss Lloyd," he said with a decided wink. "And Smith, good to see you, too, old boy."

"Your Majesty, as always, the pleasure is mine." Joseph bowed, but not nearly as deeply as the other men had, and certainly not within reach of Philip's bow.

"Did you find the books you required?" The prince seemed to be addressing Joseph, but his gaze was entirely on Constance.

He was a pleasant man, she thought, watching his face as he spoke. Certainly not handsome, with his bulging eyes and round face, his rather sparse whiskers and his rather too-full waistline. His accent was unique, almost guttural. He pronounced his 'r's with a Teutonic growl, remarkably foreign-sounding, although he was, of course, born in England. His father, Prince Albert, had been German, and the prince himself had been isolated as a boy, forbidden to play with British children his own age.

"I did find the books, sir," Joseph said. He did not address the Prince as Your Majesty, and for a moment Constance feared he would be reprimanded.

The prince took no notice.

"Excellent, Smith. I'm glad to hear it." Then he turned his full attention to Constance. "And Miss Lloyd, how are you enjoying your stay?"

"Very much, Your Majesty." From the corner of her eye she saw Philip glance towards them. Instead of walking in their direction—she was, after all, speaking with HRH—Philip stepped over to Viola, who was standing by herself near the fireplace.

"I am heartily glad to hear it, Miss Lloyd. My wife told me that she was able to locate some special flowers for you, is that not the case?"

"It is, Your Majesty." She smiled, and he returned the smile. "It was such a wonderful surprise. I hadn't been able to enjoy the scent and sight of dogwood since I was a girl."

A liveried servant stood in the center of the room and made a single tap on an enormous gong. "Your Majesties, ladies and gentlemen, dinner is served."

"Well," said the prince, placing his, and then her empty sherry glass on a silver tray. "Shall we?" He crooked his arm, and it took a moment for Constance to realize his meaning.

The Prince of Wales himself wished to escort her in to dinner.

They led the way, the others falling in ascending social rank. She could not help but giggle.

"And what is so funny, Miss Lloyd?" The Prince

inquired, leaning forward to hear what she would say.

"In all honesty, Your Majesty, I fear what I was thinking may not be appropriate to share with you."

"Oh, then do, you must! I will be terribly disappointed if you do not tell me immediately what caused you to laugh."

"Is that a royal order?"

"It is indeed! Under penalty of . . . well, something wretched and vastly unpleasant."

"In that case, Your Majesty, I confess that I find it highly amusing that I am walking with you at this moment, at the head of so many venerable peers."

"That was it?" He seemed disappointed.

"Not precisely, Your Majesty. I just thought that, as a governess, the last time I entered a room at the head of so many people, it was in a nursery."

"Well, I do hope we are a better behaved lot, Miss Lloyd."

At that precise moment a gentleman backed loudly into the dinner gong, causing it to clang into a marble-topped table.

"I'm afraid I have my doubts, Your Majesty," she muttered.

Before she could elaborate, the prince stopped just over the threshold to the massive dining room, threw his head back, and roared with laughter.

No one else had heard what Constance said, although eyebrows were raised in silent question, and the Prince's obvious delight with his partner was duly noted. Only one member of the party smiled along with HRH's genuine pleasure with his lovely companion, and that was the Welshman, Joseph Smith.

8

The first part of the meal passed in a kind of silver-plated blur, as dish after dish swept by her. There was an enormous epergne, with arms holding dozens of candles, all flickering and reflecting off the wood and silver. It was a sprawling, grotesque monstrosity that resembled a beast struggling from the sea in Greek mythology, and it obstructed her view of the other side of the table. The ocean theme seemed to be echoed throughout the first course, where platters of fish, their glazed eyes eerily mimicking the expression of more than one of the guests, were offered at speeds faster than the creature could have traveled in life.

The silverware, china, crystal, and napkins, while of extraordinary quality, were quite plain, no gold flocking or ornate designs. Lady Trent, the woman for whom tea was an apparent celebration of the mundane, was rendered speechless once again by the sheer quantity of the sights. It was similar to watching a cat following the reflections of a chandelier—her expression was nothing short of perplexed wonderment.

The food came in quick succession, always beautifully served, always with a sauce that, no matter what its color or content, seemed to taste merely warm and salty.

And in time, the conversation turned surprisingly salty as well.

Constance attempted to avoid being the center of attention, but the Prince, sitting just three people away from her, was constantly drawing her into his conversation. Princess Alexandra, catching only a few occasional words or phrases, was unable to understand much of the dining room buzz, but seemed content to focus on the guests to her immediate left and right.

Prince Edward, in the middle of eating a rather large tenderloin of beef, suddenly spoke up in a voice loud enough for all of the guests to hear.

"I say, Miss Lloyd said the most confoundedly funny thing as we entered the room this evening."

She swallowed, and instinctively glanced over at Joseph. He was four seats away, his expression bland. Philip was across from him, behind the mythical centerpiece. All she could see was the top of his head and the motion of his right elbow, which seemed to be working with startling rapidity to keep wine at his lips and the food from being ladled on his plate.

The Princess had heard her husband. "Do tell us, Your Majesty, what Miss Lloyd said."

Heads swiveled from the Prince, on one end of the table, to the Princess, on the opposite end, then back to the Prince, like spectators at a lawn tennis match.

"She said, just as we walked into this very room, 'I believe this gathering is as ill-behaved as any group of children I encountered as a governess!'" Then the Prince, his face red with repressed mirth, barked with laughter.

Constance's mouth opened just slightly before she

shut it again. By then, everyone was staring at her with bewildered frowns. Snatches of conversation filtered into her mind.

"What is *that* supposed to mean?"

"Bloody hell, what was amusing about that?"

"Bloody hell, what did she bloody well mean?"

"What sparkling wit, what?"

"She *is* an American, you know."

Joseph leaned forward, his expression still neutral, and raised both eyebrows at her before settling back into his chair.

"Tell us, what did you mean, Miss Lloyd?" The Princess, perhaps confused and blaming her inability to detect any humor in the statement on her faulty hearing and her not-quite-perfect English, searched the faces of her guests. She seemed relieved to find confusion in their features. Only the Prince, still chortling to himself, seemed in high spirits.

"Yes, Miss Lloyd," said Abigail Merrymeade. "Do explain. I'm afraid the rest of us are not as clever as either you or the Prince."

Lady Merrymeade's husband, apparently exhausted from the journey, was sitting next to Constance. He was perhaps the oldest man she had ever seen, a mere sketch of a man, the walking memory of what he had once been. Even at this early hour, with the commotion of dinner, he had fallen fast asleep. His closed eyes and occasional snort were the only features that separated him from most of the other diners.

Then a strange thing happened. Abigail Merrymeade looked directly at Joseph, a stare of both intimacy and challenge. Constance knew at once that she was the one, she was the woman who must have broken his heart. A single glance at Joseph confirmed it. His lips were set so firmly they were almost white, and she could see his hand clench his napkin.

"Well," stated Philip from behind the centerpiece, stammering in his attempt to help her. "My dear fiancée means that, in America, the children are not nearly as well behaved as they are here."

How much sherry and claret *had* he consumed?

It was all she could do to keep from ducking beneath the table.

Constance began to open her mouth to explain when Joseph piped up to try and change the topic of conversation. "Miss Lloyd and I had quite an adventure as I was escorting her to Hastings House."

If possible, she would have given every item of clothing, including the ones she was wearing, if the floor would show mercy and swallow her within the next half minute. Could this meal get any worse?

"Do tell, Smith." Philip's voice was eager.

"Well." Joseph carefully avoided her eyes. "When I escorted her from Cowes to Hastings House, we were held up by cutthroats. Only Miss Lloyd's quick thinking and steady aim with a revolver saved us."

"Mr. Smith," countered Constance. "I believe you are leaving out your own part." She turned to the other guests. "You see, he managed to disarm and disable some men lurking in the bushes. Had it not been for Mr. Smith's bravery and ability, I would not be here myself."

"What?" The prince was so riveted, he put down his fork. "Do you mean to tell me that you both were involved in a life-threatening adventure?"

Joseph nodded hesitantly. "Well, Your Majesty, at the time I don't believe we realized the true danger. But the point is that Miss Lloyd was worth any five men when it came to handling the situation."

There was a hum of excitement. Philip—nodding to the manservant with the claret, who obligingly refilled his glass—looked at Viola, who immediately glanced away from him.

"Do tell us all, Smith!" The Prince's voice boomed across the table. Joseph hesitated, and again leaned towards Constance. "I am afraid, Your Majesty, that I promised Miss Lloyd I would tell no one of the adventure. I am a man of my word."

"Fat lot of good that does me," Constance muttered under her breath.

"Miss Lloyd," the Prince commanded. "Please give Smith here permission to relate the tale. I am well disposed to hear an adventure."

"Well, Your Majesty," she began, twisting the napkin between her fingers. "I'm afraid Mr. Smith has been overly generous with his praise."

"Balderdash!" The Prince pounded a meaty fist on the table, causing the centerpiece to rumble and the crystal to vibrate. "Smith here is nothing if not honest. To a fault, I might add. It's most bothersome to get any information from him at all."

"That is because Mr. Smith has many secrets," purred Abigail Merrymeade. Constance had an unexpected, happy image of Lady Merrymeade being consumed by the centerpiece.

Joseph merely addressed Constance. "Miss Lloyd, with your permission, may I relate the story of our adventure? Or, rather, our misadventure?"

Constance had no choice but to acquiesce. And Joseph, who thus far had demonstrated a remarkable ability to use words sparingly, proceeded to weave the tale with such wondrous skill, Constance herself was completely caught up in the narrative.

He left nothing out, from the oysters that had made him ill to her shooting the hat off one of the thieves, and finally, in a description that defied logic but was fully accepted by the audience, he recounted her turning the tables on the thieves, forcing them to run away in fright. He merely mentioned his own part in passing.

"In short," he concluded, "Miss Lloyd forced nine armed men to throw down their weapons and flee in terror from both herself, a beautiful lady wearing a stylish traveling suit, and a pigment manufacturer disabled by an unwholesome mollusk."

During the tale no one had moved. Even the servants, fully absorbed by the account, had allowed the meats to cool and the ices to warm. At the conclusion, Prince Edward chortled in delight.

"Excellent, Smith! Well told, well told indeed!" And then he motioned to the head butler, who, in silent understanding, made a subtle gesture to the other servants. In the briefest of moments, champagne flutes were followed quickly by cork-popping and the pouring of Charles Heidsieck's wine.

"Let us have a toast," announced the future King of England. "To Constance Lloyd, a most welcome addition to any gathering, and a veritable flower amongst women."

As everyone but Constance raised their glasses, except for old Lord Merrymeade, who had started to drool discreetly from the left side of his mouth, their faces reflected a turbulent resignation. They all recognized that she was the new favorite, the chosen one. Joseph Smith, with his poetic and flattering account of their adventure, had kindled the romantic spark within the Prince, a man who had grown to adulthood with little but his imagination for companionship. The desire to live and experience such enticing dangers and triumphs had always been out of his reach. Such excitement had always been kept safely at bay.

Constance Lloyd, the exotic American beauty, was the personification of his still-vigorous boyhood dreams. Through her, perhaps, he could experience the daring exploits that had so long been denied him.

Joseph Smith's words had elevated her from the ranks of a comely dinner companion to that of number one object of desire. This was not the first time the Prince had singled out a woman upon whom to cast his robust attentions. If she desired, after she was safely married to Philip, she would be invited to join a revolving cast of women, including the infamous "Skittles" of bowling alley fame.

In that single toast, Constance realized that she had just made a tableful of potential enemies.

Joseph Smith, sitting four seats away from the flower amongst women, silently cursed his own ability to tell a story.

When the women withdrew to the parlor after dinner, the men remained behind to smoke, drink port, and discuss all things of a masculine nature. It was an understood truth that men required time by themselves to utter their baser sentiments, to speak their less evolved or cultured concepts. And it would never do to insult or in any way frighten the ladies with those manly notions.

"I say, that Miss Lloyd has a most damned attractive wardrobe, does she not?" Lord Trent smiled as he accepted a fragrant cigar from the butler. "And a most fetching hairstyle, what?"

"Indeed she does," agreed Lord Collins, swirling the port and admiring the liquor fingers suspended on the side of the glass. "What would you call that hairstyle?"

"I daresay it's of a classical nature, much like one would see on an ancient urn," offered another gentleman, snipping the tip off his cigar with a tool from his watch fob. "The ribbons contrast nicely with the color of her hair, though."

Throughout the conversation, the prince simply smiled, as if eavesdropping on lavish praise of his personal attributes. Philip was busy with his port and preventing the butler from removing the last of his claret and champagne before he had time to swallow each last drop.

Joseph Smith, only vaguely aware of the other men's discussion, ran a finger along the rim of his snifter and wondered how he could have been such an absolute fool.

"So tell me, Miss Lloyd, what sort of artillery do you favor?" Lady Collins inquired, accepting a cup of tea.

"In all honesty, Lady Collins, that was a lucky shot indeed that I let off on those men. Nothing more."

Constance was very aware of the open stares of the women now that they were away from the men. There was challenge and speculation on all of their faces. The only exception was Princess Alexandra, who was unfailingly cheerful and polite. At one point Constance detected a sympathetic smile from the princess, for which she was more than grateful.

"Once I heard of a man in Africa," continued Lady Collins. "He shot a tiger right between the eyes, then ate the meat. A rather glorious image, is it not? Man triumphing over the wild and all that."

"Have you ever shot anything alive?" Lady Merrymeade asked Constance.

She suddenly felt ill, shaking her head and hoping that someone, anyone, would change the topic.

"Come, come, Abigail," said Viola. "I believe Miss Lloyd is rather tired of this topic. Let us speak of other things."

"Don't be modest, Miss Lloyd." Abigail Merrymeade did not even make a pretense of selecting a sweet or holding a cup of tea. She sat directly across from Constance, her hands braced on the arms of a chair, her eyes unwavering. "I know Joseph very well. Very well indeed. And I have never heard him speak so. He was a veritable gusher, was he not, Lady Collins?"

"I should say so, my dear. Miss Lloyd, did you ever fire arms in your war?"

Constance felt as if her stomach had been kicked. "I, well . . . That was a very long time ago."

"Not really," said Lady Merrymeade. "A few short years, in actuality. But to return to the subject, Joseph was quite taken with your talents, Miss Lloyd. Whenever I see him in a setting such as this, I am so very aware of his background."

"Whatever do you mean, Lady Merrymeade?" asked the Princess.

Abigail paused slightly, but continued. "What I mean, Your Majesty, is that Mr. Smith is so very much out of his element here. He was not to the manner born, so to speak."

"My husband enjoys his company a great deal," replied the Princess. "Mr. Smith is very knowledgeable in science and technology, which is of great interest to the Prince, just as it was to his father, Prince Albert."

"Not to mention, Your Highness, Mr. Smith tells a ripping good yarn!" Lady Barrington added. "And he is most handsome. I always feel a man should be as handsome as possible, and both Lord Hastings and Mr. Smith seem to me to be the very models of masculine beauty."

"And they are such close friends," Viola said with a wink towards Constance, an acknowledgment of the successful change of topic. "I have known Mr. Smith for years and years, ever since Philip used to bring him home for school holidays. Even then they were quite a striking pair."

There was a murmur of agreement. Abigail's stance remained firm, and Constance suddenly did not feel well.

There was malice in her eyes, Constance thought. Genuine malice.

"Miss Lloyd, getting back to the guns, you must do the fair sex a favor by joining the shoot tomorrow morning!" Lady Barrington suggested.

"No, really . . ."

But the princess had heard. "Oh, what a splendid idea! Please, Miss Lloyd, do take a crack at it, will you not?"

"What if she is a truly awful shot, and kills one of the men?" another woman said.

"That may not be such a bad thing," said Abigail Merrymeade, with a tone light enough to evoke giggles from the women, but with an unmistakable, chilling undertone.

Constance watched, realizing she could not possibly excuse herself until the prince returned with the men, and the royals retired.

"I really—" began one woman. "Oh, heavens, I hear the men coming!"

"Why, that was no time at all," said the princess.

The only woman who seemed undisturbed was Lady Trent, who was reverently touching a curtain. Earlier she had occupied herself with examining a porcelain bird from a shelf.

The men entered in a cloud of smoke, in spite of the fact that they were no longer smoking. They had inhaled enough on their last puff to discharge a stream of fumes for the next quarter hour.

The princess organized card games of poker, whist, auction bridge, and chow chow for anyone who was interested, while others gathered in clusters to talk, or retired to a corner to read a book or simply enjoy the comfort of the large room.

Philip sat in a chair and, along with Lord Merrymeade, fell into a sound sleep.

"Constance." Joseph was behind her. "Please forgive me."

She took a deep breath and continued to examine

book spines from the shelf. Not knowing what to say, she did not reply to his statement.

"Do you think I should give Byron another shot? I've never really . . ."

"Please, Constance."

His voice was so urgent that she faced him. His expression was tense, the scar on his left cheek seeming more visible than before. Perhaps it was the glow of the candles. Perhaps it was the set of his features.

She very much wanted to ask him how he came about getting that scar. Had it been in childhood? Had it occurred more recently? It must have been painful, although now it was so very faint that it was hard to detect in most lights.

"Constance, look at me."

"I am."

"No. Your mind is elsewhere. I am trying to apologize for the story over dinner. You know that I would never do anything to hurt you, never. But I got caught up in the tale, carried away with my own words. Are you listening?"

"Joseph, I don't feel well."

Immediately, he held out his hand to steady her, very gently, so as not to attract any attention.

"What is wrong?"

She was beginning to feel faint at the thought. "They want me to shoot tomorrow, want me to shoot with the men. But I can't. I can't. Because of what happened during the war. There was a Yankee. It was hot on the road, and it all happened so fast. I can't shoot a rifle for sport, not ever, Joseph. I can't, because I killed a man once."

"It will be fine," he soothed, wanting very much to take her into his arms. He somehow wasn't surprised by her revelation, as if he had known all along that she had some secrets buried. They all had secrets that needed to remain buried. "I will think of something to get you out of it."

She straightened, as if suddenly aware of their surroundings. The hum of the conversations seemed to begin again, and she shook her head. "I'm sorry."

"Don't be. Now how about giving Byron another chance? The poor fellow suffered enormously for his art, you know."

And somehow the evening passed.

Abigail Merrymeade, although engaged in a fierce game of chow chow with the Princess, managed to observe every detail of the exchange between Joseph and Constance, although she was too far away to hear anything they said. What she did glean was their intensity, the closeness, an aura about them that in no way existed between Miss Lloyd and her fiancé, the ever-cheerful Lord Hastings.

When the prince and princess reluctantly retired, Constance walked over to Joseph, who stood before the fireplace.

"Good night," she whispered.

He glanced up in the mirror over the mantel, and their eyes locked in the reflection. She was standing so close, her shoulder was almost touching his chest. And they just stared at the image of the two of them, as if it were a wedding portrait. There was something in their expressions, a breathless hope, that seemed to capture a moment for eternity.

For whatever had gone wrong that evening, the sight of Constance and Joseph side by side seemed very, very right.

9

Everyone was expected to be down in the breakfast room, if not promptly by eight-thirty, at least sometime before half-past ten. The men sported their shooting tweeds, the women were resplendent in their morning dresses—newly purchased for this meal alone, to be packed away in tissue and netting and not seen again until they left Sandringham. They dallied over covered dishes arranged on the sideboard, speaking in low voices about what the day might bring, what splendid weather for an al fresco luncheon, what game would be bagged that morning.

Constance, her hair arranged by Stella, was in the breakfast room on time, her green and white striped gown pristine and crisp. Philip was not yet down, not noticeable in itself, for most of the guests had not yet appeared.

She stood with her plate, passing by the kidneys, creamed eggs, quail, sliced pheasant, rashers of bacon, and oatmeal before settling on a roll and a cup of coffee.

"Why, Miss Lloyd, what a lovely gown," Joseph whispered next to her ear.

She smiled, not looking up at him. There was no need. "You don't think the green and white stripes make me look like a wandering window awning?"

"Well, that it does. But seldom have I seen a more attractive window awning. Butter?"

"Yes, thank you."

"And are you not going to comment on my own fetching outfit? I stitched it myself."

Now she looked at him, at the beautifully cut brown tweed jacket with leather-covered buttons. He was splendid in the morning light, his hair freshly brushed.

"Did you really make that?"

"No. But I knew the shock of thinking that I did would cause you to stand still so I could reach the eggs."

Constance and Joseph laughed, and the others glanced up with foggy expressions, not yet through their first cups of coffee or tea.

"So, Miss Lloyd, will you do me the favor of a ride this morning?" Joseph returned to the buffet.

"A ride?"

"Yes. While the others are shooting, or busy in the drawing room assassinating characters, I thought a ride would be quite the thing. Philip will join us as well—I asked him last evening, after everyone else retired."

"But don't you wish to shoot?"

"Not today. I'd rather ride, and so, I'm sure, would Lord Hastings."

"Thank you," she whispered.

"Don't thank me until you see me on a horse." He winked, and then went to the large table and sat between two other gentlemen. For a moment she just watched him, easy and amiable, able to slip into any situation, it seemed, with surprising dexterity.

And yet he had just rearranged set plans to keep her from being forced to shoot. A single thought crossed her mind.

Who on earth was Joseph Smith?

By late morning Constance and Joseph were in the stables, selecting their mounts. She hesitated, thinking that he was most likely a poor horseman. After all, he'd had little access to horses as a youth. Riding was the sort of thing one grew into, after years of practice. She was about to suggest a quiet, gentle horse when Owen, Philip's valet, arrived.

"Miss Lloyd, Mr. Smith, Lord Hastings regrets to inform you that he is not well this morning, and begs forgiveness for not riding with you."

"Oh, dear." Constance buttoned her leather glove, the riding crop in her grip. "I must go and see how he is."

"Lord Hastings wishes to remain alone, Miss. His illness is of a, well, most delicate nature."

She had an image of Philip with such an illness, and realized it was not an image she wished to pursue in her mind nor in reality. The origin of his disorder required even less imagination, as she thought of the night before, the quantity and variety of wine he had consumed. "I see."

"Convey to Lord Hastings our sincere wishes for his recovery," Joseph responded to Owen. The young man shifted from one foot to the other, as if to add more information. Then he nodded and left, thrusting his cap back on his head as he walked away.

Constance did not meet Joseph's gaze. "Well," she said briskly, "I suppose we only need the two mounts, then. Philip's is rather spirited, but he's already saddled."

"Fine. I'll take him."

"Are you sure, Joseph? We can get a more settled mount if you wish."

"No. Thank you, but Philip's will be fine. Ah, here comes the stable boy with the horses."

The groom entered, handing the first horse to Constance.

"We will only require the two mounts." Constance smiled, patting the side of her horse's face. "What a beautiful animal," she cooed, as much to the horse as to the stable boy.

"That she is, Miss. And here's the mount for the gentleman." He handed Joseph the reins of a massive black stallion. The horse flared his nostrils and snorted, eyes rolling back in his head as if with alarm, and he clamped his front hooves on the ground.

"Nice horsey," he said, standing at arm's length from the animal and backing away as it sidestepped in his direction.

"Oh, Joseph, he's beautiful as well!" Constance stroked his mount's mane. "Would you feel more comfortable with the mare?" She kept her voice low, so the stable boys could not hear. By now other guests had arrived to select mounts.

"No. This one's fine, and he's ready to go. Besides, I can't envision myself riding sidesaddle." He nodded towards the mare's back. A groomsman walked by with a bucket of oats. "Excuse me, what's this horse's name?"

"The mare, sir? Why, her name is Lyric."

"Lyric?" Constance exclaimed. "What a lovely name. What a perfect name for such a very pretty mare. Aren't you a pretty mare? Yes, you are!" She planted a light kiss on Lyric's muzzle, and the horse seemed to revel in the affection, rubbing her face against Constance's cheek.

"And the stallion? What is the stallion's name?"

"Why, sir, that is Lucifer, son of Beelzebub."

"Close friend of Satan, no doubt," Joseph muttered.

"Sir?" the groomsman asked.

"Nothing. Nothing at all." The truth was, Joesph was not particularly fond of horses. They were large, willful animals, but he dealt with them the way he did an unpleasant business associate—with little fanfare and total authority.

Lucifer pranced forward, bobbing his head, forcing Joseph to follow. As they emerged into the yard, Lucifer began to kick his hind legs backwards.

Constance led Lyric ahead. "Lucifer is certainly eager for his daily gallop," she remarked.

Joseph used both hands to keep the horse moving forward. "I've had about enough of you. You're not to act up," he hissed to the animal. The horse stopped prancing and glared at Joseph. "Yes, I'm speaking to you."

"Pardon?" Constance asked.

"I was talking to the horse."

"Oh." With the groomsman's assistance, Constance was soon on top of Lyric, adjusting her skirts and patting the animal's flanks.

Joseph watched with undisguised admiration. Her riding habit, a deep shade of forest green, closely followed the curves of her figure. The top hat, set at a jaunty angle with a bare hint of veiling, complemented her dark hair, which gleamed lushly in the sunlight.

She was all grace and elegance, far more polished than the most studied of debutantes. She turned and smiled at him, and he could do nothing but return the smile.

She was lovely.

"Come on, Mr. Smith," she called.

"Yes. Of course." He could not stop thinking of her in the habit. With determination, he began to swing onto his horse, but his mind had been replaying her smile, and he absentmindedly missed the stirrup.

"Mr. Smith, really. If you would rather . . ." Before she could finish the sentence, he had mounted the horse.

"What were you saying, Miss Lloyd?"

With great control he urged Lucifer closer to her, then pulled sharply to get the stallion to halt. Patting the horse's neck, he glanced at Constance, his eyes questioning.

"Oh," she said, once again surprised by Joseph Smith. This was a man used to riding. Lucifer was no mild pony, but a massive, even dangerous beast. It was almost as if Joseph had managed the horse by sheer force of will.

"Shall we?" Constance said, adjusting her hat with an extra pin.

"After you," he nodded with exaggerated chivalry, and she smiled, the reins and her crop balanced in her lap. At which point the sound of gunshot punctured the air, as the sportsmen on a distant ridge began their day of shooting.

Apparently Lyric, the calm mare, had not been informed of the morning's schedule. The first round of fire sent her galloping forward, the crop tumbling to the cobblestone ground of the stable, the reins slipping over Lyric's neck.

Before either Constance or Joseph had a chance to react, the horse bolted through the open gate, leaving it swinging on its hinges.

"Damn it," Joseph spat as he kicked his heels into Lucifer's side. The horse, startled by the sudden commotion, bounded after them, taking off the portion of the fence that had been holding the gate.

He squinted in the sun, catching a glimpse of her flying over the closest hill. She was holding onto the horse's neck, grasping frantically for the reins as she attempted to remain fastened in the sidesaddle.

"Come on, Lucifer," he commanded, and the horse—his ears flattened and eyes rolling—seemed to pick up even more speed. Within a few moments he was beside Constance.

He did not shout to her, realizing that not only was it unlikely she would hear over the thundering hooves, but he did not want to startle the horse any further. Instead, he pulled Lucifer as close as possible, eyeing a stone fence just ahead, and realizing that he had to stop her horse before they reached the wall. He had one chance, one chance only.

Leaning over to the right, he grasped Lyric's reins and yanked. The horse stopped immediately, tossing Constance to the ground.

"Whoa." Joseph pulled Lucifer to a halt and jumped down. "Constance?"

She was facedown on the grass. Gently, he turned her over, fearful of what might be revealed.

Her eyes were open, an expression of confusion on her dirt-streaked face. "This is quite embarrassing, Mr. Smith," she murmured.

He grinned, aware for the first time that he had been holding his breath. "It often takes some time to become accustomed to a new mount, Miss Lloyd." Gently, he eased her into a sitting position, brushing her skirts over her legs and removing some of the larger twigs.

"I'm not sure Lyric should be called a mount." She began to refasten her hat, but instead simply pulled it off. "I wasn't on her long enough for her to be called that." She looked up at Joseph, the set of his features and the pounding nerve at his temple. "Thank you," she said softly.

He began to speak, then stopped, his eyes still focused with an unsettling intensity. "You're welcome." His mouth formed the words soundlessly.

Abruptly, he rose to his feet, extending a hand down to her. She accepted, and he pulled her to him. For a moment they stood very still, and so close they could feel the heat of each other's body.

"Constance, I . . ." he began, then he stopped.

"Yes?"

"I have not been honest, and now I feel I must . . ."

"Ho there! Smith, Miss Lloyd!" Barreling over the hill on foot was Lord Collins. Joseph took a step back from Constance, dropping her hand. Collins had a rifle at his side. "Bit of luck finding the two of you here, what?"

"Not as I see it," mumbled Joseph. Then, in a louder voice, "Hello, Collins."

"Sir," Constance said, nodding to the other man as he approached.

"I say, have either of you seen a rather badly wounded pheasant? I shot one back there, and the blasted thing seems to be intent on playing games."

"No, I'm afraid we have not seen a pheasant," Joseph said.

"No? Pity. Thought this one was in the bag. Are you two heading back? It's about time for luncheon."

"I . . ." Constance stammered.

"Yes. Yes, we should get back, Miss Lloyd," Joseph said.

"Yes," she breathed, an uncomfortable tightness in her throat. "Of course."

"Jolly good, what? Shall we all head back together?"

"Certainly." Joseph gathered Lucifer's reins, and with only a moment's hesitation, handed Lyric to Constance.

"I'll be fine," she said in answer to his unspoken question, and he smiled.

"So, what do you think of the Queen's eldest son? Quite the chap, isn't he?"

Lord Collins walked beside Constance and Joseph the entire journey back to the stable, perfectly content with his one-sided conversation.

There was so much Constance wanted to say. But perhaps this was better, she decided. Perhaps this was really all for the best.

Constance, claiming a fierce headache—which, in fact, was the absolute truth—did not appear for luncheon.

Stella offered to bring her a tray, but the mere thought of any food was more than unappealing. All she wanted to do was collect her thoughts, and try to untangle her emotions.

What had happened out there in the countryside?

Why was she feeling so peculiar, both light-headed and nauseous at the same time? It was more than just the physical shock of tumbling off a horse. She had done that on enough occasions to know that any symptoms she was experiencing now had little to do with horses.

Yet, deep down, she *knew* the reason. It was because with Joseph she had her first taste of happiness, real happiness, in as long as she could remember.

Now she again knew the meaning of joy, of delight, of taking pleasure from every waking moment. For the first time in over a decade she was thinking of the future, not living an hour-by-hour existence, not measuring out her laughter in teaspoons.

The reason was apparent, and a sick feeling twisted through her.

She had fallen in love with Joseph.

And she was engaged to be married to Philip.

"Oh, no," she sighed, flipping onto her back.

The feelings had been coming on slowly, but then, like a boulder rolling down the side of a mountain, it seemed that everything was accelerated and nothing could stop the emotions. She had never before been in love, although she had loved. Now she was completely, utterly in love—with her fiancé's best friend.

Granted, it was an odd friendship. The two men seemed to have very little in common other than shared schooling as children. But still there was no denying the bond, no dismissing the power of their fondness. She could never come between them, nor would she wish to.

Nor could she. For the simple fact was that Joseph Smith held her in no regard. He liked her, of course. There were some moments when his sentiments seemed to go beyond like, but then he would pull away, realizing his error.

That's what he was going to tell her that morning, before Lord Collins arrived. And that is why he had said it was better this way. How humiliating.

And so she would marry Philip, and see Joseph every few months when he came into town. He would marry, probably sooner rather than later, and then he would bring his family. His wife would be blonde, perhaps. She would be elegant and clever and she would watch Joseph, observe his mood changes, place her hand over his when he said something amusing at the dinner table.

He would place a shawl about her shoulders when the evenings grew cold, his hands lingering longer than need be. She would touch his hair, the thick glossy hair, and her finger would drop to his lips and she would trace their delicate outline with tenderness, and his eyes would close at the feel of her touch.

She hated his wife.

Suddenly Constance sat up. She needed to take a walk, to stop tormenting herself with these thoughts.

Dressing quickly, without disturbing Stella, Constance brushed her hair and pinned it up, splashing cold water over her eyes to keep her tears from becoming too obvious. Her gown, a pale yellow silk brocade, was far too lovely for moping about, and by rights the image that she saw of herself reflected in the swing mirror should have cheered her.

Instead, she shrugged and left the room, roaming through the halls, musing at how very much wandering through unfamiliar corridors she had been doing lately.

Sandringham was, indeed, impressive. She yawned, and then smiled in spite of herself.

Here she was, Constance Lloyd, up until the month before a governess in a modest household on the Isle of Wight, yawning her way around the Prince of Wales's home. The absurdity of the situation was extraordinary, and her steps began to regain some of their spring.

And then she saw him, a figure stooped over a threshold. There was no mistaking the jacket, or the reddish glints in his hair. It was Joseph.

It was as if her mental recognition had called out to him. His head snapped up, and at once he was standing up.

"Miss Lloyd." He nodded uncomfortably.

"Mr. Smith," she returned, giving a regal inclination of her own head. Now was the time to begin behaving as she should.

She started to walk past him, very aware of how he was staring at her. Glancing down at his feet, she saw a leather case and a stack of vials, some utensils, and bits of cloth. Looking away, she continued her stroll, then she stopped.

"What are you doing?" Her curiosity won out over her best intentions.

"I am standing in the hallway. You missed a nice luncheon, by the way. The Prince consumed an extended family of quails."

"Where has everyone gone?"

"Some are upstairs napping. Others are milling about on the lawn. I'm afraid Collins has gathered a party to search for his pheasant, so the countryside is not entirely safe at the moment."

She tried to hide her grin. "The poor pheasant is going to perish of exhaustion before his wounds." Then she sobered. "Thank you again for this morning."

"You are welcome. Are you feeling well?"

She nodded. "Better, thank you. Where did you learn to ride like that?"

"I know, I'm not the most polished of horsemen, but . . ."

"No! No, I mean you are excellent. Really."

He seemed pleased. "I, well. I don't know."

With a shrug, he brushed off the topic.

She was about to continue down the hall when she paused. "What were you about to say this morning? Before we were interrupted. You started to say something."

"Was I? I don't recall." Yet she could tell by his expression that he knew precisely what he was going to say. "Philip was not down at luncheon."

"He wasn't?"

Joseph shook his head. "I understand Viola brought a tray up to him."

"That was kind of her. I believe they are good friends. I mean, it is wonderful that Philip has such a good friend."

"So am I, Constance. I am also his friend. And yours." He extended his hand. "Perhaps it would be best to simply forget all about this morning. And about what happened in the library as well. Friends?"

She nodded. "Friends."

Why did she have an urge to cry? She did not want to leave him, not yet. Just a moment longer. Just a few more moments alone.

"What are you doing there?" She gestured to the leather case and vials.

"Nothing. Just standing here."

"No. I mean with this reticule, portmanteau, or whatever it is. Tell me, what are you doing?"

The smile left his face. "Please, Constance, do us both a favor and forget about this as well."

"Now you have my interest! I refuse to leave until you confess all." She peered down at the case. "What are you doing? Putting something there, or taking something away?"

"I am serious. Please, Constance, go on now."

"Hmm. Whatever it is, you're doing it on the sly."

He did not reply.

"What about the servants? Do they know what you *are* doing?"

"Good-bye, Constance. Go away. Now."

"Wait a moment." She stared directly into his face. "You *are* serious."

"Yes, I am."

"This won't get you into trouble, will it?"

"Not if you remain silent."

"Joseph, this sounds dangerous." She took a closer look at the vials, and he stepped in her way. "I just don't want to see you getting into trouble."

"Nor do I."

The hallway was very quiet, muffled by carpets and thick walls. They were alone.

He was staring at her, his expression unreadable. There was a vein at his left temple that began to throb, and she watched it, unable to pull her gaze away. She had noticed it before, that morning at the inn, when he had helped her to her feet. Very slowly, she stepped toward him, and touched the vein with her finger.

Again he remained motionless.

"There is a vein right here," she said softly. "It seems to be beating."

He did not blink. "It only happens when I'm—" he swallowed "—when I'm agitated."

"Are you agitated now?"

The nod was so subtle, she would have missed it if she had not had her finger on his temple. "It feels quite odd."

Her eyes focused on his, and, for a moment, held before she dropped her hand.

"Be careful, Joseph. Please be careful."

She began to walk away.

"And you, too, my . . ." He paused. "My friend."

She did not look back, but even without turning around, she could feel his heated gaze on the back of her neck, and it was with relief that she finally turned the corner.

10

Do you draw, Miss Lloyd?"

Abigail Merrymeade bestowed an uncharacteristic smile upon Constance. There was something unnatural about the expression. The rest of her features seemed pained by the turn of her mouth, as if one of them had betrayed the set rule of perpetual disdain.

The women were just gathering in the salon for afternoon tea. Most of the men were still in the fields, gloating over the day's kill or enjoying their refreshments in the carpeted tent.

"No, Lady Merrymeade. I am afraid my talents do not run to drawing, though not for want of trying."

Perhaps Abigail was simply attempting conversation, Constance thought as she returned to the oversized atlas she was examining.

"Do you work needlepoint or embroider?"

"Well," Constance said, tracing the route of the Mississippi River with her finger, "I have attempted to do both, but I fear the end results have not justified the effort."

"Perhaps music is your forte, Miss Lloyd."

Constance gave a noncommittal shrug. "I do enjoy music."

"What instrument do you play?"

It was no use. Constance gently closed the leaves of the atlas and turned her full attention to the interrogator.

"I do play the piano, but not well. Only children's tunes, really."

"Come, come, Miss Lloyd. We are amongst friends here. I feel you are holding out on me."

"I am not holding out, Lady Merrymeade. I play the piano, a bit."

Lady Trent, who had been examining a watercolor landscape, turned to Abigail and Constance. "The piano is a lovely instrument. Have you seen the exquisite piano in the music room?"

"No, Lady Trent. I did not take note." Abigail turned again to Constance. "So you play the piano? How very extraordinary. I did not realize that a governess would play the piano. I can only assume you learned this talent as a very young girl." The tone of her voice indicated that Abigail disapproved of Constance as a child.

"I did." She wore the yellow silk gown she would have worn at luncheon, not feeling the need to change, since no one other than Joseph had seen it.

"And tell me, will you entertain us by playing the piano at Sandringham?"

"I'm afraid not. I'm only current on nursery tunes."

"How amusing, Miss Lloyd. I suppose being a governess, playing the piano, and becoming betrothed to the second son of a duke has given you ample opportunity to hone your storytelling skills."

"I do not tell stories on a regular basis, except for the pleasure of children. Are you interested in hearing one?"

Lady Collins managed to hide a giggle by turning it into a convincing cough. "Excuse me."

"How droll." Abigail again attempted to smile, but the result was a simple display of her protruding, discolored teeth, which she ended before the full effect of the expression could be appreciated.

Viola Rathbottom entered the room. "The princess will be down shortly," she announced.

"Oh, Miss Rathbottom," Constance said. "How is Lord Hastings?"

Viola blushed as Abigail smiled. "I don't know what you mean, Miss Lloyd."

"I understand that you were kind enough to bring him a tray for luncheon. Thank you. I myself was not feeling quite well, so I was not much good. Is he feeling better?"

Viola seemed relieved. "Yes. Yes, indeed, Miss Lloyd, I do believe he is beginning to rally. Sorry, I didn't quite understand what you meant before."

Constance bit her lip, watching as Viola sat next to Lady Trent. Abigail continued to smile.

By the time the princess arrived for tea, it was just after six in the evening, and the men were returning from the field and from their various activities. Constance could hear Philip's voice as he laughed at something the prince said, although Philip alone seemed to find the remark humorous.

Hearing his voice in the hallway, Constance had a sinking feeling in her stomach. That was her future husband, the detached chuckle, the disembodied voice. Intellectually, she realized the fact, but emotionally, the thought was almost unbelievable.

In a curious way, she felt she knew him less now than she had before they ever danced at Cowes. Then, when she would watch him ride by on his horse, she imagined his character, adding a personality to fit his appearance. As a result she had felt close to him, but in truth she was close to her own image of Philip.

It had been so different with Joseph. Like peeling an onion skin, she was learning about him gradually, and every layer revealed more depth and strength of character.

He had been able to control Lucifer with sheer strength and force of will, rescuing her in the process. He handled most things in the same way, she realized, through strength and desire.

"Miss Lloyd? Lady Collins was asking you a question. You seemed to be a million miles away." Lady Trent smiled.

"I'm sorry. Could you please repeat the question, Lady Collins?"

"It was nothing important, Miss Lloyd. I was just inquiring whether you and Lord Hastings had set a date for the wedding."

"The wedding. Yes. Well, we have no fixed date, Lady Collins. The Duchess wished to wait until after this visit to set a date."

Viola paused, watching the exchange while pretending to be interested in a stereoscope of the Coliseum in Rome.

"I would imagine the date will be sooner rather than later." Lady Trent beamed. "Ah, young love. How glorious it is, is it not?"

Again, Constance smiled in reply. Lady Trent came closer to the mark than she could have ever imagined with her comment about young love. The way she felt, glorious it was not.

The prince chose Abigail Merrymeade to be his escort into dinner that evening, and she accepted the honor with studied elegance, only the distinct brightness in her eyes indicating that she was both surprised and gratified by his selection.

The princess, who had been listening politely to a description of the day's kill, went into dinner with the gentleman on her left, who happened to be Philip.

Constance was alone for a moment, and then Joseph was at her side.

"Shall we?" He crooked his arm towards her.

"Of course. But we do have plenty of time. All those with rank will proceed us, and since we are but plain Miss Lloyd and Mr. Smith, we might as well do something useful."

"You are right, Miss Lloyd. Shall we write a novel?"

"Well, we do have the time. But how about something more useful? Perhaps we can find a cure for the common cold."

"Or ascertain why men fight wars."

"Maybe we can discover a way to make politicians incorruptible."

"And to make week-old fish taste like sugarplums," he laughed.

She was very aware of his body, of the warmth of his arm against hers. Glancing down at her, he seemed about to speak but stopped himself.

"Joseph," she whispered.

A sharpness came into his eyes, a clarity, as if he was seeing her without the obstruction of details, without the mundane aspects of her features. Instead, it was as if he was looking beyond features and into her soul.

They had stopped walking for a moment, and then he tossed back his head, clearing his thoughts, changing the tone.

"Here we go." His voice was rough, and he was looking straight ahead.

They were seated next to each other at dinner, although she was compelled to engage in a lengthy discussion about quail eggs in aspic with Lord Trent, and how to slice the eggs so they do not remind one overmuch of glaring eyes. Halfway through the fish course, she realized there was something on the bottom of her plate, a piece of paper.

At first she assumed it was part of a cast-off menu card. The menus were of a cream color, however, and even in the flickering candlelight of the enormous epergne she could tell the paper under the plate was flat white.

Something clicked in her mind, a warning bell. Very slowly, she inched her foot over to Joseph's and tapped his boot with her slippered toe. He gave no indication of the movement, other than a light return tap.

The prince was recounting a rousing tale of English triumph in the Crimea, a story he had told many times before to the same people assembled, not a few of whom had actually been at the event. He had the floor, and held it firmly as the other conversations dwindled and all heads were turned to his end of the table.

"So the colonel and his second lieutenant, both suffering from scurvy, ignored their wounds . . ."

Joseph's eyes focused on Constance without moving his head. She pulled a corner of the paper towards her, so he could see it. With no expression, he gave a slight shake. Clearly, he had no idea what it was.

The settings had been prearranged, so someone had wanted her to get the paper.

"And then he rose to his feet, and with his last bit of strength . . ." The prince was in fine form, although even his telling of the story could not prevent him from eating, and during his dramatic pauses he would slip a forkful into his mouth.

Slowly, she pulled the paper to see what was on it. There seemed to be nothing but a series of random scribbles. Frowning, she inched more of it forward. And then she saw it.

It was an ink drawing, meticulously rendered, of a very naked man.

Joseph, who had been taking a sip of claret, began

to cough, and Constance shoved the paper back under the plate.

From the brief glimpse she'd had, the drawing was of an unclothed man dancing on top of a piano, holding a Confederate flag over his head. She hadn't seen the face, not that the face was the focal point of the work.

The prince noticed nothing, so rapt was he with his own narration.

Constance stared straight ahead, eyes unseeing. What could be the meaning of the picture? Who on earth could have possibly . . .

Abigail Merrymeade.

She glanced across the table and saw the woman, a very vague smile on her lips as she apparently listened to the Prince.

Just then a butler was at her side, waiting to remove the top dish.

Reaching up a hand, she gripped the plate with all of her strength. The butler pulled harder, not wishing to make a scene. Constance held firm her grasp of the plate.

"Madam," he hissed.

She pretended not to hear, smiling along with the other guests at the conclusion of the Prince's tale.

"Your plate, Madam. I need to remove your plate."

Again, she maintained an expression of innocence; all the while her knuckles were grown white with the effort to keep the plate.

Joseph began to choke.

Constance gasped, watching as he made the most alarming noises. The butler abandoned his quest for the plate as the table erupted in concern over the choking Mr. Smith.

"I say, what shall we do now?"

"Frightfully loud, isn't he?"

"Pound his back. That's the thing. Hit his back."

While all of this was occurring, Constance was in a panic, loosening his cravat, asking for help. Finally their eyes met, and with unmistakable emphatic significance, he blinked downwards, toward her plate.

"Oh," she whispered, and while the ladies rose to their feet and fanned him, and the men began taking turns clapping him between the shoulder blades, Constance slipped the paper from under her plate, folded it under the table, and tucked it into her sash.

Almost immediately, Joseph seemed to recover.

"Thank you. Yes. Thank you, sir. No, no, I have quite enough water . . ."

The meal concluded on schedule, the baffled Prince at one end of the table, his unflappable wife at the other, and the happy butler, at last in possession of Constance's fish plate.

"Poor man," sighed Lord Collins. "Somehow, I just don't think that Mr. Smith is having such a success of it this weekend, what?"

"No, indeed," agreed his wife. "The poor chap seems to have a bit of a thundercloud over his head. Dearest, do me a favor, will you?"

"Of course."

"If Mr. Smith attends tomorrow's shoot, do try to stand well away from him. I do not like the idea of that man armed with a weapon."

"I will, my pudding. I will indeed stay away from the unfortunate man."

The knock on Constance's door awoke her well before dawn.

Sleep had eluded her for most of the night, and it was a surprise that sleeplessness is every bit as unpleasant in sumptuous surroundings, with goosedown pillows and soft linen sheets, as in a tiny governess's room with a slanted ceiling.

She pulled on her dressing gown and paused. Perhaps she had imagined the knock. Perhaps it had been a dream.

The second knock was just slightly louder, and more insistent.

Before she turned the doorknob, she paused. There had always been below-stairs whisperings about the goings-on in country houses. It was understood that the host and hostess would fix a blind eye on the midnight visitings that were so routine, and even assist the cause of adultery by arranging to have amorous couples located within convenient reach of each other. Their respective spouses were usually engaged in their own diversions.

But in the darkness of the old, drafty hallways, guests were known to get lost and confused. There was a story making the rounds of a certain MP who waited until the assigned hour, crept down the hall, slipped into a room, and jumped into the bed itself, yelling "Cock-a-doodle-do!" at the top of his voice.

Unfortunately, his lady love had changed rooms without informing him of her plan. The MP ended up in bed with a very startled archbishop.

The only awkward moments came when a husband or wife, tiptoeing down a carpeted corridor after a tryst, would pass each other. It was understood that the usual polite greetings could be dispensed with in such cases.

Clutching her wrap with one hand, she opened the door. And there stood Joseph, completely dressed.

"Joseph?"

"I . . ." He just stared at her for a moment, and in spite of her robe, she was aware of an odd sensation of having no clothes on at all.

"What are you doing here?" she whispered. It was quite possible, even probable, that the house would begin stirring soon, and that other guests would be returning to their own rooms before sunrise.

"I am leaving," he said. "I just wanted to say good-bye. I didn't want you to think that I would leave you without saying good-bye."

Constance stammered in confusion. "What do you mean? How can you leave before Sunday?"

"I must. An urgent message was delivered to me after everyone else retired."

"Does this have anything to do with your little vials?"

He said nothing, but his eyes conveyed his meaning. The subject was not to be spoken of.

"Joseph." She reached out her hand, suddenly very aware that she might not see him again until she was married. "I will miss you," she said simply.

The words were so very inadequate, so meaningless compared to the tumultuous emotions that seemed to choke her.

"And I," he stopped and grasped her hand, "I will miss you as well. I wish you the greatest joy, Constance. With all of my heart, I wish you nothing but joy."

He kissed the back of her hand, his lips pausing there for a moment longer than necessary.

"Good-bye," he whispered.

"Good-bye, Joseph."

He began to walk, and stopped suddenly. "Oh, I almost forgot. A parcel should be delivered here to you tomorrow, at the latest by Monday. It's a delayed engagement gift."

"Thank you." She smiled.

He seemed about to return to her side. Instead he fixed a tweed cap on his head, adjusting the brim over his eyes, and nodded once before he left.

Constance watched him until he turned the corner. Even then, she remained in the same spot, as if willing him to return.

11

Not many of the guests came down for breakfast the following morning. The breakfast salon, its sideboard laden with all of the delicacies expected, was all but empty when Constance entered just before nine.

For a moment she paused, uncertain if she had wandered into the wrong room, or perhaps the clock in her room had been pushed ahead, like so many other of the clocks at Sandringham.

"You are not mistaken, Miss Lloyd. We are all but abandoned this morning." Lord Collins greeted her from his position at the long table.

"I do hope it was nothing I said." She smiled uncertainly. She was exhausted after staying awake all night, thinking about Joseph, about his expression as he stood in the hallway, and about his back, broad and strong, as he left.

Lord Collins barked a peculiar laugh as he rose to his feet. "Nothing you said could account for this, my dear. My valet mentioned that some of the guests are feeling rather ill this morning."

"Really? I did not realize last night's revelries had taken so many prisoners."

"Apparently that is not the case. It seems another illness has taken hold during the night. Tell me, Miss Lloyd, did you eat all of your fish last evening?"

"The fish? Yes, I believe I did eat most of it."

"I was curious. Lady Collins had her full portion, and does not feel well today."

Constance poured herself a cup of tea. "I do hope she improves."

Lord Collins waved a hand, not bothering to put down the bread he was eating. "Not to worry, my dear. I appreciate the sentiments, but it does seem that whenever we attend a royal weekend, one or both of us ends up ill."

"Really?" She sat down across the table from him.

"Indeed. Is this your first visit to one of the royal homes?"

She nodded, and he continued.

"I believe the most diseased of the places is Windsor. Both Lady Collins and myself suffered from typhoid fever about two weeks after our last visit there. Others came down with it as well, and Lord Ashberry—did you know him? A fine man, although given to riding his horses too hard. Well, the upshot is that old Ashberry died."

"Poor man," she said distractedly. There was something odd about the situation, but she was unable to put the pieces together. Something was very wrong.

"Well, we can rest easy that we are not at Balmoral. Now that place is a cesspool of illness. It's a wonder the royal family survived their holidays there."

"Balmoral," she repeated.

"Yes. In Scotland. By the way, Miss Lloyd, did you see any cream up there? I seem to have missed the cream."

"I, yes." She stood and retrieved the cream.

Scotland. That was where Joseph had gone. And the vials, his leather portmanteau. He had a complete knowledge of chemistry. And, not incidentally, he had little regard for the aristocracy.

Her teacup began to rattle, and she pushed it away.

"I say, Miss Lloyd, you are looking rather peaked yourself."

Was it possible that Joseph was responsible for these illnesses?

She thought back on some of their conversations. He had liberal leanings, to be sure. But was he an anarchist?

No. Impossible, she thought. Then she recalled the passion with which he spoke of making the world better for the underclass. And those strange men, Walker and Crimmins, who appeared out of nowhere to send him off to Scotland.

Brown. That was another man's name. Brown.

"Lord Collins, please forgive me." She smiled. "I'm afraid I'm not feeling well myself."

"Go on then, my dear. Take care of yourself."

With a light nod she left the breakfast parlor.

"Now, let's see," Lord Collins muttered. "Was that a ham I saw next to the creamed eggs?"

Guests began leaving Sandringham just after noon.

Although most were scheduled to leave that afternoon, the departing times were moved up by several hours. Hatboxes and trunks and gun cases were stacked in the hallway. The valets and lady's maids bustled about, their footsteps soundless on the carpets. Carriages were brought to the front entrance, and there was a great deal of mumbling amongst those leaving.

"Must go back to town," said Lord Trent. "Frightfully full schedule, you know."

"My youngest seems to have caught cold, and is

calling for me," explained Lady Barrington. No one pointed out that her youngest was well into his forties.

Lord and Lady Merrymeade were also awaiting their carriage. Lord Merrymeade sat in a corner chair and closed the translucent lids of his eyes, and within moments he seemed to be enjoying a deep slumber.

Abigail Merrymeade looked at Constance through the netting of her fashionable hat. "And where is dear Mr. Smith?"

Constance almost slipped and said that he had left earlier. Instead she shrugged. "I don't know, Lady Merrymeade. I have not seen him since last evening."

She hated to tell a lie, small though it was.

"How fascinating. One can only assume that he is among the dearly departed."

"Excuse me, Lady Merrymeade. I need to find my fiancé."

In truth, she hadn't seen Philip all day, and while he had not been foremost in her mind, guilt prodded her to seek him out.

Philip entered the hallway with Viola and Owen, both men pale and hesitant in their steps. Philip's whiskers, however, were splendidly brushed, and his boots polished to a high gloss.

"Philip, how are you feeling?" He truly looked miserable.

"I have been better," he admitted with a small smile. There was something fragile about his appearance that made her want to take care of him.

"We'll get you home in no time, no time at all," she soothed, smiling at Viola.

It was while she patted his hand that she realized why her affection for him seemed so familiar. He was like one of her charges, one of the children she had cared for as a governess.

Stella appeared with some questions about packing, and Constance was relieved to have something else to think about. The last thing she wanted to dwell upon was the realization that in marrying Philip, she was simply trading one position as a guardian for another.

Word of the incident at Sandringham spread quickly through the inner circles of London, where it was the talk of the fashionable clubs, of the best drawing rooms, and during walks and rides in Hyde Park.

Not that such an event was unusual, for many country house parties were cut short by unknown illnesses. Several years earlier, a great assembly of peers intent on a week of shooting grouse was canceled the day after the guests had arrived, and by the following week more than a dozen of the guests had died, including valets and housemaids.

But the Sandringham affair was different. Not only did it involve a royal residence, but it had occurred in the home of the Prince of Wales, the future King of England.

Rumors began to spread that, unlike other country house illnesses, the events at Sandringham may very well have been intentional. No one had noticed a foul odor that weekend, which was usually a sign of stagnant, putrid water.

Other bits of gossip were supplied, mostly by eager speculators who were not in attendance those few days. Although most of the guests were well known to the Marlborough House set, there were a few newcomers.

One was the American woman; a governess, by all accounts comely enough, but something of a mystery. Her intended groom, the youngest son of the famous Mole Man, was known mostly from secondhand accounts of his exploits, antics that continued well into manhood. Nothing particularly sinister was seen in the two, although they were indeed a curious pair.

The single individual who prompted the most intense contemplation was the wealthy Welshman, Joseph Smith. Although he was a familiar sight at the clubs in London, and at balls and parties, no one seemed to really know that man. He was a puzzle, that one. He was always nearby, yet nobody could claim true intimacy with the man. The exception was young Lord Hastings, who was known more for his ability to ride a horse while fully intoxicated than for any astuteness of character.

And Lady Merrymeade, when pressed on the issue, had mentioned that Mr. Smith had been the first to leave Sandringham that weekend. He was long gone well before dawn, for she herself had seen him leaving from her window.

Questions were raised, first as whispers, then in louder voices, and finally as carefully phrased editorials in the more common newspapers. How had the man really amassed his vast fortune? Where did he come from, for intrepid reporters could not find any details of his early life. Even at Oxford, there were dons and tutors who recalled him, but they remembered a serious young man who read theology.

How did a theological scholar become a manufacturer, a financial success, and a chemist as well? He seemed extraordinarily familiar with the most recent scientific discoveries, ones that were being written about in France and Germany. There was something terribly odd with Mr. Joseph Smith.

There seemed to be only one logical explanation: he was being funded. An organization or, more likely, a foreign power was funneling money into Joseph Smith's company, and he was in turn using the proceeds to finance a diabolically clever scheme to wipe out the royal family.

There were even more serious rumblings, and one newspaper actually printed a front page story about

190

Joseph Smith being arrested for high treason, complete with an engraving of a gentleman in a full beard being lead away by rough-looking London bobbies. Upon closer examination, it would be revealed that the man in the etching was, in fact, a doctor who had been accused of murdering his wife four years earlier. No matter. The headline said it was Smith, so most of London believed it to be Smith.

Unfortunately for the newspaper, the account proved to be false.

But then something just as sensational happened.

Joseph Smith seemed to vanish from the face of the earth.

Philip was becoming more and more involved with his campaign.

After he had fully recovered from the Sandringham weekend, he seemed to be in a fury of activity, always dashing through Hastings House with a distracted expression on his face, usually followed closely by his friend Mortimer.

On occasion, he would run to his room without speaking to anyone, using a back staircase and telling Owen to go away and bother someone else. It wasn't until Constance caught a glimpse of him that she understood the reason for his haste and secrecy. He was, in fact, covered with egg shells, tomato bits, and great yellow gobs of raw egg yolk and shiny, gelatinous white. A lettuce leaf dangled from his shoulder like a vegetable epaulette.

She assumed his speech had not gone as well as one would have hoped.

Philip had also enlisted the help of an outgoing MP to assist with the campaign, although the Honorable Charles Beckersby seemed far more interested in catching up on his sleep than in actively guiding Philip. And his opponent seemed to be faring even worse than Philip when it came to the popular vote, for Mr. Jones—the Liberal candidate—was routinely disguising himself with odd hats and eyeglasses to avoid being attacked by the masses.

The real advantage Philip had was his family's money, and the simple fact that much of Ballsbridge was dependent upon the Hastings estate for their existence. That alone all but guaranteed Philip's success.

And when the polling finally began, an event that took place over three days, Philip took an early lead and never fell behind. He was now a Tory MP, and the household celebrated.

For Constance, however, nothing really changed. Once again, her days had fallen into a tedious routine, punctuated by interminable meals and stilted conversations with Philip's family. The only person with whom she felt completely comfortable was the duke. He alone brightened her day, and she had taken to sharing tea with him every afternoon in his underground lair.

And then she would retreat to her room, or walk on the grounds if the weather was fine. At least when she had been a governess, there had been the unexpected behavior of the children to brighten the day.

One afternoon, just before tea, she was in the library when there was a knock on the door.

"Miss Lloyd? Excuse me," Stella bobbed. "There is a most odd-shaped package that has just arrived for you, express from Sandringham."

"Sandringham? I wonder what it could possibly be. May I see it, please?"

She nodded, and in a moment returned with a rectangular object, several feet long and wrapped in thick, brown paper.

Constance examined the label. "It's not actually from Sandringham. It was sent there for me after we had left, and was simply forwarded from that place. There is no return name or address."

She reached for a letter opener to slice the string and pull apart the brown paper. The moment Constance saw it, she began to laugh, simply because she did not know how else to react.

"What is it?" Stella asked.

"It's a writing desk, a lap desk. It was my mother's, and it was ruined. He had it repaired."

"Who sent you a desk?"

"Joseph did. I mean, Mr. Smith. My God, you can hardly see where it was splintered. Look, Stella. Even in the light, the grain looks perfect. How on earth did he manage to find someone to fix it?"

She touched the wood, wondering at the smoothness, at the way it looked even finer than before. Slowly she opened the lid, and the crystal ink bottles, filled with inks of all colors, glittered. There were quill pens and two gold ones, and a fresh bundle of paper, elegant sheets with her initials on the top.

"Is it nice, miss?" asked Stella.

"It's beautiful." Again she touched the soft wood; even the inlay felt like velvet.

"Well, isn't this a surprise," said Stella, repressing the urge to grin as she looked at the expression on her mistress's face. "This is quite a surprise."

"It is, indeed." When Constance opened one of the compartments, she noticed something folded. Tucked under a drawer was an envelope.

"I've never seen the like," Stella added.

"Um, it's lovely. After tea I'll go up to my room and write." She did not want anyone else to see the letter. It was hers, from Joseph. No one else should see it.

Carefully she placed the note back in the writing desk.

"Well, I believe I'll go downstairs now. Are they all below?"

"Why, yes, Miss Lloyd. Will you be joining the others today?"

She really wanted to skip tea altogether, or at least visit with the duke rather than Dishy, the duchess, and Philip.

Instead of making an excuse, she simply smiled. "I think today I should join them."

Together, Stella and Constance left the room, the desk, its note and secrets hidden out of sight.

12

Someone else was in the red room for tea, along with Philip, the duchess, and Cavendish.

Constance heard a woman's voice, soft and languid yet fully audible from down the corridor. It was a voice she had heard before.

Just then the door opened and Philip emerged, his face red, as if he had just been through some terrible ordeal.

"Philip?"

He turned partially, careful not to slow his progress. "The rally. I don't want to be late." He gave a half-wave, then disappeared around a corner.

"Miss Lloyd? Is that you?"

The duchess had heard her, and there was no other choice but to enter the red room.

Stepping into the room, Constance first saw the duchess, a look of delight on her face such as had not been seen since the triumph of the Sandringham invitation. Dishy sat in his usual chair, a folded newspaper in his lap and a dollop of whipped cream from a cake dotting the corner of his mouth.

"Miss Lloyd, we have thrilling news!"

The third person in the room was Viola. She smiled from the blue and gold wing chair.

"Miss Lloyd already knows, your grace."

"You told her about your engagement? How on earth did you two meet?"

Constance was about to say at Sandringham, when something stopped her. Viola gave an almost imperceptible shake of her head.

"Oh, we met . . ." Constance began.

"On the grounds beyond. Miss Lloyd was strolling in the orchard, and I was there doing a watercolor."

"Yes," Constance agreed. "It is such a pleasure to see you again, Miss Rathbottom. And how did that watercolor turn out?"

"Not well, I'm afraid. It rained just after you left, and all of my oaks ran into the apple trees."

"And who says a little rain is not destructive?" Constance looked at Viola, trying to decide why her visit to Sandringham was being kept a state secret. It would have made the duchess delirious with joy to know that both of her future daughters-in-law had been with the prince and princess. Perhaps the secrecy was because Dishy had not been issued an invitation.

"Indeed. How very right you are, Miss Lloyd. Sometimes, even mild acts of nature can be dangerous."

The conversation was beginning to take a most cryptic turn. "I'm afraid I haven't properly congratulated you." Constance turned to Philip's brother. He nodded once, then flipped his newspaper over to read the other side.

"Well, it seems no introductions are needed today," said the duchess.

"I have heard so much about you, Miss Lloyd," Viola began. "It is so nice to meet you properly."

"Yes, it is. The introduction by the . . ."

"Orchard. It was by the apple orchard."

"Of course. That was less formal."

"My cousin, Lady Merrymeade, was at Sandringham at the same time you were, I believe."

"Oh, yes. I did have the pleasure of meeting Lady Merrymeade. She is also quite a capable artist. The talent must run in your family."

Viola seemed perplexed. "Did Abigail draw there? That is unlike her. Anyway, I have always admired her drawings. How often I've wished I could have her talent."

"She is nothing if not talented," Constance agreed.

The duchess asked Viola to pour the tea, which she did easily, with no show of nerves even before the august duchess. Constance could not help but admire her.

"Philip seemed to be leaving in a great hurry," Constance mentioned, taking a sip of tea.

"Yes. Yes, indeed he was."

"Well, it's no wonder he doesn't want to be with you, Viola," Dishy said. Constance turned in surprise, wondering if she had ever heard him make a comment unless absolutely pressed to speak.

Viola looked down. "What a kind thing to say, Cavendish."

"Come on. You did nothing but torment the man for years and years. Remember when you put him in that pit with all of the spiders? He would be there now, by God, if that scruffy little Joseph Smith hadn't been visiting from school. He was the only one who noticed Philip was missing."

Viola set down her tea. "It was most amusing. It was all my idea, I must confess." She turned towards Constance, her suddenly uneasy manners clashing with the false lightness of her words. "You see, Miss Lloyd, I am known as something of a wit in the Marlborough House set. It was I who placed the soap in the cheese dish last year during the London season. And it was I who put the ink bottle over the doorway at the Martin-Smiths' shooting party."

The duchess's face was set in an expression of bafflement. She glanced at her son, who did not return the favor. Instead he crossed his legs and yanked his trousers down at the ankles, taking great interest in something contained in the paper.

"My dear," said Dishy, still focused on the paper. "Perhaps you had best not tell Miss Lloyd of your varied career as a social wit."

"Nonsense. I will explain, Miss Lloyd. She will find this amusing. I did torment Philip, well beyond childhood in fact. But the wretched boy would never so much as look at me. So my antics grew rather outrageous, to the point where, by the time I came out, I was considered quite hopeless."

Cavendish cleared his throat and seemed to want to leave very much. Even the duchess seemed taken aback, attempting to maintain an expression of amusement, and looking briefly at Constance.

"One time I even—"

Cavendish put down the paper. "Please, Viola. This is quite enough."

"Well, I must say that I am something of a black sheep in my family. But now that Dishy and I are engaged, they are all happy." She smiled. "My engagements to Dishy always make them happy."

Constance looked at the duchess, who in turn looked at Dishy, who shrugged. "One day, Viola, you will learn the fine art of silence."

"I have no doubt, dear Cavendish, that you are just the man to teach me." Viola said it with such a sweet expression, it was almost impossible to find fault with her on any count.

As the tea continued, Constance could only wonder how on earth these two people could ever find happiness. The odds seemed against them taken alone, as two separate entities. And together, they seemed perfectly impossible.

For a long while she sat simply on the bed in her new room, the gold room, where she had been elevated after the triumph of the Sandringham invitation.

Darkness fell, and Stella appeared to light the lamps and a small fire.

"Would you like a lie-down, Miss?"

Constance did not respond at first but finally she shook her head, and Stella left with a slight bob and a perplexed expression on her round features.

There was a knock on the door.

"Come in," she whispered. The door opened, and the Viscount Cavendish, her writing desk in one hand, came into her room.

"Sir." She rose to her feet.

"Please," he began. "Please. I just wished to bring this up to you."

"Thank you." She took the desk and placed it on her bed. She had forgotten all about it since tea.

"I do not wish to intrude upon you, Miss Lloyd. But I do wish to apologize for this afternoon. Viola is rather high-spirited, and I believe she is worried about our impending union."

"I understand that is quite common," she said flatly.

"Yes. For us it is, at any rate. We have quite a record when it comes to engagements. I will see you at dinner then."

He gave a brief bow, and she nodded once before he began to leave. He paused at the threshold. "You must think this a curious household. But, in our own way, we just do the best that we can, all of us. I do hope this day has not led you to think we are a peculiar lot."

"Don't worry, sir." She smiled. "I can assure you that anything that was said today did nothing to alter my opinion of you."

He smiled as he went through the door, but the smile faded and he seemed about to speak again when Constance waved him on.

"I must dress for dinner," she said sweetly. And he left.

Again she paused for a moment, looking at the closed door. Then she opened the lap desk, running her hand against the silken wood, and reached into the drawer where she had put the note from Joseph. At first she thought she was simply mistaken, or looking in the wrong place.

But soon one thing was painfully obvious.

The note was gone.

Dinner was more pleasant than usual, mainly because Viola's presence at the table deflected the bulk of the duchess's scrutiny from Constance, and Viola was a lively addition. Another difference was that Philip was there, arriving late after his rally, yet managing to change into a dinner jacket and polished boots in time for the meat course.

Viscount Cavendish was also markedly changed, not in his attire but in his attention to Constance. He was kind, addressing comments to her.

Once Philip was seated, the duchess waited until his plate had been filled before she spoke.

"Well, as we all know, dear Cavendish and Viola are to be married."

Philip looked down at his plate, giving no indication of any emotion.

"And since Dishy is the heir, and will inherit, it is only right and just that his marriage should proceed that of his younger brother. I believe six months would be appropriate. After all, the main thing is that Philip is known to be betrothed. The election is won. There is nothing to be gained by a hasty marriage."

For the first time, Constance had a genuine urge to hug the duchess.

Viola straightened in her chair. "No, your grace. You are all kindness, but I do not believe that Dishy and I should be first. Philip was engaged before we were, so by rights they should go first."

Philip put down his knife and fork. "No."

His mother blinked. "Excuse me?"

"No, Mother." Philip straightened.

"What do you mean, 'no'?" The duchess seemed uncertain as to how to react.

"I mean, a marriage is for two people to decide, the bride and the groom. No one else. Certainly not the groom's mother."

"Don't be ridiculous, Philip," said his mother. "In the scheme of things, you must realize that their marriage is of greater significance than yours. Dishy is the eldest son. Had you and Miss Lloyd been betrothed for any length of time at all, well, I could see your point. But as it stands, there are but a few weeks between the engagements. And if you count the three times they were engaged previously, well, they go first."

"Four times," corrected Viola. "Don't forget the engagement at the Christmas ball."

"Heavens, yes. I always forget that one." The duchess smiled again, finally feeling back in control. "Or we could have a double wedding."

"No. I refuse." Viola looked over at Constance. "I mean, there is really no rush. The main thing is for all of us to get to know each other, is it not?"

"You've lived next door for all of your life," Dishy said. "How much more could you possibly learn about us? You already know more than anyone outside of the immediate family. Actually, you probably know more than anyone at all."

"Pardon me, dear Viola." The duchess took a rather aggressive stab at her filet. "I am still the duchess."

"Why, of course you are, your grace." Viola smiled graciously. "In my mind, you will always be the duchess."

"Miss Lloyd." The duchess turned. "What do you say?"

"Well, I . . ."

"Why are you always such a bully, Mother? Dishy and I can handle it. But why must you be such a bully to Constance? To Viola as well." Philip pushed back his plate, which moved his wine glass with such force the wine sloshed over the side.

"Philip!" snapped the duchess. "That is most unkind and unnecessary."

"I disagree, Mother, I fear it is kind compared to what I am thinking, and necessary considering the situation. Dishy, why are you opening yourself to further humiliation? She has used us all of our lives. Haven't you had your fill of her game?"

"Stop!" The duchess slammed her palm against the table. "You are excused, Philip."

There was complete silence in the dining room. No one made a move.

"I said, you are excused."

"I thank you, Mother, but I did not ask to be excused." Philip reached for the claret and poured himself another generous glass.

The duchess glared at her youngest son. "Leave this room before I . . ."

"Before you do what, Mother? Put me over your knee? Send me to bed without pudding?"

"Before I send you from this house!" The moment the words had escaped her mouth, her face flushed.

"Then do it, Mother."

"Philip," began Cavendish.

"You stay out of it," Philip shot, pointing his finger at his older brother. "I am thirty four years old. I am now a Member of Parliament. I am sick of it, heartily sick."

Constance was suddenly filled with a sense of pride for Philip, like seeing a younger brother climbing a long-feared tree. Or when Wade had enlisted in the army. "What are you sick of, Philip?" she coaxed, surprised by her own voice. He turned to her, his expression growing softer as he did.

"I am sick of being used. I am sick of not doing what I wish, of pleasing others—mostly you, Mother." He looked briefly at his mother, then back to Constance, and finally to Viola. "I will speak plainly. It was originally Mother's idea that I find a bride before the elections. And so, as usual, as I have always done, I complied with Mother's wishes."

"Philip, this is not the time nor the place to—" Cavendish began.

"On the contrary, this is precisely the time and place."

"There," said the duchess with satisfaction. "You have said what you wish, Philip, and we are all impressed. Please sit up straight, you're slouching again. Now let us continue the meal in peace. I saw in the *Court Circular* that . . ."

"It was not my original intention," Philip restated. He hunched over his place setting. "I was petulant and resentful, and I apologize to you, Constance, before everyone here. I did not treat you as a person, I treated you as an impediment. An impediment to what, I don't know, but I behaved badly. I should apologize before the world, but this is a start, the beginning of a life made of truth and not lies."

"Philip," his mother warned, "I requested that you cease this conversation. It is most inappropriate."

"So is a grown man performing for no one but his mother," he snapped. "I'm sorry, but the weekend at Sandringham woke me up, so to speak."

"Why is that?" Constance was intrigued. This was the first conversation of substance she had ever witnessed at Hastings House, and most certainly the only time she had really caught a glimpse of the real Philip.

He steepled his hands together, almost as if in prayer. "I saw what I would become. And I finally saw what Joseph was, especially compared to the other men. I've teased him for his seriousness for years, and then I saw him with the others, and for the first time I was ashamed. He has passion, drive, something to aim for. The rest of them seem to live for the next shoot, the next meal, the next season. I've been the same way, lacking focus, drifting from one gathering to the next, intoxicated more often than not. But I believe I may resolve it. And the irony is that it took Constance to show it to me."

"You are talking nonsense, Philip. You always talk nonsense after a few days with Smith," sniffed the duchess. "Yes, we have benefited from his financial insight. Still, he is not quite the quality one would wish."

"Mother, he has all but saved this estate, and you know that full well. The truth is, after much thinking, I realize I do wish to be an MP, the very best I can possibly be. This will not be a hobby. And further, there is something else I would like to do."

"What?" His mother leaned back impatiently. "What could you possibly do, my dear?"

"I believe I could have a real talent."

"In what, for God's sake?" Cavendish began to rise from his seat, but sat back down. "You read English Literature at Oxford, barely passing, I might add. Since then you have become an amusing companion in the best drawing rooms in England. What grand occupation has your training prepared you for?"

"Yes, Philip. What great talent are you withholding from the world?" the duchess asked. Then she rubbed her temple, her voice calmer, almost gentle. "I am sorry, Philip. But you astonish us all. Thus far you have shown neither talent nor interest in anything."

"Whatever it is you enjoy, you may do it when Parliament is not in session," Dishy pronounced.

"But why must one select one interest? Joseph has several avocations, and combines them with great satisfaction. As far as I know, he has never been bored or at a loss for something to do. And look at my situation—we have spent hundreds of pounds on this election, and I won. But I will receive no salary." He cleared his throat and ran a thumb along the rim of his wine glass. "But I earnestly believe that, as a painter, I could earn a respectable sum."

"A painter!" Dishy cried. "My God, Philip, are you insane?"

"A painter?" His mother looked from face to face in utter confusion. "As in one who paints the trim on a house?"

Constance and Viola remained silent, and both smiled.

"And what find you so funny, Miss Lloyd?" barked the duchess when she saw the expression on Constance's face.

"It all makes sense now," Constance said, looking

at Philip. "I'll wager you were painting all along, even at Eton. And when Joseph decided to manufacture something, he used what he had been familiar with because of you. He made pigments."

Philip nodded. "He pilfered my stock time and again for his experiments. Good God, if you knew the foul smell of burning paint."

"Well, you may paint when Parliament is not in session," repeated Dishy, pleased to have made his point. "Besides, you probably have not done it in years. Perhaps you had a middling sort of talent as a student, but as an adult, well. We all know how childhood talents are rendered useless in adulthood."

"That's not exactly true, Dishy. I have been painting steadily for well over a decade, in London. I use part of Joseph's London laboratory as a studio to paint. It's a horrid little place on the other side of the Thames, off Waterloo Road. I believe he remains there simply to torment me, but it's been splendid, absolutely splendid."

Cavendish straightened his tie. "I had no idea, Philip. No idea whatsoever. No one did."

"That is not quite true," Philip said.

"I knew," said Viola. "And so did Joseph, and, of course, the duke."

"Father?" Dishy cried.

"Who?" the duchess asked.

"My father, the duke. The man who lives downstairs with all the tunneling. Joseph told him years ago, and it was a good thing, because I had to have some place to put all the finished canvases."

"How on earth did you get them there without our knowing?" Dishy inquired.

"The tunnels, of course." Philip took a sip of wine. "There are some entrances to his tunnels way out on the grounds, far beyond sight of the house. The servants would never tell, of course. They are his own personal army. Whenever I would come for a visit, I would take the back road and deposit my canvases below, then come round the front."

"You did all the paintings in your father's corridor?" Constance asked.

"Not all of them, but quite a few. He has a rather annoying taste for the masters, and I am unable to paint that fast."

"The dog in the tea room?"

Philip laughed. "Sampson. Yes, Constance, I did that one."

"It's marvelous, absolutely wonderful! And Viola. Of course you painted Viola." Constance glanced at Philip, who was staring at Viola. He looked at her with a peculiar expression, and with a jolt she recognized it—love. Philip was in love with Viola.

"We will discuss this matter later," the duchess said, but with less bluster than she had used before.

Constance's head began to pound as the conversation at the table continued. She needed time to think, to sort out all that had happened. Finally she stood. "Please forgive me. Once again, I am not feeling well."

"Well, that is certainly most understandable, Miss Lloyd. I am not feeling well myself." The duchess gave a meaningful but brief glance at her youngest son.

Philip also stood. "May I help you?"

"No, please. I'm sure I shall feel better in the morning."

"Good night, Miss Lloyd," said Viola. She suddenly seemed very tired as well.

There were more good-nights, and at last Constance was able to retire to her own room.

Joseph. Where was he? Was he safe, in some sort of

danger? Perhaps that was what the missing note had said, information on where he was. And perhaps he needed her in some way.

And now there was Philip. Did he even realize he was in love with Viola?

She felt as if her life was out of control, spinning away faster than she could possibly hold on.

"Oh, God." She slumped on the bed. "Think," she urged herself.

And suddenly, it all became clear. She could not stay at Hastings House, not even another day. She had to leave that very night.

Unwittingly, she had been the cause of chaos in the household. She owed it to everyone, especially Philip, to leave.

Where would she go?

To find Joseph. To help him. Perhaps he would not want her, but that mattered little. There was no choice for Constance—she would find Joseph.

Stella entered to help her undress, and Constance thought of telling her, of giving her a note for Philip to explain and apologize. But Philip would simply come after her, and the situation would be an even bigger mess. No, she could not tell Philip.

The duke? He would be sympathetic, to be sure. But she couldn't put him in such an awkward position. It would be unfair to unburden herself, to ease her own conscience at the expense of his.

This was something she had to do by herself.

Once again, Constance Lloyd was completely on her own.

13

London was the logical place for Constance to begin the search for Joseph.

Philip had mentioned that Joseph's residence in town was off Waterloo Road, east of the Thames. So that is where she would go. That is where she would begin.

Then she began to realize the magnitude of the undertaking.

Every step she could foresee was fraught with barriers. The first, and by no means the greatest, obstacle was simply getting to London. She could not walk, of course, even if she knew the way. If she could procure a horse she could ride, but once in London that would necessitate a stable and food for the animal, as well as food along the way. If she could get to the nearest station, she could take the rail cars. That would be her best option.

Another crimp in her plans was the very real issue of money. No matter how she chose to travel, it could not be done free of charge. The safer and more convenient the option, the more money it would cost. The stark reality was that beyond the estate gates she would need some form of currency, and she had not so much as a farthing.

Her mind was churning as she paced the room. Perhaps it was because of her own overworked emotional state, but she imagined she heard someone crying, a woman sobbing in some part of the house. It was a heartbreaking cry, a sound of utter hopelessness and despair.

She thought of the servants, for the cry seemed to be that of a young woman, but their quarters were far beyond earshot. No sound could possibly reach her from where the housemaids lived.

A thought struck her: The place was haunted. Perhaps the ghost of a long-ago woman, forever trapped in the unforgiving walls, had returned to lend comfort. Maybe the woeful spirit was warning her to leave now, before she herself became a miserable soul, with no hope in this world or the next.

"Nonsense," Constance said aloud to herself.

The wrenching sobs continued, but she ignored them, partially from common sense. Partially from the very real fear that she would join the mysterious woman in a flood of tears.

Opening a drawer, still going over the issue of money, she pulled out some undergarments to pack, placing them on the bed before realizing she did not even have a portable bag in which to put her clothes. The journey to Sandringham had been made with trunks and valets and coaches. The only items she could carry would be the tin bucket from the duke and her writing desk.

There was a knock on the door. After only a slight hesitation, Constance opened it.

It was Viola, in a billowy white night wrapper,

holding a candle. Her nose was red, eyes moist from crying.

The mystery of the midnight weeping had been solved. The surprise must have been evident on Constance's face.

"I do not wish to shock you, Miss Lloyd," she whispered. "But may I enter and have a talk with you?"

Constance nodded, simply because she had been caught off guard, and no other option had presented itself in her mind in time to prevent the woman from intruding.

Without waiting for her hostess to speak, Viola stepped into the room and closed the door behind her. Immediately, her gaze shifted to the bed. "So, are you planning a journey, Miss Lloyd?" She placed the candle on a chest and waited for an answer.

"No, no. I was just . . ."

Constance's voice trailed off, and Viola sighed. "Forgive me." She closed her eyes. "I seem to have made something of a habit out of being rude. Something about this house makes me so disagreeable, I find it hard to tolerate myself. Which makes things rather awkward, to say the least."

"May I help you with anything?" Constance asked, at a loss from both the nocturnal visit as well as the odd behavior of Cavendish's fiancée. "I did not realize you were spending the night here. I assumed you would be going to your own home."

"I made an excuse of feeling rather ill myself. You see, I was hoping to get the chance to speak to you in private."

"Was that you I heard crying?"

"Good Lord, you could hear?" She looked about the room. "This old house carries the noise, doesn't it? Yes. I do confess that was me."

"Are you feeling better?" She could think of little to say. "Is there anything I can do to help you?"

"I'm not sure. You see, well. This is quite difficult for me. I've never come to anyone for help before, not like this."

"But you have the advantage of knowing the topic," Constance attempted a light tone. "Please, just say what you wish to say."

"I understand you were a governess."

For a moment Constance just stood, staring at Viola. "Yes, I'm afraid that is true. I was a governess for well nigh unto a decade, so there you have it. Your curiosity is satisfied." She began to pass Viola to open the door for her, hoping the woman would leave her alone.

"No, you misunderstand." She tied the belt at her waist in a nervous gesture, almost fluttery, then untied it again. "I just want to know about you."

"I will be more than delighted to discuss my history at another time, but at the moment I—"

"Are you in love with him?" Viola blurted.

"Pardon me?"

With more confidence, she took a step forward. "I asked you if you are in love with him. That's all I need to know."

Constance crossed her arms and glanced towards the bed, where her clothing sat in silent accusation. And then she saw her writing desk, the gift from Joseph. This had gone on too long, far too long. She could no longer pretend.

"Yes," she admitted, closing her eyes for a moment. "Yes, I am very much in love with him."

"Oh." Viola's voice was nothing more than a small puff, and her shoulders slumped forward. "Then, well. I am sorry for the intrusion. And I wish you every happiness." She swallowed and reached for the candle. "May you and Philip be very happy," she said softly.

"Wait." Constance stepped towards her. "You inquired if I was in love with Philip?"

Viola nodded, her lower lip straightening as she attempted to smile.

Should she tell her? Constance watched the other woman. Again, a sense of being trapped by falsehoods, although well-intentioned ones, rose in her throat. This could not continue. She would be gone soon, it no longer mattered.

"I am not in love with Philip."

Viola did not move. "But you just said you were."

"No. I meant Joseph."

"Joseph Smith?"

"Shush! You'll wake the entire house!"

Viola clamped her hand over her own mouth, her eyes staring straight ahead. Then she began to laugh.

"Well, I am glad I could provide you with such amusement," Constance muttered.

Viola waved her hand, but continued laughing silently, her shoulders shaking. With her expression so natural and unguarded, the change in the appearance was quite astounding. The guarded stiffness was gone, and she was again as she was at Sandringham, as she would be forever in Philip's painting of her—a genuinely pretty young woman free of artifice.

Constance relaxed, and even smiled a bit in return. Viola's giggling was indeed an infectious relief.

Finally Viola took a deep breath and ran a finger under each eye to wipe away the tears. "Forgive me," she said at last. "I seem to be falling apart. It's just that, well, you see, I *am* in love with Philip."

Constance's mouth opened, and Viola grinned.

"I always have been, ever since he threw a rock at me when I was five years old."

"Well, if that won't inspire love, I don't know what would," Constance stammered. She raked her hand through her dark hair. "You're in love with Philip?"

Viola nodded. "Desperately so."

"Then why are you engaged to Cavendish?"

"I suppose for the same reason you're engaged to Philip. No choice, really. I have spent years making a complete fool out of myself to get Philip's attention, but, as you can see, it hasn't worked. Even that horrid trick that I played on him when we were children was yet another attempt to get Philip to notice me. All it managed to do was instill a lifelong fear of spiders in the poor man. All of my pranks were to get him to notice me. Even if Philip became angry, well, at least that would have been something, now, wouldn't it?"

"This is taking me a while to comprehend."

"I know. It's quite a mess, isn't it?"

"Here, let's sit on the bed." Constance pushed away her clothing, and the two women settled on the edge.

"So you are in love with Smith?"

Constance nodded. "I didn't realize how very much until today."

"Do you have any idea of his whereabouts?"

"No." She paused before continuing. "In truth, I was planning on leaving tonight to try to find him."

"Leaving? Tonight? How on earth could you do that?"

"I'm not sure." The small dimple appeared just below her lip. "The reality of the situation was just sinking in when you came."

"Do you have any idea where he could be?"

"Not really, although I was going to go to London. Philip said he has a laboratory off Waterloo Road, so I thought I would start there."

"I don't know." Viola bit her lower lip. "I should doubt very much he would be in London. No one's seen him for days, and I would imagine that he would have a beastly time hiding from anyone in town at the moment."

"I know he was in Scotland recently. Perhaps I could find him there."

"Miss Lloyd, Scotland is a big place. We need more to go on than a man by the name of Smith and a country. Do you have any other names he might be associated with?"

Constance wavered. She did not know this woman, not really. Perhaps it was an attempt by one of Joseph's enemies—whoever they were—to get material to use against him. Although she had little enough solid information to offer, it was a possibility.

"Oh, come on, Miss Lloyd." Viola wearily rubbed the back of her own neck. "I'll be frank—my only hope of forming any sort of relationship with Philip, other than the unfortunate one you saw this afternoon, is to get you happily away from here with Joseph Smith. Don't you see? Anyone else, and Philip would move heaven and earth to find you. But Smith, well. Smith just happens to be the one man whose happiness Philip would choose over his own. But . . ."

"But what?"

"How does Smith feel about you? I am living proof that a woman may very well feel she is the ideal mate for a man, and he may never know it. Does Smith in any way return your affection?"

"I, well . . ." She thought of his expression, the way he had looked at her in the library at Sandringham, when he came to her room to bid her good-bye. "I believe he does feel something," she concluded. "He has indicated a certain fondness for me. And he sent me that writing desk."

Both women glanced over at the lap desk, and Viola smiled.

"Well, from Smith, that is the equivalent of a

declaration in the *Gazette*. So now what are the names that might connect you with Smith?"

Again she hesitated.

"Please," Viola urged. "I will be perfectly honest, Miss Lloyd. I am forced to marry Cavendish because my parents have lost much of their wealth. Unlike the Ballsbridge estate, our estate was small, and held to land which has become all but useless. My younger brother will inherit all, and my parents have given me the choice of accepting Cavendish, or becoming a governess myself."

"You would become a governess?"

"I have little alternative. I will turn thirty in less than a month. The estate cannot support us much longer. I have very little choice."

There was absolutely no doubt in Constance's mind that Viola was being honest. It was a humiliating thing to admit for anyone, but at least when Constance had been forced into the position, she had not had to do so in front of all the people she grew up with in Richmond. At least she had not had an audience for her social ruin.

"And at this point," Viola continued, "I believe I would rather be employed as a governess than endure a loveless marriage."

That was it. That was the very crux of the matter, the very heart of why Constance could not possibly continue at Hastings House.

"Can you imagine," Viola whispered, "what it would be like in five years' time? Now I can pretend politeness to Cavendish, all the while thinking of Philip, comparing their gestures and smiles and the way they sit a horse. But if I marry Cavendish, well. I believe I will lose my mind. By then it wouldn't matter, I suppose, because I would have already bartered my soul."

"Crimmins and Walker," Constance announced.

"Excuse me?"

"I don't know their Christian names, but two gentlemen of Joseph's acquaintance escorted me to Hastings House after we were waylaid by highwaymen."

"Oh, yes! Cavendish told me about it! Jolly good, Miss Lloyd. Jolly good indeed." Then she sobered. "Crimmins and Walker. Well, that is something. Any other name?"

"Miss Rathbottom?"

"Please, call me Viola."

"Viola. I must be honest with you. I've seen the way Philip looks at you, at Sandringham as well as here. And I would bet just about anything that he is at least as much in love with you as you are with him."

"You are joking," said Viola, her eyes indicating that she very much wanted to believe that Constance was sincere.

"I do not joke about such things."

Viola took a deep breath. "Dear God, I hope you're right."

"Brown."

"Brown?"

"Yes. I just remembered the other name connected with Joseph. Crimmins and Walker seem to have some association with a Brown, John Brown, I believe. One of them slipped the name in the coach."

"John Brown. That's not really . . ." Suddenly Viola stopped. "John Brown? Is this John Brown the connection to Scotland?"

"I believe so. And the coachman mentioned a large man in a kilt speaking to Joseph before he collected me for the journey here."

Viola's eyes grew very wide. "And where again did he collect you from?"

"Cowes. On the Isle of Wight. What is it?"

"Cowes. And was the Queen by any chance at Osborne House at the time?"

"Why, yes, as a matter of fact, she was. Viola, what's wrong?"

"I believe I can tell you where Smith is."

"Where? Please don't keep it from me."

"I saw the *Court Circular.*" Her voice was hollow with astonishment. "The Queen is going for her holiday at Balmoral in Scotland."

"What on earth does the Queen have to do with this?"

"My dear Miss Lloyd, John Brown is her private manservant. Whatever Smith is engaged in, it has something to do with the Queen of England herself."

"Queen Victoria?" She could barely get the words out. *"That* John Brown? The man from all of the pamphlets, from the cartoons in *Punch?"*

"Queen Victoria," Viola confirmed. "The Queen, and John Brown."

Somehow, their own problems seemed very small indeed.

It wasn't until Constance was on the train to Scotland on the London and NorthWestern line, and then on the twenty-mile coach ride from the station to Balmoral, that she actually had time to think. And her thoughts centered on the sheer impulsiveness of her journey, as well as the improbability of it succeeding. She wondered when she would be missed, if those at Hastings House would be relieved or alarmed. Probably a little of both, she concluded.

With Viola's help, she had penned a note to Philip, just a few lines. Using her newly restored writing desk and the fresh paper and ink, she thanked him for everything. But she did not love him, and he deserved something more. Indeed, she concluded, she felt certain he was not in love with her—and one day soon, she knew he would find joy with the woman he loved, the woman who would love him forever in return.

That last bit had been Viola's addition, and in hindsight Constance winced at the melodrama. But it was too late to be changed.

On the train she thought of the old duke, and hoped her sudden departure would not cause him worry. She knew the duchess would be too busy counting the silverware and examining the jewel boxes for missing items to concern herself overly much with the missing fiancée. She had placed the engagement ring in the center of her dresser, so the duchess should be pleased.

Above all, she thought of Joseph.

It had, indeed, been a most extraordinary twenty-four hours.

Everything had happened with astounding haste. It seemed as if, from the moment Viola had appeared at Constance's door, the world had tilted upon its side.

After they had figured out the probable identity of John Brown, the plan unfolded quickly. Viola slipped back to her own home and managed to procure almost fifty pounds from various hiding places in the house, including her mother's secret money pouch hidden behind a marble bust of Queen Anne, and returned through the Hastings House side entrance with traveling clothes, a small portmanteau, and a train schedule.

"Viola," Constance said. They had been addressing each other by their first names for well over twenty minutes by then. "I honestly don't know how to thank you."

"Please," Viola replied, examining the train schedule. Finally she looked directly at Constance. "The faster I get you out of here, the better chance I have at marrying the right brother."

The smile faded from Constance's face. "What am I doing?"

"You're going off to find the man you love."

"This is madness."

"No, it isn't." Viola grabbed her wrist. "Madness is me marrying Cavendish. Madness is you marrying Philip."

"There is no guarantee that Joseph even wants me, none at all."

"Perhaps. Just as there's no guarantee that Philip will want me."

"And there is absolutely no guarantee that he is at Balmoral, for heaven's sake. If the London reporters can't find him, how can I be expected to?"

"For one thing, my dear Constance, unlike the London reporters, no matter how audacious they may be, you have a more urgent need to find Joseph Smith than they do. You are on a quest for love, which is far more potent than any reporter's assignment. And you are right—we don't know how Smith will respond when you do see him. There is no guarantee on any of that. But I'll promise you this—one thing I *can* guarantee is that you will be miserable if you don't go after him."

That was true. Everything she said was true. But was this the right way to secure a chance at happiness?

"I am not certain if this is the right course," Constance admitted. It was such an unexpected relief to have someone to confide in, someone with whom to unburden herself. She had not had such a friend since Mrs. Whitestone.

No. She had not had such a friend since Joseph.

"What other course is there? For God's sake, Constance, we are both of us running out of time. Do you realize that if we do not do something now, we will forever pay the price in misery? And it would be nothing more than what we deserve, exactly what we would deserve if we don't at least try."

"I'm not sure . . ."

"Perhaps you are not sure, but I am." Viola lowered her voice. "I will make up some story, anything. I'll say I took you to Rathbottom Grange."

"Rathbottom Grange?"

Viola grinned. "Dreadful, isn't it? That's the name of my home. Now you know why I wish to marry Philip—so I will no longer bear the name Rathbottom." Again she became all business. "No matter. I will write a note to say that we left early this morning for Rathbottom Grange. By that time he will have received your note, the one releasing him. I know Philip—he will wait some time before he comes after you. He'll wish to think, to figure out what to do. That will keep all of them at bay, and when Philip comes round to see you—and I have no doubt he will once he draws up a battle plan—I can do my best to entertain him."

"What on earth will I say to him? I mean, when I do see him."

"By 'him' I assume you mean Smith."

Constance nodded. Her head had begun to pound fiercely. This was all so very improbable.

"Let's just get you to Scotland first, Constance."

"I mean, how shall I explain my sudden appearance? 'Hello, Mr. Smith. It is so lovely to see you. I just happened to be skulking about the royal residences of Great Britain, and what a coincidence that you happen to be here, sir.' Can you imagine?"

"Well, you will have hours on a wobbly train to come up with something glittering and brilliant. But if we do not get you to the station soon, it will mean nothing."

"How will you explain your absence, Viola?"

That man was John Brown.

The very man she was there to see, to find out where Joseph was.

The carriage let her out just at the base of the Balmoral path. It wasn't an unusual request. The coachman assumed Constance was perhaps another lady to visit, or an elevated lady-in-waiting to the queen. She paid the man and he drove off, only slightly perplexed by her desire to walk the rest of the way instead of being driven.

She took a deep breath and clutched her bags, a small reticule and the portmanteau borrowed from Viola. She had packed the duke's bucket, this time with no comforting tea cakes, for good luck.

And as she walked up the rugged path, it did occur to her that if at any time in her life she needed a bit of good luck, it was, most certainly, now.

14

Now that she was within sight of Balmoral, after trudging the rocky, windy path and fending off insects the size of small mammals, she was not sure what she should do next. In reality, she had never really anticipated getting this far without being stopped by some burly guards or hidden agents of the queen. As far as she could tell, there was little or no security on the grounds. There were caretakers, men walking about with rakes who would tip their caps, women with buckets or baskets who would smile with broad, red faces and scurry on. But unlike Osborne House, there were no soldiers posted. Balmoral looked just like a large, well-tended private home rather than the current residence of the most powerful monarch in Europe.

She began walking towards what seemed to be the main entrance, all the while waiting for someone to jump from the shrubbery to halt her, to grab her by the waist and wrestle her to the ground.

No one did. Her path was unimpeded, and one of

the men with a rake even pushed aside a pile of trimmings for her to pass with less trouble. With only a slight hesitation, she marched up to the house.

And then she was grabbed.

Instead of protesting, or being frightened, she was almost relieved.

"Who are ye, woman?" a man's voice growled next to her ear.

"I am here to see Mr. Brown," she replied as calmly as possible, realizing that her feet were no longer touching the ground, and she had an overwhelming sensation of being clutched by a large, tipsy sheep. She felt enveloped by the scent of damp wool and whisky.

"And what be yer name, woman?" The hold seemed to lessen on her, and she was again able to draw a full breath.

"I am Miss Constance Lloyd. Actually, I am here to see Mr. Joseph Smith, if you happen to know where he is."

"Shut up."

"I beg your pardon!" She turned to face the voice, but he would not allow her the freedom to move. "Sir, you are not behaving as a gentleman should."

"I never claimed to be a gentleman, woman," he barked. "And you are trespassing on the property of the Queen of England."

"I know that," she hissed with as much force as his hold on her would allow. "I am not a complete idiot."

"The evidence thus far points that way, woman. Now if I let you down, will you behave?"

"Of course I will. Why, I never."

"What is that accent?"

"I was wondering that myself, sir. You seem to have a very broad Scotch accent."

"You know nothing, woman." He dropped her to

her feet, and finally she saw her abductor. He was enormous. Not in height, for he was actually no taller than Joseph or Philip. It was his build that lent him an overall impression of hugeness.

His face, when her eyes finally reached it, was quite attractive, the features strong and regular, the skin tanned and just beginning to weather like worn leather. He wore a peaked cap with an emblem pinned to the left side, and a beautifully tailored blue jacket and bright white shirt. But it was his kilt, with a sporran covered with so much shaggy fur she expected it to bark, and heavy wool socks that caught her eye, mainly because of the circumference of his legs.

They were massive. She had seen oak trees with less sturdy trunks. Never before had she seen legs of such obvious strength, including on beasts in the zoo and the occasional elephant foot umbrella stand. The man's legs were human, but just barely.

"I'm speaking to ye, woman." He crossed his arms. Perhaps because of the well-cut clothing above she had not realized that his arms were every bit as broad as his legs.

"I believe, sir, you are the largest man I have ever seen."

For the first time he smiled, and Constance realized, with something of a jolt, that the Highland giant was as handsome as he was large.

"Why, thank ye. But I am a Scot, not Scotch."

"Excuse me?"

"Ye said I had a Scotch accent. Maybe I do, but Scotch is whisky. A person such as myself is a Scot, woman."

"I do beg your pardon."

"And where were you a lass?"

"Where was I a lass? Oh, in Virginia, sir."

"Then you are indeed Miss Lloyd." He bowed. "John Brown at your service, woman."

"*You* are John Brown?"

"And what were ye expecting—a mountain goat?"

"Forgive me." She extended her hand. "It is a pleasure to meet you, sir."

"And you, woman. Smith has told me about you."

"Is he here? That's why I came."

Brown stepped back and gave her a painfully obvious head-to-toe appraisal. Slowly he raised one of his hands to his face and stroked his whiskers, rich brown just beginning to turn gray, his eyes narrowing.

"He told you nothing, did he?"

"Mr. Smith?" she asked.

Brown nodded.

"No, Mr. Brown. Unfortunately, he told me nothing. So when those rumors began circulating about him, that perhaps he was in some sort of trouble, well, I decided to try to find him. I thought I could be a help. Why are you looking at me like that?"

"Like what, woman?"

"You're looking at me as if I might be a threat to national security."

"That is exactly what I was thinking meself." He continued to toy with his whiskers. "You are betrothed to another man, are you not?"

"Well, actually . . ."

"And before that you were a governess, were you not?"

"Well, yes, but—"

"So your man allowed you to leave by yourself and trot about the Highlands on a fool's errand to find another gent?"

"No! No, it's not like that at all!" Then she clasped her hands. "He doesn't know where I am."

"Yer man?"

"I do not have a man, Mr. Brown. I do not have a man any more than you have a woman."

She knew the moment she made that comment that

she had made a mistake. A glint sparkled in his eye, and a slow smile spread across his mouth.

"That is not what I meant, Mr. Brown, and you know that very well." Drawing a deep breath, she looked away towards the mountains. For a moment she just watched them, the low clouds that floated around the tops, the lush green and the brilliant purple and yellow of the autumn flowers. "My God, it's magnificent here."

"So it is."

She turned back to him, and the smile was gone now. "Sir, please. Do you have any idea of where I may find Mr. Smith?"

"Nay."

"Nay?"

"That's what I said, woman. Nay."

"So I've come all this way for nothing?"

He shrugged. "Not necessarily. Would you be wanting a pot of tea and a scone?"

She smiled. "Thank you, Mr. Brown. That would be lovely. But may I ask you something first?"

"You may ask me anything ye wish, that's for certain. I may not answer, but you may ask me anything ye wish."

"What is Mr. Smith up to? And is he in any sort of danger?"

"I won't tell you his business. I have no right, none at all. But you'd be daft to think he's not in danger. Daft indeed."

She closed her eyes for a moment. "Thank you."

"Tea, is it?"

"Tea it is," she agreed, and he offered his arm as he scooped up all of her luggage with the other.

Tea was in the servants' quarters. After being among the upstairs folk at Hastings House and Sandringham, it was a great relief to be below, with people who judged her as she was. Unfortunately, they judged her as an unstable woman from the American South who had journeyed across Great Britain to find a man who had vanished, and who was not in any way her intended husband. Still, considering the bare facts that Brown presented, they were most obliging indeed.

She was unable to make much sense of the pecking order of the servants, other than with Mr. Brown, who seemed to command a lairdlike reverence from the other staff. He brought her into the kitchen, then went to a separate corner of the room where he began preparing a tray with all of the somber ceremony of a High Church Eucharist.

"Tea for the queen," whispered an older woman wearing a lace mop cap with quaint lappets.

It wasn't until Brown left that conversation flowed freely amongst the servants. She loved hearing their gentle chat, the beautiful lilt of their words, the warmth that was so obvious amongst the Highlanders. A few words were directed towards her, and she noticed when they did, they inevitably spoke slower and louder.

Even on the cold stone floor, the kitchen sitting area radiated comfort.

"So, is it Smith you're looking for?"

It was the old woman in the mop cap. Constance nodded, and the woman looked back at her teacup. "He's a good man, Smith is."

"Yes, he is," she ventured. "Has he been here lately?"

The woman was about to answer, but there was a sharp tongue-clicking from one of the undergardeners.

"I can't recall," the woman said with such little conviction that everyone in the room knew she remembered precisely when she had last seen Smith, what he had been wearing, and the weather that day.

"Oh. I see." Constance carefully crumbled a bit of scone.

"Why would ye be wanting to find him anyway?" a young housemaid asked. She did not seem more than seventeen years old. "Brown says yer betrothed to the son of a great duke."

All Constance could do was shake her head, wondering herself what had possessed her to run away to Scotland. Suddenly the idea was hopelessly absurd, comical, really. Constance Lloyd, former governess, had narrowly escaped the luxury of Hastings House, where a man who loved her—or at least believed he did—wished to bestow upon her his riches and his name, to hide belowstairs at Queen Victoria's retreat and hope against hope to win the love of the Welsh dye-maker, Joseph Smith.

Narrow escape indeed.

Her shoulders began to quake with laughter, and the servants glanced at each other uneasily. They had seen more than their share of peculiar behavior since the arrival of the Queen more than fifteen years before. They and all their royal lot were an odd bunch, to be sure.

"Are you all right, Miss Lloyd?"

The lack of sleep and simple worry about Joseph had worn her down. She was in a strange land, looking for a man who may not want to be found. The laughter suddenly dissolved into tears.

It was hopeless, utterly hopeless.

"Miss? Would you like a drop of whisky to ease you?"

That struck her as singularly funny, that in her moment of despair, she should drink whisky. Images flooded back to her: memories of the war, and old

Mrs. Witherspoon's son, who sold everything the family had of value for Yankee whisky. Perhaps he had something there, good old Purvis Witherspoon. The thought again made her laugh, but she was not really laughing but crying.

And then she could not stop. Everything she had so carefully stored away for years came into the open, from the stench of death in her front yard, to the openmouthed shock of the Yankee's face when she shot him in the neck, the seasickness on the ship to England, the fear and absolute terror she would fight to squelch at night so she would not lose her mind.

None of it mattered now.

Everyone seemed to be shuffling about the kitchen with great purpose, her vision smeared with tears. Someone handed her a linen handkerchief, and soon another when the first one became so damp with tears. They were all talking loudly now, over her head, no longer attempting to disguise their conversation about her. But she didn't care, and couldn't make sense of their words even if she tried with all of her might.

"There, there, Missy." Someone patted her hand.

"The thing is," she said, her voice broken, as if she had been in the middle of the most normal discussion in the world, "the dreadful thing is that I love him, and I don't know where he is, or if he's well or hurt or sick or needs me. If only I knew. If someone would tell me, you see, I would just go away."

A strange silence descended over the kitchen, but Constance did not notice. Instead she pulled at the soggy handkerchief and continued talking, almost to herself.

"I haven't seen him since Sandringham, and I don't know how I can continue without knowing . . ."

Then someone's hands were on her shoulders. "My dearest, dearest girl."

She straightened, and then realized the servants had left.

"I had no idea, none at all that your feelings for Hastings were so very deep." The voice was masculine and familiar.

And when her vision cleared, she was looking directly into the eyes of the Prince of Wales.

"Your Majesty." Constance rose to her feet and dipped into a curtsy.

"My dear, when there are no others about it is perfectly fine for you to address me as 'sir.'" He was wearing his deer-stalking tweeds and smelled of roast beef.

"Please forgive me," she stammered.

"No, I will not! For had I not come in this way, through the kitchen, instead of the long way, I would never have known how you feel about Hastings. My feet were wet, you see." With his mouth he made a peculiar motion, as if removing something from his teeth with his tongue. The great waxed mustache rotated in exaggerated, synchronized motion with the mouth. "So why, then, are you here?"

"I . . . well . . ."

"Foolish, impulsive, romantic girl! I understand completely—you wish to make the young buck follow you." He clapped his hands, as if applauding a happy moment in a play. "Shall we let him know where you are, or let him stew? This is a delightful diversion. Absolutely delightful."

The prince was exceedingly pleased, and bounced on the balls of his feet as he spoke.

The misunderstanding had gone too far already. "Your Majesty, I did not realize you would be here. I heard you were in town."

"Yes, I was. I was in town until yesterday morning. But I came here to . . . well. I did have some business to conduct, and I needed to . . ."

233

"Miss Lloyd." The voice was unmistakable. John Brown stood in the doorway, or more accurately, cast his shadow over the doorway to the kitchen. "Your Majesty." He nodded very slightly to the prince.

The prince simply glared.

"I beg your pardon, Your Highness, but Miss Lloyd is weary from her journey. Mrs. Robinson has been kind enough to ready a room for her."

"Not in the servants' quarters." The prince stiffened.

"Yes, Your Majesty." Brown had the ability to address the future king in a manner that would suggest very different words indeed. "She will be more than comfortable in the fine little room."

"This is outrageous, Brown." The prince's voice was even, the anger kept just barely under control. "She is to be moved upstairs immediately. She is my guest, not a resident of the servants' hall."

"If I may, Your Highness." Brown glanced down at his fingernails, buffing them lightly on his kilt. "Miss Lloyd is a single lady; at the present time she is not married, however well-bred and delightful she may be. Further, she has yet to be presented to the queen at court. Therefore, she cannot possibly be an official guest at this royal palace."

The prince made a sort of gurgling sound, but no actual words were produced.

Brown continued in his calm, even manner. "You must see that, at this point in time, especially with your dear wife the princess yet in town, Miss Lloyd, as an unexpected guest, will remain where she is."

The prince's face turned an astonishing shade of red, and again he made an odd sputtering noise. Without looking at Constance, he kicked a small wicker stool, wincing at the unexpected pain when the stool tumbled against his shin, and then marched out of the kitchen. His shoulders were very straight, and from the rear the only indication of his displeasure was the distinct set of his cap, which he had shoved over his ears.

After he had exited, she turned towards the Highlander.

"Thank you, Mr. Brown."

He smiled, an expression of both warmth and sympathy. The smile vanished almost immediately, and if she had not seen his teeth so clearly, she would have thought she had imagined the smile.

"You must forgive the queen's eldest son." Brown did not attempt to conceal his disapproval. "His manners are not yet as polished as one would hope. It is a situation we are at present attempting to redress."

The other servants began to come back into the kitchen one by one, none of them speaking, but all, at their own rate, glancing at Constance, offering small nods of reassurance and understanding.

She felt a perfect and utter fool, but accepted the kindness of the servants. Even below she was on display, not quite fitting in, just as she had always been.

When had she last felt at ease, completely herself with no critical glances or judgmental silences?

With Joseph. Even at Sandringham, she had felt untroubled and comfortable when he was nearby. Even spending the night in a roofless, damp inn, she had felt safe with Joseph, free to say what was on her mind, free to allow her emotions to surface.

The question was, now that she knew what it was to be with him, how could she ever survive without him?

The room Mrs. Robinson had prepared was tidy and clean, and far more comfortable than any of the grand places she had slept in recently.

There was nothing but a small bed covered with a colorfully stitched quilt, a single ladder-back chair, and a washstand in the room. The small fireplace held a cheerfully burning flame, and the window was covered with a starched white curtain.

It was more than perfect.

There wasn't even a chest of drawers or a closet. Instead, a pegboard painted moss green served to hang garments.

The sun was just going down when she sat on the bed, intending to simply think. There was no point in staying at Balmoral. Perhaps she could ask Mr. Brown some more questions to determine where Joseph could be.

Drowsiness crept through her limbs, and she placed her head on the pillow, just to think further. The pillow held a fragrance of pine and fresh air and glacial streams, a scent of the outdoors. Even from her small window in the servants' quarters, the beauty of the land filled the room. A mountain nearby seemed to be an almost unnaturally intense shade of green, with gray rocks and clumps of earth dotting the side and mist gathering at the peaks.

Every corner was filled with a clean, bracing perfume, as if the pure breeze enveloped everything in its path. She closed her eyes, again to make her thoughts clearer.

And then she was asleep, dreaming of a waltz. She was being swirled and held, a face indistinct above hers, lost in a blur as the music became faster and faster. She wore a golden-colored silk dress with large hoops and a low-cut neckline. It was of a style that had been out of fashion for a decade or more. Her mother had worn such a gown when Constance was a child, and she recalled the feel of the silk, the way the gaslight reflected off the material, the bone crinoline and the swish of petticoats, the scent of lavender.

At her throat, in her dream, she wore a cluster of bay leaves, a custom she had abandoned in the past few weeks. The point of one of the leaves scratched and nudged her neck, making her uncomfortable.

The dance continued, and her partner pulled her to keep up with the band, her arms aching at the joints as she tried to protest, but no words came from her mouth. The music grew louder and faster, and then she was falling, falling, the skirt gathering the wind as she came closer to the ground. She was alone now, but still the music continued, building and rolling as her legs were swinging in the air.

The ground was no longer a polished dance floor, but a field of sharp, broken rocks. There were already bodies on the rocks, twisted and bloodied, some men dressed in uniforms, some women in ball gowns.

Then a hand was over her mouth.

She struggled against the hand, and realized it was a man. Her partner? No, this was something different . . .

This was no longer a dream.

Again, she tried to cry out, but this time her voice was stifled by the hand. Her heart was pounding with such force she could not hear his words, could not distinguish the voice in the night.

The fire had long since sputtered out, leaving the room in complete darkness.

"Constance, stop . . ."

He pulled her closer, and with all of her strength, with every fiber of her being, she kicked out her leg. Her knee slammed into his abdomen, and his hold on her finally loosened. She was about to scream out for help when she heard his voice clearly.

"Christ almighty," he moaned. "I think I'm going to be sick."

She stopped, his breathing ragged, and reached up to touch his hair. It was soft and thick in the darkness. Her hand traveled down to his cheek, clean-shaven . . .

"Joseph?"

"Aye," he groaned. "So now you know the name of your victim." He coughed, and she could hear him roll onto his side.

"Joseph! It's you!"

"Stay away! For mercy's sake, stay away . . ."

"No, I didn't mean to hurt you. Oh, Joseph, I've been looking for you, that's why I came up here." He emitted a strange moan, and she tried to pat his shoulder, but instead patted the side of his face.

"Ouch," he said.

"I'm so sorry. I was having a bad dream."

"I gathered." His breathing was more even now. "My God, Constance, you have quite a kick to those legs."

"Where have you been?" Her hand remained on the side of his face, and she could feel the smoothness of his skin, the warmth.

"Just now I was in indescribable pain."

"How did you know where I was?"

"Brown showed me to your room. Christ. I believe you've rearranged some inner organs."

"Sorry. So you were here the whole time. I wonder why Brown didn't tell me earlier?"

"I just arrived. Interesting."

"What is interesting?"

"You seem to have located a muscle I did not realize I had."

"Sorry. But then, where were you?"

"I was working at my lab in London. Which leads me to ask—what on earth are you doing here?"

"I was looking for you, Joseph. I was worried."

"You did not have to worry. Did Philip send you?"

"No."

"Does he know where you are?"

"He probably does, at least by now. I left him a note."

"Excellent. Then we'll return you right away to Hastings House. I'm sure . . ."

"No."

"No?"

"I'm not going back there."

"Now, Constance, I know the duchess is overbearing, but in time I feel confident that you will manage."

"Is that what you think this is about?"

"I . . . Constance. No. Tell me."

"I am no longer engaged to Philip."

He drew in a long breath, and she continued. "It was all wrong, Joseph. For so many reasons, the main one being that I do not love him, nor does he love me. He's in love with Viola."

"Viola? You're mad, Constance. Viola Rathbottom has been the bane of his existence ever since I can recall. If you had any idea of the stunts she has pulled—"

"I *do* have an idea. She told me, confessed everything the night before I came here. It was all to get Philip's attention."

"It worked. He hates her."

"No, he doesn't. He loves her, but he's been so busy responding to her ink pots on people's heads and slivers of soap on the cheese dish that he hasn't had the chance to realize it himself."

"What about Dishy?"

"The only reason she agreed to marry him was to avoid becoming a governess. That is why she has not been able to marry him before. She had always hoped that Philip would claim her instead."

"I need to let this sink in. This is extraordinary, absolutely extraordinary."

"Think about the way they look at each other. Have you ever seen it? At Sandringham it was all they could do to keep their eyes off each other."

"I had assumed he was just wondering if he had to

duck from her." Idly, he stroked her hand. "I just realized something, Constance. He's been sketching her for years. The laboratory we share is filled with drawings and paintings of her. I just assumed it was because her face was so familiar to him. Bloody hell, I believe you're right! I'll be damned. Viola and Philip."

He shook his head, and after a while began to chuckle. "Really, Constance, if you had seen her as a child, all arms and legs, but she always wore a big floppy ribbon in her hair. We called it her disguise. Others thought she was a girl, but the two of us knew better—she was a French agent, intent on killing us all. She had a slingshot and the sharpest collection of rocks you've ever seen. Tried to hit Philip once, but she got my cheek instead."

"Is that what that scar is from?" She smiled, reaching up to touch the side of his face. "I always imagined it was from a duel."

"It seems it was, in a fashion. She was fighting for him. How very extraordinary. She was fighting all along, and we never realized it."

She ran a hand through her hair, which had come unpinned during her sleep and the struggle with Joseph.

"Did you have a pleasant journey?" His voice had a peculiar quality, his breath caressed her neck. What a peculiar question, she mused.

"Yes. Yes, I did, thank you." It was hard to remember what his question had been.

In the darkness she reached up and again touched his face, slowly at first, then, as she realized they were closer than she had expected, she explored the softness of his features. Once her finger ran down his cheek, she paused, and as she stroked his mouth, his hand grasped hers.

"Constance," he whispered.

240

"Joseph." She bit her lip, as if to withdraw her voice, and everything she was feeling.

And then his lips were upon hers.

It was lost then, the world as she knew it thus far. His hands cupped her face, reverently and with a gentleness she had never experienced.

"Joseph," she began again, but her utterance was silenced.

She was so very aware of his body, of the heaviness as he weighed down upon her, of every intake of his breath. The closeness was miraculous, the intimacy astonishing. Yet so comfortable, so relaxed.

He began to speak, and suddenly she wanted to hear nothing of his voice, honeyed as it was to her ears. All she wanted was to experience him, to feel him, to be with him.

Everything about him was perfect, his scent, the scent she had only garnered in fleeting glimpses before, now she could savor and inhale and glory in his fragrance. Her hands grasped his arms, and she was surprised for a moment at the roll of muscles there, at the rush of emotions that were released upon that touch.

Her gown. He unbound it with a facility she would not dwell upon, and then she felt his hands upon her flesh. Instead of being frightened or embarrassed, she was relieved. Now she could feel him, now she could feel his hands upon her skin.

She grasped his earlobe within her teeth.

The rest was a whirl. Of hands, and breath, and the feel of precious skin. In a world beyond all else, he was there.

Her breasts were touched with such delicate care, she felt herself grow weak.

"Constance," he breathed.

And then she was lost, in his touch, in his scent, in his feel.

In him.
And then she was lost.

They were still in the darkness, his features yet masked in the night.

He smoothed her hair, pressing a lock against his lips before speaking. "We should not have done that. I should not have done that. We should have waited."

"I wanted you," she breathed. "More than anything, no matter what happens, I wanted us to." She planted a kiss against his chest. "May I ask you a serious question?"

"You are trying to change the subject."

"Will you promise to answer me truthfully?"

After a long sigh, he spoke. "As truthfully as possible," he hedged.

"Joseph, is what they're saying true? That you are trying to poison the royal family?"

He was silent for a moment before he spoke. "To tell you the truth, I don't have to."

"Oh, my God, what do you mean?"

"You've tasted the food at Sandringham. The French cook is already intent on completing the job."

"I am serious, Joseph. Those vials you had, your knowledge of chemistry. I've heard you speak on republican topics with great passion."

"You've also seen some of the more notorious London gazettes, have you not?"

"A few," she began.

"I believe I will sue the one that ran the picture of the murdering physician and implied it was me. I'm far, far better-looking than that fellow. And I don't have a beard."

"Joseph, please stop joking. I must know. What are you doing? Why are you working with Brown? Why did you disappear?"

He cleared his throat, and she could tell he was

about to make a glib reply, when he halted. "I'm not certain if this is the right thing, if I should tell you. It's a burden. I'm offering you fair warning, it's a heavy burden. Do you still wish to know?"

"Of course I do!"

"Very well. I am telling this to you not so much for my own sake, but for Brown's. There are people who would be delighted to witness his downfall."

"I do not give a jig *why* you tell me, just tell me." She sighed.

Languidly, his thumb stroked her cheek as he spoke. "Brown contacted me several months ago. He had heard of my interest in science, especially in the realm of disease prevention. He sent me a note to meet with him last spring, and it seems he felt comfortable with me, a fellow Celt."

"What did he contact you about?"

"As you know, there have been more than a few attempts on the queen's life, the assorted anarchist with a gun, that sort of thing."

"Luckily, unlike our Mr. Booth, your madmen seem to have rather poor aim."

"Something to be grateful for. But Brown worried that our madmen may have abandoned firearms for something less obvious and more thorough."

"What do you mean?"

"I will go back a bit. In recent years, great scientific discoveries have been made in the field of medicine. Your Civil War did much to add to our knowledge. Until a few years ago, the notion of germs and disease was unheard of. On the field, surgeons would amputate a limb after sharpening their knives on their boots, and wonder why, after a successful operation, the patient would die. They were killing their patients, not with the blade itself, but with disease from their unwashed hands and the very instruments they employed to help save lives."

"That is very much along the lines of your notion, is it not? Preventing disease through hygiene and purification of water?"

"Exactly!" His fingers folded over her hand, and it felt so very right. "So, Brown had heard of my ideas—the servants' network is more highly evolved than any espionage system in the world—and asked me to take samples from all of the royal residences, specifically water samples. You see, there have been illnesses, even deaths, of guests after staying at a royal residence. The prince himself, as you'll recall, almost died three years ago."

"I remember the thanksgiving celebrations—they were astounding."

"Right. So the Queen became ill last year, and Brown began thinking—is this a coincidence? Is it just bad luck that has the Queen's family ill so frequently?"

"What about her husband's death?"

"That was another thing. It always bothered Brown that Prince Albert succumbed so quickly to typhoid fever."

"But that was before the medical discoveries."

"It was, but it may have given someone an idea."

She shook her head in confusion, and he continued. "We know that typhoid fever can be passed from one person to another. What if you *wished* to infect someone? How would you go about it? You could taint the water supply, of course. And many of the royal homes, like other homes, have terrible drainage systems. Water stagnates and gathers disease. Brown wanted me to check out the homes and see if there were any suspicious signs of tampering. Thus the samples."

"What sort of samples?"

"Again, water mainly, but paint—which you caught me doing at Sandringham—and soil, food, fabric, just about everything you could imagine. I'm working on a way to get air samples, but so far I have not found a reliable method."

"Joseph, why didn't you just come out and say that to begin with?"

"Because we did not wish to give ideas to any budding John Wilkes Booths out there, Constance. It's a terrifying notion. In theory, one could ransom an entire city's water supply. No, it would not do to have our notions made public. And another thing . . ."

He did not speak, as if wondering whether he should continue.

"You can trust me," she said softly.

"I know. That I know. I just don't know if it would be safe to tell you the rest. Already I may have placed you in peril."

"So there can be no more harm done, can there? Please, Joseph. This isn't fair."

"Well . . . we believe, that is, John Brown and myself, we suspect that we know the individual behind the scheme."

"So why don't you tell the police and have him arrested?"

"Because, well, damn it, it's the Prince of Wales."

Her jaw dropped, and she shook her head in confusion. "The Prince of Wales? Impossible! Why would he want to poison his own family? My God, why would he wish to poison himself?"

"He has no intention of doing either. Let me clarify—he wishes to frame someone for the alleged crime, once it has been discovered. I believe his valet is the real culprit behind the scheme, not Bertie. The valet and Brown have been at odds for years, and he planted the idea. The prince is pretending very studiously that he has no knowledge of it. At least, that is my theory."

"But he's the future king! How can he do this?"

"He is a future king who longs for respect from his mother. She will not allow him to govern anything except for the social set. He's frustrated and bitter, and he's turned his anger towards the one person who has the respect and attention of the Queen, everything he so longs for . . . John Brown. In his mind it is John Brown and John Brown alone who stands between the prince and the queen."

"Does the Queen herself know anything about this?"

"Of course not. And mind you, the Prince has no desire to actually harm anyone. That is why I was invited to Sandringham. He wants me there as a control. I believe he's not a little afraid of his own valet. No, all the Prince wishes to do is eliminate Brown, to get him neatly convicted of treason. Unfortunately, his valet is more reckless."

"So the Queen has no idea of what is going on under her very nose."

"As far as I know, she does not. But she trusts Brown above everyone. He would not worry her, though. He considers this his business, and his alone."

"And yours."

"Well, yes. And mine."

"Do you collect a fee for this service? I mean, your reputation, even your life could be at stake."

His laughter filled the small room. "No. I'm afraid that on this account, I have proven myself to be a very bad businessman indeed. That was part of the reason Brown contacted me rather than some poor professor. Not only would I already be asked to attend functions where I could easily do my work, and Brown slipped me a few invitations himself, but he knew I would not require a fee. And no one would think my presence odd. No one, that is, except for me."

"And, therefore, he could keep the project between the two of you, without having to inform the Prime Minister or anyone else."

"Correct. Although now, I suppose, it is a secret shared by three, not two."

"Thank you," she whispered. "Thank you for telling me."

"You are welcome." He leaned back, relaxing as if for the first time. "You know, I really feel better now. Relieved that you know everything. I did not want you to think ill of me."

"I would never think ill of you."

"I . . . thank you." He shifted on the bed. They did not speak for a long moment. Yet both were keenly aware of the other's presence, of their bodies being inches apart, touching in other places, feeling the warmth in each other.

He was leaning against the headboard of the bed. Slowly, she slid beside him and rested her head on his chest. His arms encircled her, and he kissed her forehead gently, leaving his lips against her skin, his breath feathering her temple.

"What are we going to do?" she whispered against his shoulder.

At first he said nothing, then he took a deep breath. "I need to finish this, not only for Brown's sake, but for the sake of the future king. He's been ill-advised, and that is no fault of his. Yet he will be king, and must realize that intrigues of this sort are absolutely unthinkable."

"But after that is resolved, what will we do?"

"I can make no promise, Constance. I have no idea what will happen, where this will lead to. I'm doing the best I can, but doing it blindly. I can only say that . . . I feel, well. I've never before . . ."

"Yes?"

"Good night, Constance."

She realized he would not say anything else, not tonight. Already he had confided in her, told her more than she ever imagined, given her more than she had ever dreamed possible.

"Good night," she whispered. "Good night." Then, more softly, she added, "I love you."

There was no response, and she only smiled, grateful at last that she had been given the chance to tell him.

"Damn him," she muttered again.

He was gone by dawn. She awoke, ready to embrace Joseph and life and the world, and he had vanished, leaving a note and a flower. Nothing more.

Constance was fully awake now, all illusions of romance had dried up with the morning dew.

It was a beautiful rose.

A very slight smile touched her lips as she picked it up, wondering where he had managed to get a perfect red rose in the middle of the Highlands, in the middle of autumn. She touched the bloom to her nose, and the fragrance was exquisite, the petals like perfumed silk.

"Damn you," she repeated, but with less inspiration than before.

Finally, she picked up the note. There was no name on it, just a piece of folded paper.

Bracing herself, she opened the note.

"C—I will be back. —J."

Then, at the bottom, *"And I love you, too."*

"Damn you." She grinned at last. And she wondered when he would be back, and hoped it would be soon, very soon.

15

The rest of the household awoke early in the servants' wing of the castle, the sounds of footsteps rushing up and down the halls and clicking on the back staircases, brooms hastily sweeping the floors and hearths, the laughter as the morning meals were prepared for the guests above and eaten by the staff below. Noises that never filtered to the main portion of Balmoral were deafening in the uncarpeted, whitewashed rooms where the staff worked and lived.

Constance put the pillow over her head, but still the sounds came through.

Had last night been a dream, she wondered. Had Joseph really been there?

He had. She could detect his scent on the sheets and the pillow case, a scent that was now mingling with bread baking below and the Highland mist.

And there was his note, just beyond her reach, and the perfect red rose. The thought of him made her stretch and smile as she slipped out of bed.

She dressed quickly, running a brush through her

hair and pinning it with more speed than care, and went below.

A few "mornings" greeted her, and others smiled and nodded. On the large, broad table were loaves of bread and pots of jam and butter, coffee and tea.

"Is Mr. Brown down yet?" Constance asked of a young man with pale hair. He stopped chewing for a moment before he replied.

"Aye, he's been down and up again. The Queen is feeling poorly, so we're not likely to see Mr. Brown till nightfall."

Suddenly the day was not quite as glorious as it had seemed just a few moments earlier. The Queen was not feeling well. Of course, it could be something simple.

Or the prince and his valet were about to make their move.

She had a peculiar, disjointed feeling of not really belonging there, no matter how friendly the servants were, or how pleasant their morning banter was. Constance knew too much, understood far too well that the daily routine might be shattered at any moment. They all had tasks to perform, useful chores to complete, mundane things that seemed terribly important now.

Her appetite gone, she left the kitchen without eating, but no one seemed to notice. Back in her room, she straightened the handtowel by the washstand, smoothed the cover on the bed, and folded all of her clothes back into the portmanteau.

Again she went downstairs, aimless and feeling her nerves fray.

"Why don't you have a turn about the grounds, miss?"

It was the cook she had spoken to before, a sympathetic-looking woman wielding a large wooden spoon that seemed to have become an extension of her arm. She pointed towards the window, dripping white batter and wiping up the drops with her apron.

"Go on, miss." She smiled. "It will do you good to have a brisk walk about."

Constance nodded, realizing that she was very much underfoot in the kitchen. She left without even going back to her room for her bonnet.

The morning air was bracing without being terribly cold. She walked towards the rear of the house, appreciating the barely tamed beauty of the grounds and the wild landscape beyond. Just being in that setting was a restorative, a soothing balm for the soul. It was the sense of being a part of a grander scheme, something bigger than anything man could create, that put life in perspective.

The hem of her skirt soaked up the water from the grass as she walked, but it didn't matter, not really. There were wild flowers and armfuls of heather to gather, and the further she went from the house, the more splendid the scenery became.

"Good morning." The male voice seemed to come from nowhere, and she was startled. "Forgive me, I did not mean to surprise you."

A slender man wearing a somber black frockcoat and a tangerine-colored vest rose from a stone bench. About his neck on a chain were a pair of eyeglasses. He moved with difficulty, and Constance noticed a silver-handled cane propped against the bench.

"Oh, please, do not trouble yourself," she said quickly, and he seemed both relieved and embarrassed as he returned to his seat.

There was something familiar about the man, whose hair was unnaturally black, especially in contrast to the pallor of his complexion. His skin was dry and covered with a web of lines, but no deep wrinkles, and his lower lip protruded even as he smiled.

"Ah. Now I understand. Now I understand perfectly."

"Excuse me?"

"You were on a mission of love, were you not?"

"I . . . well." There was something so comfortable about the elderly man that she was at her ease. "I suppose I was, although everything is a bit of a muddle now."

"Ah, do not say that. Are you both alive?"

"I'm afraid I don't understand."

"I said, are you both alive, you and your gentleman?"

"Why, yes," she answered. "Yes, of course."

"Then any problems that arise can be solved."

"That's a very optimistic approach to life," she said. "But some problems are quite tangled, are they not?"

"Nonsense. May I tell you a little story?"

"I wish you would."

He chuckled and shifted on the bench, gingerly moving one of his legs over. "Gout," he confided.

"I'm sorry. Is there anything I can do to help you?"

"Not at all, my dear. And as painful as the condition is, I have had a splendid time acquiring the disease. Now where were we?"

"Gout?"

"No. I was going to bless you with a tale. Many years ago, there was a very young man. He was something of a fop, of a dandy, and he had great charm but very little sense."

"That seems to be an over-used combination."

"Indeed. Now this young man was one step away from debtor's prison. He had made something of a name for himself by writing popular novels, you know the sort, with a great deal of romance and wickedness, but the wicked are always punished in the end so that the churchgoers will not take offense. There was a woman he knew, she was a rather silly thing, he thought, and she was a dozen years his senior. She was also recently widowed. But he was determined to marry the silly widow."

"For the money?"

"Partially. At first, in fact, that was the main reason for wishing to marry her. By then he had managed to avoid prison by winning a seat in the House of Commons. He won by the very skin of his teeth, I might add. But as you probably know, an MP cannot be arrested for debt. Still, he was determined to marry this widow, mainly because he said he would, and also because she demonstrated a certain reluctance."

"Because of his poverty?"

"No. Because of his character. You see, he was a flighty young man, always engaged in unsuitable affairs with amoral women. She had no desire to become yet another of his conquests. And she had always fancied the thought of marrying someone with a title. This young man was honorable only in the sense that, as an MP, that distinction was automatically placed before his name."

Constance smiled, and the man patted her hand with one of his large, dry ones.

"There were so many obstacles that the young man simply forged ahead, writing to the widow and addressing each letter 'to my dear wife.' Finally she gave in, and they were married."

"Was it a good match?"

"Indeed it was. Many years later, someone asked the woman if it was true her husband had married her for her fortune. And she replied, 'Yes, he did. But he would marry me a second time for love.' And she was right, he would have."

Constance was silent for a while, pondering the old man's words. "What a wonderful story," she said at last. "And it's true?"

"Every word. And the interesting thing is that the young man was eventually given a title, and so the widow got everything she wished, and so did the young man."

"How wonderful. And how I envy them. They were able to find the happiness they were seeking."

"Yes. Yes, for the most part they did." There was a strain in his voice, and she looked over at her companion. His gaze was fixed on a distant mountain, although she suspected he could not really see much beyond the bench. "It will soon be two years since I lost her, my Mary Anne."

"You were the young man." She was not really surprised. It simply made more sense now. "I'm so sorry for your loss, sir."

"Yes. Thank you." He took a deep breath and turned towards her. "So, how can your troubles compare to ours? And we triumphed in the end. How can your story be more misguided and impossible than mine?"

"Well, in that light, I must say all is well. I must be just feeling a bit anxious."

"That is a very small problem indeed, madam. Should you doubt his feelings, well, that is one thing. Should you question the union in any way, that is quite another. But on those points you are secure. No, that is no trouble at all."

"It is odd, but until very recently, I was engaged to another man. The son of a duke, in fact."

"There are many sons of dukes floating about, my dear. Even princes. Look at Prince Chitter-chatter himself."

"Prince Chitter-chatter?"

"Forgive me, that was impolite. But I refer to the Prince of Wales." Suddenly the older man crossed his arms and examined her with his eyes squinting. "God forbid, that is not the object of your affection, is it? I will lose all faith in mankind if you tell me you followed Chitter-chatter to Scotland."

"No! No, not at all!" She began giggling at the thought, and the man joined her, laughing heartily. For the first time she noticed that his teeth were artificial, and not terribly well done. "No. It is just that he is not here, and I am lonely."

"So where is he, your love?"

"I don't know."

"He's bolted, has he?"

"I wouldn't say bolted. He has gone away for a while."

"If I may be bold, perhaps I can do something to assist you?"

"You, sir?"

"Yes. I am not without connections, my dear. And there is no greater goal worth fighting for than true love."

"You are entirely too generous . . ." she began.

A footman appeared as if, it seemed, from nowhere.

"I beg your pardon, but your presence is requested by the queen, my lord."

"Yes. Yes, very well. I will be along presently." He stood unsteadily, and Constance assisted him.

"Thank you, my dear. I believe this good young man may help me back to the house."

"Yes, my lord."

They fumbled with the walking stick, and the footman took his other arm.

"It was a delight to talk with you. I tire of politics, and do so enjoy conversing on love and youth, two things I once had in abundance and will forever long for anew," he said to Constance. "And pray forgive me for not introducing myself—I am Beaconsfield. I am to quit this very afternoon, but should you need me, I am on Downing Street in town."

"Beaconsfield," she repeated numbly. "Lord Beaconsfield." Of course. That is why he had looked so familiar. She had seen etchings of him in the London papers, but had never seen the real man. Beaconsfield.

"And your name, my dear?"

"Forgive me," she mumbled. "Lloyd. Constance Lloyd."

"Miss Lloyd, I thank you for the pleasure of your company. And may all go smoothly for you and your gentleman. Good morning, my dear."

The servant and the old man left together, and Constance sat heavily on the bench. Beaconsfield. It was unbelievable, astounding. Constance Lloyd, former governess, had just passed the larger part of an hour with Lord Beaconsfield, better known by his given name of Benjamin Disraeli . . . the Prime Minister of England.

By the time she returned to the castle, the servants' quarters were in an uproar. Instead of the smoothly running, if slightly hectic, machine she had left earlier in the day, it was a chaotic mess. A large bowl dropped to the stone floor in the kitchen as Constance entered, but that was barely noticed.

The moment she entered, one of the cooks shouted, "She's back! Tell Mr. Brown she just came back!"

"What's happening?" Constance asked.

"Everything has come apart, that's what happened! People are coming and going, the prince is in a fit over something or other. Everything has come apart." The cook gasped.

A gardener came in, clumps of mud on his boots, took one look at Constance, and fled.

"I'll fetch Brown," he said over his shoulder.

"Is anyone ill?" Constance turned towards a trio of housemaids, who ran from her when she addressed them.

"No one's ill," said the cook with an ominous nod.

"Will no one tell me what has happened?"

"Mr. Brown will tell you . . . he will—"

"Woman, where have ye been?" The unmistakable baritone of John Brown threatened to shatter the window glass.

"I was outside, taking a turn on the grounds. Good Lord, what in heaven's name has happened?"

He took her by her arm, raising her above the ground as he pulled her aside.

"That hurts, Mr. Brown."

"I do not mean to harm ye, Miss Lloyd," he said between clenched teeth. "I need to speak plain. Smith has been arrested."

"Arrested? On what grounds?" The world seemed to tilt.

"He was arrested on the grounds of high treason."

"Treason?" The words were strangled. It was impossible.

"Aye, treason. But lass, before . . . He requested I tell you something."

"Treason," she repeated numbly, unable to reconcile the plain word with the appalling reality of the meaning.

"For God's sake, woman, you must listen to me. I don't have time for this." He slammed his hand against the frame of the door and she jumped. "Before he was arrested, he asked me to tell you he is very sorry, but has reconsidered whatever he said in his note to you. He says his words were an error, and that you will understand his meaning, and he is sorry if he has harmed you in any way."

"What? I don't understand. I can't think."

"Blast it all, woman, he does not love ye!"

"No, no. That is not true." Rubbing her eyes, she tried to gather her thoughts. "He said that only to protect me. He doesn't want me to wait for him, but I will."

"Are ye daft? I just told you he spoke to me before he was arrested. *Before* he was arrested! Listen, woman!"

"No. I am sure you are mistaken."

"I do not have the time to play the nursemaid," he growled, and stalked out of the room.

16

As Constance watched John Brown's retreating back, a sense of outrage suddenly welled within her.

"Wait a moment," she shouted, stunned by the force of her own voice. Brown turned slowly, one of his thick eyebrows arched in disbelief.

"You can stop this." She stepped toward him. "You alone, Mr. Brown, know that Joseph has not been engaging in treasonous plots. Why did you not do something to prevent this? Why haven't you done anything at all?"

Brown glanced over his shoulder, and when he was assured that no one else was listening—they were all too swept up in the activity of the prince and prime minister's sudden and unexpected departure, requiring an extra meal to be prepared immediately—he spoke.

"The very worst thing I could do now, woman, would be to side with Smith. There would be no hope then. Do you not understand?"

"But you two were working together, to secure the queen and her family's safety. Surely there is proof of that."

Again he grabbed her arm, pulling her into a back pantry. His voice was fierce and rough. "You are the one who does not understand. They are using Smith to get to me."

"Who?"

Brown's humorless laughter snarled close to her ear. "Do you not know? Most would gladly attend my hanging, and if that is not possible, my downfall would satisfy. Did you not see that pamphlet?"

"I heard of it." She squirmed under his hold, and he loosened his grip, although he did not release her.

"Let me refresh your memory. It was a slanderous bit of defamation that indicated the queen and myself were married. They called it 'The Empress Brown.' Never mind the woman has her husband's clothes laid out every night and morn, as if he were alive yet. Never mind she sleeps with a life-sized photograph of his head and shoulders over her bed, a photograph taken after his death. There are those who resent my access to the Queen."

"I know. Joseph told me all. But still, you should be able to stop this."

"Is your head cracked, woman? She is the Queen of England. Those who wish to reach her, and you know very well who I mean, must do so through me. Is that not cause enough for resentment?"

"But she needs you," Constance said, her own face not six inches from his. "She must have someone to trust, and since her husband's death, she turns to you."

Brown shook his head. "Aye. That is how I see it, as does the Queen. I have no wish to become a king, for Christ's sake. But there are those in her own family who see me as a threat to their own power. And those not in her family who see me as a dangerous foreigner."

"Then so am I," she whispered.

"Aye. You are at that. And so is Smith. But you have an advantage in being a woman, and a good-looking one at that, and being an American. Smith and myself are seen as loathsome Celts. He has more of a chance alone than with any help from me. That I know."

Finally he let go of her arm.

"How was he arrested?" Her voice was weary. "Why?"

"Because he was found on the grounds of the queen's residence. They had meant for me to be found, for me to be seen tampering with the water. Instead, they found Smith."

A sudden hope took hold. "What about the queen herself? She can speak out for Smith!"

"No. She does not know what he has been doing. I kept our plan from her, not wishing to make her uneasy. She knows nothing of this, nor will I tell her, not while she is unwell."

"What can we do, Mr. Brown?"

"I don't know. The best thing I believe we can do is stay away from him, as far away as possible. I would have gone after the man myself if I thought it would help him, if I thought that would not only hasten his destruction."

"Then tell the world," she urged. "Tell everyone what has been happening."

"Aye. And think of what would happen, think. To proclaim it would again add to his end. To come out against the prince would not only be suicide, it would indeed be treason."

She crossed her arms protectively, as if fending off any more blows. "What can we do?"

"The best thing you can do is to go away. The best thing I can do is act as if there is nothing amiss, nothing at all."

"There must be more we can do. I refuse to accept this."

"There is naught to be done for Smith now. He alone can get himself out of this. Any help from us will be a hindrance."

"I can't possibly do that," she whispered. "I love Joseph."

"You must forget about him." Brown's voice softened with a gentleness she had not thought possible from him. "He does not love you, lass. This is hard, I know, but it is true. Go back to America. He does not love you."

"No. You're wrong. You don't know him as I do."

"I know him better, lass, for we are of a kind, Smith and myself. We are loners. We prefer solitude to society. We travel through life without family, with few friends. The sooner you forget about him, the better off you will be—as will Smith. Your future is elsewhere. Forget about all of this, for both of your sakes."

"I can't."

"You must, lass. We all have our share of heartache. We all do. Some more than others. The best thing you could do, not only for yourself but for Smith, is to leave. You're only drawing attention to him by remaining. And deep down, you know I speak the truth."

A horrendous sense of clarity washed over her. He was right. "Good God." She clamped her hand over her mouth and looked up at Brown. "What have I done?"

"Now we'll have none of that." He patted her arm, but she did not notice. "I'll have someone take you to the station. There should be an afternoon train to the south."

"What have I done?" she repeated.

Brown watched her slowly walk towards her quarters upstairs, her turquoise eyes filled with tears, and heard her breath catch as she attempted to withhold a sob.

"The question is, lass," he mumbled to himself. "What have *I* just done?"

Philip met her at the Ballsbridge station.

The shock of seeing him would have been far more potent had she not just spent the journey crying into her handkerchief, rendering her numb with exhaustion. Everything Brown said was ringing in her ears, over and over like hollow drumbeats, assailing her with the truth.

The great statesman Disraeli had been wrong about this. He had assured her that all would go well as long as both parties were alive.

And in a matter of minutes, she had discovered that she would have no future with Joseph.

In a way, Disraeli was fortunate. Although he was grieving the loss of his wife, at least he had decades of joy upon which to reflect. And he could share his grief at the loss openly, and everyone would understand his sorrow.

Constance had precious but scant moments to treasure, a touch here, a press of his hand there, a look, a kiss. No matter how potent her loss, she would be forced to bear it in complete silence. No one would know what might have been, had life been fair.

"Constance." Philip's tone was gentle. His attire was as splendid as ever, every bit as elegant, with his dark blue frockcoat and black lapels. But his expression was vastly different. He seemed . . . happy. Relieved. Relaxed.

"How did you know I would be here?"

"I received a wire from John Brown at Balmoral. You look about done in, I'm afraid."

"Philip . . ." She didn't know where to begin. "You read the letter I left for you."

"Yes, I did. I must say you caused quite an uproar at the noble House of Hastings."

"I am so sorry. Please, I did not mean . . ."

"No. You misunderstand." Philip ran his hand through his hair, then looked down at her. "I was furious when I first read your note. I stormed about, kicked table legs, cursed the skies, made a string of meaningless vows about getting even with you, about justice. That sort of thing."

"Philip." She shook her head slightly.

"But then I went for a long walk, and this ancient barouche pulled alongside of me. It was Viola. She played the part of the good neighbor, and, well. She is not the person you think she is, Constance."

"She isn't?"

"No. She is compassionate, warm. She let me talk and ramble, and I told her things I've never told a soul. I told her things I didn't even realize until I said them aloud in that barouche. In short, by the end of the ride I realized that I was in love with her—always have been, I suppose. You were right, Constance. I do not know how I will ever thank you, ever repay you in a million years. You were right."

"I am so happy for you, Philip. Really, I am."

"Well, everyone seems rather pleased except for Dishy. He's thundering about now, but less than usual, and certainly less than at the end of their last engagement."

"How wonderful." She smiled weakly.

"Yes, well. Now what about you? What can I do to help you? Anything. I will do anything."

"I don't know. I suppose I should find another position."

"As a governess?"

"It's what I know. I think perhaps I should go home."

"To the Isle of Wight?"

"No. I should really go home, to America. But I'll forever be grateful for the offer of marriage. You and your family have shown me nothing but kindness, and have gone to a great deal of expense for me. I promise I will repay you the cost of the clothing."

"Constance, please. Come back to Hastings House for as long as you wish. You need not decide your future now, at this moment. Rest a bit, then you will see everything clearly. "

"That's just it, Philip. I do see everything clearly, and I must leave. Is that the train to London?" She pointed across the tracks.

"I believe so. Why do you ask?"

"I have a few things to settle there, then perhaps I will go to Cowes to rest for a while. Mrs. Whitestone may be kind enough to put me up for a few days. And then I'll go home."

"You can't just leave. You have people who care about you here. Reconsider, Constance. What do you have across the ocean? No family, no position. Don't be hasty."

"There is great opportunity there, I hear. Maybe I'll go up north, New York or Boston. The nation is rebuilding. The very worst will be that I become a governess there, now that people are able to afford them again. I've been gone a long, long time. I believe it might be time for me to go home at last."

"Constance," Philip began. Then he stopped and gently pulled her aside. "Why should you begin your struggle once more?"

"No," she smiled. "I need to go home."

Finally, Philip handed her the portmanteau. "You may change your mind, you know. And if you do, you may come back."

"Thank you."

"You should not travel alone. Please allow me to accompany you."

"No, thank you. It doesn't matter, not really. I'm a hardened spinster, Philip. No one will take notice of me."

"Where will you stay? In London, I mean. You said you would go there first."

"I . . . to tell you the truth, I had not thought that far ahead."

"I have a townhouse in Knightsbridge, just off Hyde Park. Do you have a piece of paper?"

In her reticule she had a pencil and paper, and Philip scribbled the address. "I will wire the house-keeper, so she will expect you."

"Thank you. You are kind, Philip."

"No. And forgive me, but do you have any money?"

"I have some, yes. Enough to get me to London and then to Wight."

"Here." He reached into his jacket. "I have some notes. Take them."

"No. Please, as it is, I will not be able to reconcile what I owe you. . . ."

"Owe? You owe me nothing. I am the one who owes you everything. Here. I insist."

Reluctantly, she allowed him to slip the notes into her reticule.

"Thank you."

"You are welcome. Here, let me take you to the car."

In silence he walked with her back to the train, and helped her into the cab. He handed the leather case up to her, and the door clicked shut behind her. As the train pulled from the station, she wondered if she had just made a mistake.

And then she smiled. No. This was the right thing, if not for her, then most certainly for everyone else.

Constance had not been to London for several years, since the last journey she had made with the Whitestones to purchase clothing for their eldest daughter's coming out. If possible, in those short years it seemed that London had become dirtier, the streets more mired with horse manure and human waste, and after a few moments in the outdoors, Constance's garments had acquired a patina of soot.

It wasn't until she was well on her way to London that she counted the money Philip had given her, and gasped. It was over two hundred pounds, more than she had made in four years as a governess. Added to the money from Viola, even with the amount she had spent on train fare, she had over two hundred and thirty pounds.

It was more money than she had seen in her entire life.

From King's Cross station, she hired a carriage to take her to Knightsbridge, where the housekeeper greeted her cheerfully. She explained that she was already preparing the place for his return to London, since he would soon be there for the opening of Parliament.

After a restless night's sleep and a wonderful breakfast she could barely eat, Constance set off in another hired hack.

There was but one place she had to go in London. Joseph's studio, the place where he did all of his experiments. There would be proof there, she knew, that he had been taking samples to test, not planting poison at the royal homes.

Philip had said it was off Waterloo Road, and she was determined to find it as quickly as possible.

Both foot and carriage traffic were slowed because of confusion in directions, coaches stuck in the mud of the streets, their drivers shouting to each over the twitching ears of the horses. The costermongers crossed at will with their carts, not caring about interrupting traffic, only concerned with peddling everything from wilted produce to painted dolls and musical instruments and live kittens. Their voices rang loud over the constant din, all crying out their wares in competition with the other peddlers and the street sounds.

A gypsy band played on a street corner, and a crowd gathered to hear their fiddles and guitars and tambourines, and watch the rainbow swirl of a dancer's skirt. Men maintained expressions of dignified boredom, while women with their hatboxes or paper packages talked excitedly, their bonnets touching like duck bills, or plumed hats sweeping against each other.

Newspaper boys stood on their hard-won corners, shouting out the headlines of the latest editions. She had the driver buy three papers, but none of them had any mention of Joseph and his arrest.

"How odd," Constance said, wiping the still-tacky ink from her fingers. His every movement has been suspicious and newsworthy just a few days before, and now that he had been arrested, there was not a single comment. Perhaps the news had not yet reached London, she reasoned. Perhaps Brown, with his casual airs, had lead the reporters astray.

The carriage crossed the Thames to the east side over Waterloo Bridge. The stench of the river was almost overwhelming, as thick and unpalatable as the sludge in the water itself. The river was filled with debris, bits and pieces of lives that were no longer of use, with crockery and furniture and cart wheels. A three-legged chair floated by, and at the river's edge was a young boy with ripped trouser knees attempting to lure the chair to him with a stick.

Constance asked the driver to turn down Waterloo Road, and he looked at her with mild alarm; clearly he was not pleased with what he saw nor with the direction she had requested. This was not the fashionable side of London. The pedestrians no longer carried packages or seemed to be walking with any great determination in any direction at all.

All of the buildings on the lane looked similar in their lack of ornamentation and detail. Constance asked the driver to please wait, and she descended to the street. The driver seemed to be poised to assist her, but after one look at his surroundings, he remained perched on his bench.

Feeling conspicuous, she approached several of the buildings without success. Finally, just as she was about to give up hope, she came to a small building. Her knock was answered by a young man.

"Pardon me," she inquired. "I am looking for the laboratory of Mr. Joseph Smith. Do you know where it may be?"

"This was it, miss," the young man said.

"This is it?" She had found the place! "May I please come in? I am a friend of Mr. Smith's, and—"

"I said, this *was* it, miss. It is no longer."

"I don't understand."

"Mr. Smith is no longer using this location. He took everything with him. He's gone now."

"May I please see where the lab was?" Perhaps there would be some sort of clue, something that would help clear his name.

"I'm afraid not, miss. Someone else has let the location. I wish you a good day."

The young man closed the door, and she heard the distinctive sound of a bolt sliding into place.

She had to think. She had to find something else to do. Although she would never see him again, she had to somehow help Joseph before she left England forever. That was the very least she could do.

"Did I do well, sir?" the young man asked.

The older gentleman nodded. "Very well, lad." For the boy's troubles he was given a gold sovereign, more money than he had ever seen at one time.

"Thank you! Thank you, sir!"

The young man left, allowing the gentleman to stay in the laboratory, examining vials and samples and notes that the previous occupant, Joseph Smith, had left behind.

No matter what the turn of events, it seemed highly unlikely that Mr. Smith would ever be returning to his East End laboratory.

Very unlikely indeed.

The gentleman smiled before removing his hat and coat.

Very unlikely indeed.

17

There was only one place left to turn.

Constance dressed with extra care the next morning, aware that her plan was audacious and perhaps not entirely sane. Again there was no mention of Joseph Smith in the morning paper, although by now she was well aware that meant little. It simply proved that the London reporters were not nearly as clever or well-connected as they fancied themselves to be.

Before leaving the house in Knightsbridge she sent a note to Harriet Whitestone in Cowes, requesting that she please be allowed to come for a brief visit. After that task was completed, there was nothing to delay her mission.

She comforted herself with the simple fact that whatever transpired, she would soon be leaving England forever, and therefore need never see these people again. No matter what she did, an ocean would soon be between Constance and the rest of the country.

Her destination was but a short walk from the

townhouse, another address on the West End. Everything was vastly different on this side of the Thames—the smells, the sights, the people. Everything was respectable and decent and good, or at least had the cunning to appear so.

She approached the somber house on Downing Street warily, every ounce of her strength devoted to propelling her forward. It was no easy task. The numeral "ten" was indicated in polished brass, large but subdued at the same time, as if to say, if you needed to ask whose residence it was, you need not bother to knock.

Well-dressed men milled about the address, some with expressions of bright optimism, others with tired and worn faces, men who had once held great hope but were now accustomed to defeat and frustration. They stood in tight clusters, elbow to elbow, encouraging each other as they intimidated everyone else.

The men stepped aside as she passed through them, all silent, a few winking and nudging their companions. She hit the brass knocker with more authority than she felt.

The door opened. "Yes, ma'am?" A footman in a powdered wig answered. He did not seem to be quite awake, much less capable of communicating a message.

"Yes." She straightened. "I wish to see Lord Beaconsfield."

"I am afraid he is indisposed at present." The man possessed the remarkable ability to speak without altering any feature except for his lower lip, and that seemed to move with great reluctance.

The door began to close, and she placed her foot over the threshold. "Forgive me. I was just a guest at Balmoral with Lord Beaconsfield, and I did wish to inquire after his health."

The man's eyelids opened just slightly wider. "If you wish to leave a card, you may do so."

"I have no card. At least, not with me. I must have left them back, um, at the palace."

She smiled with what she hoped passed for confidence.

The door began to close again.

"Please, do tell Lord Beaconsfield that I wish to speak to him about the same matter."

"The same matter?"

"Yes. We spoke at great length in Scotland about a specific matter." Glancing behind her, as the others stepped closer to catch her words, she whispered, "I would prefer not to mention the topic. It will do neither myself nor Lord Beaconsfield any credit."

The drowsy eyes opened just a bit more. "Indeed. And your name, ma'am?"

Would he know her name, she wondered? The unmitigated gall to assume the Prime Minister of England would take time out of his day to discuss a personal matter was more than impertinent. It was very nearly unforgivable.

But then again, unforgivable would best describe almost every action she had performed within the last two weeks.

Soon she would leave the country, she reassured herself.

"My name is Miss Constance Lloyd."

The door closed, and this time she did not prevent it. All she could do now was wait and hope, just like the dozens of other people who were on Downing Street with urgent business. Perhaps their business would be considered life or death.

Well, so was hers.

After a few minutes the other men seemed to grow accustomed to her presence and speak freely amongst themselves. She heard bits of conversation on grazing violations in the west and of high local taxation in the south. One man was complaining bitterly about the high taxes on French wine.

The door opened, and all gathered fell silent, waiting to hear who had been selected for an audience.

"Miss Lloyd?"

Constance stepped forward, passing men who offered her looks filled with both curiosity and resentment. She alone was allowed entrance to Number Ten.

"Please make yourself comfortable," the footman said with doleful solemnity. She sat on a red cushioned couch in the hallway, and again she waited.

Other gentlemen emerged from a room upstairs, adjusting their cravats and dusting their hats as they descended the staircase. They spoke in hushed tones, unable to express their true opinions of what had just transpired until they were back at their clubs or perhaps a local public house.

She shifted her gloves from one hand to the next, counting the spokes on the banister, thirty-four from what she could see, and the stripes on the hallway wallpaper, one hundred and twelve. At last she was summoned.

"This way, Miss Lloyd," the footman said with a bow.

She followed him up the staircase and to the left, where a door stood slightly ajar. He spoke without entering the room.

"Miss Lloyd, my lord."

"Miss Lloyd? Do come in," came the parched voice she recognized from Balmoral. "Forgive me for not escorting you myself. The gout."

She entered his office, and he rose slightly from behind his chair. His desk was covered with papers, and there was a general air of orderly chaos.

"I am pleased to see you looking so well, Miss

Lloyd," he said as he eased himself back into his chair.

"Thank you, and you are looking well also," she said, although it was far from the truth. His skin had a greenish cast to it that did not seem at all healthy, and there were dark circles under his eyes. As with the natural light in Scotland, his complexion seemed to be worsened by contrast with his overly black hair. The color would have been remarkable on anyone, but on a man of his age and coloring, it was all the more apparent that his hair had been both dyed and curled. A single lock fell rakishly, and incongruously, over his forehead.

"Now, relieve me from affairs of state, my dear, and regale me with affairs of the heart." He pushed aside his papers and smiled.

"Well, my lord," she began. "If you recall, when last we met we were discussing a certain matter, and you concluded that as long as both parties were alive, the case was not hopeless."

"Yes. Yes, I do recall saying those words, and still heartily believe them." As he spoke, he placed a hand over his mouth and turned away for a moment. It was then she realized his false teeth had slipped.

Gathering her composure as he slid his teeth back into place, she spoke as soon as he was finished. "My lord, the problem is that one of the parties may not be alive much longer."

"Good God, are you ill?"

"No. I am not the one in danger."

"Then it is your young man. I am grieved to hear it. What is the nature of his illness?"

"The nature of his illness? Well, my lord, you see, he is suffering from being wrongly accused of treason."

The expression on the Prime Minister's face would have been comical if the situation was not so dire. She gave him a brief summary of all that had transpired, including Joseph's name and the involvement of John Brown. And she mentioned the prince and his valet.

Disraeli listened, and after she had finished speaking, he folded his hands slowly on top of the desk.

"My dear, I appreciate the courage it took for you to come here and plead Smith's case. But to be frank, I have heard nothing of this. I was at Balmoral when this supposed event transpired, yet was not apprised of any such situation."

Constance was completely stunned. But from his manner, and the surprise on his face as she revealed the more startling details, he was being utterly truthful.

"Where is he then?" she asked, shaking her head. "And why would Brown tell me a falsehood?"

"My dear, you may not be aware of the nature of most Highlanders. Rumor and gossip are chief enjoyments for them, regardless if the stories are true or false. Brown may have fallen victim to such a tale, and related it to you before he found that it was just that—a tale."

"But what about Joseph?" An awful notion began to enter her mind. It was so terrible, she could barely breathe.

"Is it possible that your affections for him are greater than his are for you?" He spoke barely above a whisper, but his words seemed to blare in her ears.

"I hadn't thought of that until just now." She clenched her hands. After the night at Balmoral? Was it possible?

She closed her eyes, remembering how she had behaved. No better than a brazen hussy. Worse. How he must despise her.

And then another thought crossed her mind. He must have put Brown up to the story. It was a desperate attempt to get rid of her, to lose her once and for all, for she was so determined he knew he had to make the tale brilliant.

How he must loathe and pity her.

She had been a fool, and worse. Constance Lloyd, who had always tried to behave well, had gone to Britain to show the English that an American could demonstrate every bit as much decorum and taste. And look what she had done.

How ashamed her parents would be if they knew, but thank God they were beyond such cares. For the first time since their deaths, she was grateful they were not here to see what a folly their daughter had made of her life.

"Miss Lloyd? Are you well?"

"Yes. Yes, I am well, thank you." She stood unsteadily. "I must not keep you any longer, my lord. Thank you for your kindness. Thank you."

Constance left the office, her gaze straight ahead, her entire being steeped in humiliation and disgrace. She did not see anyone—the footman, the Prime Minister himself as he walked her partially down the hall.

She did not see the older man on the staircase as she passed him. He looked behind as she continued her descent, pausing for a moment before he continued.

"So, you are the new prime minister?" the gentleman said with a broad smile. "Pity. I wonder how the deuce we will ever survive."

"Ballsbridge! By God, it's good to see you in town again! How are your tunnels?"

"Very well, sir. I added a new ballroom below the apple grove."

"Splendid! Come in, come in. When I heard you wished to see me, I cleared the afternoon for a late luncheon. I beg you, wait a moment. These new teeth are giving me a devil of a time."

"A shame. And I thank you, sir. The matter I've

come to see you about concerns that young lady who just left, and a certain young man."

"Come in," he repeated. "By God, Ballsbridge, it's good to see you in town again!"

Cowes, Isle of Wight
November 1874

"Are you sure you wish to go through with this, Constance?" Harriet Whitestone asked once more, pouring another cup of tea in the parlor. "This seems such a drastic measure."

Constance smiled at her friend. "Not really, Harriet." It still felt strange to call her former employer by her first name. "I am just going home, that is all."

"But you are not going home at all. You are going to New York City, a place as strange to you as India would be."

"And if I had managed to secure a position as a governess in India, I am sure I would be going there as well. Really, Harriet, this is all for the best."

"I'm beginning to wonder if I did the right thing by writing you those glowing references."

Constance laughed. "Of course you did! I can't thank you enough. The Colonel and his wife sound wonderful, even if they are Yankees."

"Well, at least they are wealthy Yankees." Harriet stepped forward and touched her friend's shoulder. "Why will you not even try to contact Mr. Smith? This is so unlike you, Constance. You have always been so bold with what you want."

"Too bold, I'm afraid," she murmured to herself.

"Pardon me?"

"Nothing, Harriet. No, I cannot write to Mr. Smith. It is over, it did not end well for me, but hopefully it will end well for him."

"There was a mention of him in the paper yesterday."

"Was there?" She tried to keep her voice neutral. "And what did it say?"

"Not much, really. It seems he has been asked to head some governmental committee to address the problems of urban poverty."

"Really? How wonderful. He will enjoy that a great deal, I'm sure."

It hurt to think of him. It filled her with extraordinary pain to hear his name, but at least he was well. The prime minister had been right, the rumor of his treason charge had been groundless. She had made a complete fool of herself by pleading for the life of a man who was not in danger, only attempting to escape the unwanted advances of a governess.

All in all, the past few months had been an utter catastrophe.

"Oh, and there was something else of interest. A Lord Merrymeade passed away in his sleep. Did you not know that gentleman?"

"Yes, yes, I did." She thought of Abigail, and wondered if she would again pursue Joseph. That would make sense. At last they could both be happy.

"Constance, what is wrong? Are you not feeling well?"

"No. I'm fine, Harriet. Are there any more scones?"

The two men sat in the walnut-paneled splendor of the club, each sipping a brandy and soda from fine crystal tumblers.

"So, it's done, then," said Joseph, rubbing his temple. He had been plagued with headaches of late, fierce and unrelenting headaches that nothing seemed to ease.

"Yes. It is done, my friend." Philip smiled and placed his glass on the table by his arm.

"How does Cavendish feel about it?"

"Well, as you could well imagine, he is quite put out. This has happened to him before with Viola, you know. So, I suppose he is quite used to it, but still, it is something of a sting. Thank goodness Mother had not placed an announcement in the paper yet, so he doesn't have that humiliation to contend with."

"Thank goodness, indeed," he replied. "Has your mother made any more attempts to place notices of your father's death in the gazettes? I have missed seeing his name. It's always pleasing to see someone you know mentioned in the paper."

Philip laughed. "No. She seems to have abandoned that trick for the time being, although I'm sure after the wedding, she will return to it with new vigor. Mother always needs something of note with which to pass the time. Or perhaps she will busy herself with finding Dishy a fiancée, now that his usual one will be otherwise occupied."

Joseph smiled.

"Smith, do you mind my saying something?"

"Of course not. What is it?"

"You are not looking well."

"I've been working too hard," he replied. "After the committee is set up, I'll have more time to relax. That's all it is."

"The hell it is. It's Constance, isn't it?"

Joseph shook his head, then closed his eyes. The movement was painful, jarring his headache into a new pounding.

"I know where she is, you know. She is intent on paying us back for the clothing and her transportation once she begins her new position," Philip said quietly. "Why don't you drop her a note?"

"No."

"Are you under the impression that I am angry at

you over this whole mess? I am not, you know. Not in the least. Had it not been for Constance, I would have never known that Viola Rathbottom has always been in love with me. That is why she did all those ridiculous things. You know the things I mean."

"The ink over the doors? The tobogganing down staircases on silver platters? The soda siphon battles? By the way, I saw Viola and Abigail Merrymeade in the park the other day. They both seemed to have hurt their legs. I do hope it was nothing serious."

"Hurt their legs? Oh," Philip chuckled. "Because they were limping, is that what you mean?"

"Yes, Philip. They were both very nearly lame, from what I could tell."

"No, it's the newest thing. It's called 'The Alexandra Limp,' after the Princess of Wales. It is all the rage amongst the ladies to emulate the walk. It's quite captivating, really."

"Are you mad? Are we to imitate every infirmity the royals possess? What's next—stylish whooping cough or fashionable dandruff?"

"Not a bad idea, Smith. But back to Constance, why—"

"Please stop. My head is pounding, Hastings."

"I do not love her. I do not believe I ever did, although I will always be grateful to her for all she has done. Funny, before I met Constance, I assumed I had all the answers. It took her to point me to the questions I had never even thought to ask."

"Enough, Philip. I am going now."

He rose to his feet, and Philip stood as well.

"You know, Joseph, I feel damned lucky to have had a friend like you."

Joseph smiled weakly. "I feel the same."

"So will you do me a favor?"

"I was so close to a clean escape." Joseph withdrew

his hand. "What does this one involve? Capturing a rabid lion? Tasting a new flavor of arsenic? Just tell me."

"I want you to go after Constance."

"I have done that once, Philip. I will not do that a second time. Good day, my friend."

He began to walk away, shoving a hand in his trouser pocket. Hastings would never give up. Once he got a notion in his head, it was hell to get loose.

"She saved your life, you know." Philip's voice carried down the club's carpeted hall.

Joseph turned. "I am aware of that. With the bandits. That is old news. Again, I bid you good day, sir."

"No. She went to Disraeli after you were arrested."

Joseph stopped and returned to Philip. "What did you say?"

"She went to London to plead for your life."

"I thought your father did that. I have thanked him, many times. Your father went to Disraeli."

"My father alone could not have done it, my friend. He did not have the whole story. It was by combining what Father said with what Constance had just related that Disraeli realized the whole episode was simply a squabble between the Prince and Brown run amok, and you were caught in the middle. Go on with you, Smith. You have more important things to do than listen to old news."

Philip sat again hard in his chair, and Joseph returned to his. They ordered two more brandy and sodas, and did not leave the club for many, many hours.

18

NEW YORK CITY
APRIL 1875

The McKenzie children were, as usual, in high spirits. Their joy was infectious as they ran towards Fifth Avenue, Lydia with the buttons of her gloves open, Gunther with the laces of his boots yet untied.

On most days Constance was far more efficient, always one step ahead of the children and their incorrigible ways. In truth, she thoroughly enjoyed the McKenzie children, even their occasionally dreadful manners and Gunther's lisp. The brownstone house in the East Thirties was always a bevy of cheerful activity, with Mrs. McKenzie dashing from one fund-raiser or meeting to another, and the Colonel continuously bringing home his Wall Street friends.

All who met Constance were immediately impressed with her accent, which they took to be elevated and dignified.

"She is from England, you know," she heard Mrs. McKenzie comment to a friend as they left the house for a meeting of the Unfortunate Children of the

Cruel Streets Society. "She was to marry a duke there, I understand."

"Well," her friend had replied, "better a governess in America than a duchess in England. That's what I always say."

"Indeed," Mrs. McKenzie had agreed. "You are so right, Mrs. Appleton."

Constance felt it best not to correct any of their slight misapprehensions. Just as in England, where it had been to her advantage as a governess to play the role of the half-savage American, now it did well for her to be an almost duchess.

Of course, they did not know the truth.

That very morning the final blow had arrived. Viola, the new Lady Philip Hastings, had written her yet another gossipy letter.

"Slow down, Lydia," Constance instructed as the girl skipped beyond her reach to the corner.

"Better slow down, or Miss Lloyd will put you in the Tower of London and you will die a terrible death just like the little princes. Isn't that so?" Gunther looked up at Constance.

"I myself was not responsible for that particular punishment, Gunther." His hand tightened in hers. "That was my great-great-grandmother."

His eyes widened in admiration.

They crossed Fifth Avenue to the light green oasis of the park, navigating the cobbled street, threading past the carriages and omnibuses and carts and hansom cabs, all spilling their passengers and contents onto the road. The mansions on the east side of the street seemed to shimmer in the springtime sun, all marble gaudiness and stone pretension, pressed into tiny plots of land, each house vying for attention.

"Lydia, the horse! Mind the horse!" Constance shouted as the eldest child, at nine, ran into the street.

"The Tower for sure, Miss Lloyd," muttered six-year-old Gunther.

"At the very least." She smiled. The little boy returned the smile.

The zoo in the park was filled with children, faces bright and eager on one of the first fine days of the spring. The scent of roasting corn and salted peanuts, of sticky-sweet caramels and candied apples mingled with the animal scents of the zebras and the old lion, who seemed most content just to lie on his back and snore.

When they reached the monkey cage, and both Lydia and Gunther dissolved into giggles at their antics, she could at last sit down and ponder the letter she had received in the morning post from Viola. Pulling it from her drawstring bag, she read again the essentials of the note.

. . . The most amazing thing, dear Constance! My own dear Abigail has arrived, and, as you know, she is but recently made a widow. Yet all is not sorrow and gloom here at Hastings House, and she is about to make a match with someone YOU know VERY WELL INDEED! Can you believe this? She is to become my best of friends in marriage as well as in life. I only wish you could be here to share our joy. . . .

That was enough. She was happy for Viola, of course, but to read about Joseph and Abigail was more than she could bear, even on such a beautiful day.

Gunther turned to her with a rather alarmingly accurate imitation of a scratching monkey, his lower lip jutting out as his left arm collapsed over his head to pull his right ear.

"Keep that up, Gunther dear, and you're sure to be a hit on the debutante circuit," she said.

Lydia grinned over her shoulder at Constance, and returned her attention to the animals.

Really, she was quite happy.

She was back in America, although it was an America that felt strange and foreign, the pace so fast she feared she would not survive a shopping trip to the Ladies' Mile, or even crossing Broadway. The people spoke quickly, the men behaved with manners, but they seemed rushed and not sincere. The women were all busy, no matter what their station in life.

No one seemed to sit still for a moment.

Constance found herself adapting the same behavior, not because she had so very much to do—for the McKenzies were more than generous with her free time. Instead, she found as many activities as possible, simply because, by keeping in constant motion, she was unable to dwell too much on Joseph.

During the day the plan worked well enough, and she only thought of him during restful moments, such as at the park or when she took the children to a matinee. Her mind would wander, and she would remember something he said, or an expression that once passed over his features, or recall his smile. Or his touch.

But no matter how exhausted she was, how brutally she had driven herself to help Mrs. McKenzie with some sort of do-good society in the evening hours, she would still fall into her brass bed, close her eyes, and see Joseph. His face would appear with such clarity that she could almost imagine touching it, or running a finger along the scar on his cheek. But the very idea of touching his face brought the whole situation into focus.

Never again would she touch, or even see, his face.

And now he would finally marry Abigail Merry-meade.

"Miss Lloyd! Miss Lloyd! Can I have a licorice whip?" Gunther called.

"Me, too, Miss Lloyd! Please! Me, too!" Lydia chimed in.

A tightness clutched at her throat as she saw the two children, their eyes bright with hope and joy. For she knew she would never have children of her own. Her life would be a succession of other women's children, sharing the happiness of other families until it was finally time for her to find another family with younger children to care for, to love as her own.

But never her own.

"Is anything wrong, Miss Lloyd?" Lydia stepped towards Constance, genuine concern on her open features. "Is there sad news in your letter?"

"No. Not at all." Constance folded the paper and slipped it back into her bag. "Licorice, did you say?"

They both nodded.

"Only on one condition."

Again, they both nodded.

"You must promise to be very, very well-behaved until you each reach the age of eighteen."

"We will! We promise!" they both shouted.

Constance laughed, taking each of their hands in hers. "Very well then. Let's go off in search of licorice."

And they walked away. The children did not seem to realize that the brightness of Constance's blue eyes was not caused by the anticipation of licorice.

The brightness was caused by unshed tears.

Constance carefully addressed the envelope to Hastings House. It contained her twice-monthly payment of two dollars, her effort to pay off her debt.

She calculated that, at the rate at which she was going, her debt would be fully paid by the year nineteen sixty four.

"I believe I will celebrate on that day," she said to herself as she blotted the ink.

There was a soft knock on the door. "Come in," she smiled, anticipating one of the children. She had put them to bed early that evening, exhausted as they were by a full day at the park.

"Constance?" It was Mrs. McKenzie, splendidly dressed in a sleeveless gown with peacock feather designs, shimmering in the light. In her hair she wore a single blue feather.

"Mrs. McKenzie, you look just lovely!"

"Oh, dear me, thank you. I did not come up here to fetch a compliment, but you must remind me to do so more often."

Constance stood up from her desk. "May I help you with anything, Mrs. McKenzie?"

"Yes, I'm afraid so. Now I know you've had a long day with the children, but the Colonel has brought home an unexpected guest for our dinner party, a gentleman, you see. And as nice as he seems to be, it throws off the setting of the table. And after I worked so hard to make it boy, girl, boy, girl. Would you mind slipping into something and joining us downstairs? If you have nothing suitable, I can lend you a gown."

"So I'm to eat at the grown-up table?"

"Just this once," Mrs. McKenzie laughed. "But I will insist that you help me cut the Colonel's roast for him. Will you, Constance? Will you please join us?"

"I am flattered, Mrs. McKenzie. Of course I would love to join you."

"Splendid! And do you need a gown?"

"No, thank you. I do have one that would be suitable."

"You are an absolute gem! Just come on into the

parlor whenever you are ready. Oh, and shall I send Kathleen up to do your hair?"

"Thank you, no. I'll be fine. And, Mrs. McKenzie?"

Her employer paused at the door.

"Thank you," Constance said simply.

The other woman smiled. "No, my dear. It is you who should be thanked. Come down when you are ready."

Constance descended the staircase slowly, listening to the sounds of the guests laughing in the parlor, the gentle clinking of glasses, Kathleen the maid offering delicacies from a silver tray.

It was vaguely reminiscent of the other life she had had, the one that had lasted a few short months. The house was not as grand, nor was the staircase, but the dress was one she had last worn at Sandringham with Joseph.

She had been unable to part with her gowns, not for reasons of greed or practicality, for she did not ever expect to find an occasion to wear one. Instead, she had kept them as reminders of that short spell, the interlude.

The gowns reminded her of Joseph.

She stopped in the hallway, examining herself in the large mirror beside the parlor doorway. She did not look any different than she did at Sandringham or Hastings House. Her features were the same, her hair still dark and too thick to be managed easily. Perhaps she was a little more slender, but that was it.

And her eyes. Her eyes were different.

How she envied Abigail Merrymeade.

Her gown, the silver silk she had worn at Sandringham, the one Joseph seemed to like, felt strange after her months of practical governess's attire. In her hair she had braided a faux pearl necklace. It was quite a good imitation, from one of the new stores on the Ladies' Mile.

Taking a deep breath, she stepped into the parlor. The place seemed to be filled with people, although in reality there were only twelve, including herself.

"Miss Lloyd!" The Colonel was at her side, his salt and pepper mustache waxed to perfection. "How delightful! Please let me introduce you to our guests. . . ."

Constance shook gloved hands with her own gloved hands, trying to fix each name with the proper face, although after the third couple she all but gave up. They all had similar appearances, well-fed and satisfied. The glow of the gaslights gave them all a bluish hue, making the red gowns seem purple and the white ties gray.

"And this is Mr. and Mrs. Jebediah Baxter of Albany, New York. Oh, and finally, our friend from across the pond, Mr. Joseph Smith . . ."

Constance swayed as she looked up into his eyes, for a moment wondering if this was yet another of her endless dreams. But he caught her in his arms.

"Dear me, Miss Lloyd seems quite unwell. . . ."

"Does anyone have smelling salts?"

"She *is* the governess. Perhaps this is all too much for the poor thing."

She heard the chatter and din, but it seemed far removed, a different world entirely.

"Joseph," she breathed when at last she was able.

"Constance." His eyes were steady.

"Colonel McKenzie, they seem to be acquainted already!"

"She *is* English, you know."

Her hands gripped his forearms, the solid strength there, the strength she thought she would never again feel.

"Here," he murmured. "Come over here and sit."

His voice, the familiar lilt she thought she would never again hear.

Joseph.

"How . . . why . . . oh, Joseph," she stammered.

And then he smiled, the smile she had seen so often in her mind's eye, only more glorious than she could ever have imagined because now he was real.

"I will answer each of your questions, so economically phrased. First, how. Well, Constance, by ship, as I assume you would imagine. I am doing some work for the government, investigating how you Americans are dealing with the issues of poverty, if at all. And I had some investments to look after on Wall Street. Your second question, why. Well, that is simple. Because of you."

"How . . ." she began again, then closed her eyes.

"I thought I answered that. Oh, I see. How did I know where you would be?"

She nodded.

"Simple. You have been kind enough to send Philip some money each month. We have calculated that, at your present rate, you will have paid off your debt by—"

"Nineteen-sixty-four."

"Precisely. So your return address has been on the envelopes, a very American custom, I might add. And I took the liberty of contacting Mrs. Whitestone, who told me all of the circumstances of your journey."

"All of them?"

"All of them."

The other guests had returned to their conversations, and no one took any notice of Joseph and Constance on the yellow settee. He held her hand still, her one hand clasped between his two large hands.

"I have a headache," she sighed, rubbing her temple.

"I had been having those myself, so I was hoping you would be the cure."

"This is impossible."

"No, it is not. I'm here. As long as both parties are alive, it seems to me—"

"Disraeli!" She had not meant to shout, but her voice seemed to cut through the other conversations. Everyone in the parlor stared at her, a few of the women with mild trepidation.

"It's a game," Joseph said to the assembly. "Very popular in England. It's called 'Prime Minister,' and Miss Lloyd just trumped my Gladstone."

There was a moment's pause before they all returned to their clusters, glancing only occasionally at the couple on the couch.

"You saved me, Constance. You saved my life." His voice was rough, and he leaned in toward her, his breath kissing her bare neck.

"I don't understand."

"Listen to me, and we'll never speak of this again. I *was* arrested at Balmoral."

"Joseph . . ."

"I was arrested on the grounds of high treason. It was a colossal misunderstanding, of course, but it came very close to getting out of hand. What began as a fascinating bit of business very nearly cost me my life."

"I can't think straight. Brown. He told me you did not care for me. . . ."

"I was under arrest. I know you well enough to think you would try something foolish, and thank God you did."

"You mean you didn't tell him before your arrest?"

"Of course not. But I was ready to do anything to disassociate myself from you, and just about everyone else. I did not wish you to suffer for knowing me. Unfortunately, that meant you and Brown were the only ones with the full story."

"And then I went to Disraeli," Constance began.

"But I tried to get into your laboratory for proof of what you were doing, but you had moved it."

"Not at all. Everything was in place, right off the Waterloo Road."

"But the boy there said you had quit the place."

"Indeed, because the boy there had been paid by the Duke of Ballsbridge."

"Philip's father? He left his tunnels and went to London?"

"He had gone to town with Philip's keys to do the same thing you were trying to do. The servants had told him what they suspected about my arrest—his gardener's son works at Balmoral. You know how the duke is with his staff—they told him everything, although I did not realize it at the time. He'd been replacing Philip's paint and canvases all along, and luckily he was curious to look over my own work as well. He managed to secure proof in the form of my notes, the logs I keep. But that would not have been enough to let me go free. The truth is, I needed both you and the duke, and you both came through for me. I can never repay you, never."

"Joseph." She smiled, still amazed by his presence.

"I have very good friends, better than I could ever imagine. Better, I fear, than I could ever possibly hope to deserve."

"Oh." He was there out of a sense of gratitude. She remembered then—Abigail Merrymeade. That was all. He had stopped by while in New York on other business to express a very gentlemanly sense of gratitude. "I understand you are to be congratulated."

"Well, thank you," Joseph beamed. "I appreciate it. Not every man gets off a charge of treason with nary a word to the press. I was lucky, you see, in that at the time I was arrested, the London reporters were far more concerned with the scandal of—"

"No. I mean on your marriage. Congratulations."

"Again, I thank you, although I do find this most unconventional."

"What do you mean?"

"I believe the custom is for the would-be groom to ask the would-be bride to marry him first, and then it is the pleasant duty of other people, not the would-be bride, to congratulate the happy man. But thank you."

Her head was spinning. "No. I mean Abigail Merrymeade. Are you not betrothed to her?"

The smile finally left Joseph's face. "Abigail Merrymeade? Where on earth did you get that idea?"

"From Viola. She wrote me a letter—"

"Viola?"

"Well, yes."

"No, my love. You have been misinformed. The charming widow Merrymeade is to wed none other than our own beloved Cavendish."

"Dishy!" she again shouted, and the room fell silent.

Joseph smiled toward the guests. "Another parlor game, I'm afraid. This one involves the rapid naming of kitchenware." He was greeted with blank expressions. "It's frightfully fun on a rainy day."

This time no one bothered to look surprised before they continued their own discussions.

"So, Constance, will you?"

"Will I?" she repeated.

"Will you marry me?" he whispered. "Please. Just this one last time, I'm begging you to save me. Rescue me. Marry me."

"Yes," she cried softly as he took her into his arms. "Yes. But, Joseph, you are wrong."

He pulled back and brushed his knuckle against the side of her face. She closed her eyes and kissed his hand before she spoke.

"You are very wrong. All along, it was you who saved me."

From the corner of her eye she saw the large wall mirror, and their reflection—a man and a woman holding hands, their faces so close their foreheads were very nearly touching, as if in a light kiss.

They looked so very right together, the couple in the reflection. They had always looked so very right.

The next day, everyone who had been at the McKenzies' dinner party the previous evening was still buzzing with the news. After all, it was not every day that a family lost a governess and gained a wedding invitation before the soup course was even ladled.

"And what time did he say he would be here?" Lydia McKenzie asked.

Her mother smiled. "Mr. Smith said he would come to fetch Miss Lloyd at ten this morning, and the clock has just struck ten. I am sure he will be here at any moment."

Lydia flung herself into the overstuffed chair by the window. "Oh, Miss Lloyd, he is so handsome! He looks just like a prince."

Constance laughed. "Lydia, believe me, I have seen a prince, and, thank goodness, Joseph looks nothing like one."

Mrs. McKenzie picked up her needlepoint. "I should be annoyed, Constance. Really, you are by far the best governess we have ever had."

"I am sorry, Mrs. McKenzie. I do feel terrible about this."

"Nonsense! You are going to be a very happy wife and mother, I am sure. That is far better than being a governess. And I should know."

"Really?" Constance asked.

"Really, Mother?" Lydia swung her feet over the armrest.

"Really," she concluded. "What do you think I was doing before I met the Colonel? Oh, I hear a carriage now."

"He is two minutes late." Constance grinned, pushing in her hat pin.

"Discard him at once!" Mrs. McKenzie proclaimed.

Kathleen announced Joseph, and he entered the parlor, his face an ashen white.

"Joseph, is anything wrong?" Constance was immediately at his side, and he raised his arm and encircled her in his embrace. He did not speak at first.

"Kathleen," ordered Mrs. McKenzie. "Please get Mr. Smith a glass of water. Or would you prefer whisky?"

"Water." The word barely escaped from his throat.

"Joseph, you're frightening me," Constance said, noticing the vein on his forehead was pulsing. "Are you agitated?"

He nodded, then reached into his frock coat and withdrew a telegram.

"Oh, no," said Lydia. "Someone is dead. That's what telegrams always mean. Someone has died suddenly, probably in a terrible accident or of a dreadful disease."

"Hush, Lydia," Mrs. McKenzie replied.

"Read it," Joseph said, his voice slightly stronger. "Go on, Constance. Read it aloud."

"All right," she said uncertainly, her heart pounding. "'Mr. Joseph Smith, care of the Union Club—'"

"No. Further down. Read it aloud."

Her eyes scanned the yellow paper. "Here we go . . . 'You are hereby notified of the death of the Duke of Millington.' The Duke of Millington? Joseph, do you know a Duke of Millington?"

He shook his head and gratefully accepted the water from Kathleen. "Go on," he said after a sip of water.

"Let's see, something about entails—or is it entrails? This part is smudged. Oh, here it is . . . 'notify Mr. Joseph Smith of . . .' I can't pronounce this name."

"It's where I'm from in Wales, my hometown. Go on."

"'Mr. Joseph Smith, of someplace unpronounceable in Wales, is the sole heir to the title, the estate, and all the responsibilities and privileges . . .'" Her voice trailed off.

"Joseph," she murmured. "You're a duke."

"Kathleen! Please fetch Miss Lloyd a glass of water," Mrs. McKenzie shouted.

Lydia alone glowed in jubilation. "Wait until I tell Amy Van Der Bruen that my governess is a duchess!"

Constance blinked and reached for Joseph. "I don't suppose this is another parlor game?"

He shook his head and was about to speak, when he saw her wobble, and just before she hit the carpet, he managed to catch her.

"That's okay," announced Lydia with authority. "Nobility always faints." Then she giggled, watching as Joseph gently stroked Constance's cheek, and as Kathleen brought the water and Mrs. McKenzie shook her head in wonderment.

"Just *wait* until I tell Amy Van Der Bruen!"

19

❧

St. James's Palace
London, England

Are you sure you can't go in with me?" Constance grasped her husband's hand, the three-foot train of her sumptuous gown thrown over her other arm.

He smiled down at her, his Constance. "No. You must do this alone. It's a small group, now that the Prince of Wales has taken most of the court to India with him. You will survive. God knows I did. And I had to wear knee breeches and buckle shoes."

"You looked adorable."

"I did, didn't I?"

"Just like 'Little Boy Blue.'"

"If you're not careful," he warned, "I'll take one of these feathers from your hair." He lightly touched the required plumes in the back of his wife's hair, where they were fastened with a platinum comb he had given her that morning.

"Please do. I'm molting."

The Duke of Millington's rich laugh echoed down the long gallery, where future pillars of society waited to be presented to Queen Victoria. They all turned and looked quizzically at the handsome young duke. Who was this man, they had all asked. And how could he so easily glide into society after being branded an outsider for so long?

He had been known as a hard worker, to be sure. A quiet, industrious young man working to better the lives of the less fortunate. Yes, there had been a bit of nastiness before, some confusion that had all been resolved. No one could remember just what had happened now. It had all been some error on the part of those unsavory London gazettes, no doubt.

The main point was the duke's extraordinary sense of civic duty. And now he had redoubled those efforts, and joined forces with a most unlikely individual, the second son of the duke of Ballsbridge, a newly elected MP who was showing considerable fire and flair during his debates. Together they were becoming a powerful team, a political force to be reckoned with. Not to mention Lord Hastings had become quite the find of the art world, his paintings accepted for the next exhibit at the Royal Academy.

But it was the duke himself who fascinated everyone. After the young duke had married Constance in a quiet ceremony, everyone suddenly wanted to befriend the striking couple, wondering why no one had ever taken note of the extraordinarily good-looking man before he inherited his title from a relative so distant, it took over a year for him to be located. Pushy mothers sighed over the lost chance, just as their daughters sighed over the way the duke looked at his beautiful duchess.

"Why must I wear a gown cut so low?" Constance whispered.

"For the same reason I had to wear knee breeches and buckle shoes." He allowed his hand to rest for a moment on her bare shoulder, stroking the slender line of her neck with his thumb.

Her breath caught in her throat, and she looked up at her husband. "Joseph," she said softly.

"Constance." His voice was ragged as he pretended to be examining the clasp of her pearl dog-collar necklace. "Do you think we would be missed?"

His lips began to touch her cheek, and she closed her eyes.

"Constance, Duchess of Millington!" a voice boomed from a door at the end of the picture gallery.

"The Duchess of Millington is going to be ill on her husband's shoes," she moaned.

"Don't you dare. They are the first pair I have ever owned that fit, and it took the wealthy wife of a duke to get them for me."

"Joseph, I really do believe I am going to be sick."

"There. Just follow that gentleman in the silly satin outfit. We've gone through this before, Constance. I'll be waiting for you at the other end, and then we have a ball or two to attend."

"If I don't become ill first."

"Well, yes. That would put a bit of gloom into our day."

"Joseph . . ."

Very gently he tilted her chin towards his face, and for a moment he just stared down at her. "Just remember this. I love you, Constance. I did not really live until I met you, until you saved me from a lonely existence with my books and beakers. I adore you with every ounce of my body, every portion of my soul, and I always will."

Her eyes began to mist with tears, and he grinned.

"Now, go say hello to Vicky for me." And she smiled as the lord-in-waiting ushered her into the throne room.

"Don't get ill, don't trip on the train," she said in her mind, willing herself to walk the long path to the

Queen as gracefully as possible. An attendant took her train and fanned it out behind her, and then she approached the woman on the throne.

Her first thought was that this was a mistake. The tiny, plump woman wearing a black dress and a black and blue Garter Ribbon across her chest could not possibly be the mighty Queen Victoria of England. Upon approaching, she was able to get a closer glimpse of the queen's facial features. And she realized that the Prince of Wales had similar features, only exaggerated—the small eyes, the round face, the long nose.

But the queen's coloring was lovely, as fresh and vibrant as a woman half her age.

"Don't get ill, don't trip," Constance continued to chant to herself.

As she got closer, an attendant handed a card to the lord chamberlain, who announced in a booming voice, "Constance, the Duchess of Millington."

Now came the difficult part: the curtsy. Constance sank as low as she possibly could in front of the throne, her eyes lowered as she had been instructed.

Slowly she reached her hand out for the Queen. As practiced, the queen would place her hand over Constance's ungloved one, and then Constance would kiss the queen's hand.

Something was wrong. The queen did not extend her hand to Constance.

If only Joseph was there, but he was not.

Hesitantly, worried about slipping to the floor if she remained in the position for much longer, she glanced up at the queen.

Queen Victoria was smiling.

Never had Constance seen a smile so transform a face. Instead of looking distant and lofty, she was suddenly a woman one would want to get to know, to share secrets with over a cup of tea.

"My good man Brown has told us of you."

"Your Majesty," was all Constance could say.

And then the queen leaned forward.

"Your Majesty," hissed the lord chamberlain urgently. "Don't kiss her; she is not a real lady!"

"There you are wrong," the queen said loudly enough for the assembly to hear. "She most certainly *is* a lady."

With that, she kissed Constance on the forehead.

Constance blinked, the rest of the lords and ladies gasped. A kiss was only bestowed upon a fellow member of royalty, or a peer of noble birth.

Somehow Constance managed to back out from the room without falling over the train, without becoming ill, and without fainting.

As she exited, and the door to the throne room closed, a pair of arms grasped her waist.

"Well?" Joseph asked, twirling her to face him.

"She kissed me!"

Joseph smiled. "Of course she did. She is a wise woman." With his broad back he shielded her from the others waiting in the gallery. "I hope that means you will continue to accept my kisses, now that you have been kissed by royalty."

"Oh, Joseph," she sighed against his chest. "It's over."

By that afternoon, the rumor had already made the rounds of all the men's clubs in London. The Duke of Millington had been seen kissing his wife behind a potted palm just moments after she had been presented to Queen Victoria. The tale prompted sharp comments and not a few fast remarks, but most just smiled when they heard the story.

One man, upon hearing the gossip recounted, smiled rather wistfully, and returned alone to his home on Downing Street.

* * *

The orchestra began another tune, and the dancers began to swirl on the polished marble floor. The man stood beside a white chair, where a woman of extraordinary beauty was seated. He held out his hand to her, and she shook her head.

"Your grace, I do not know if I can dance another waltz with you. It would be most improper."

"Hang it all, Constance! This is marvelous!"

"I thought you hated to dance."

"But Constance," the Duke of Millington urged. "You love to dance."

"Joseph, it is almost four in the morning, this is the fifth ball we have been to, and I will personally murder every Strauss in Vienna if I have to dance another waltz."

"Come." He held out his hand, and she smiled up at him before accepting.

Among the other dancers were Philip and Viola, who was hiding her yawn behind her fan, and Cavendish and Abigail. Constance thought it was amazing, the transformation in everyone, especially Dishy and Abigail. And even Philip's mother seemed content at last, her two sons married and her youngest making a real success of his life. The last time she had seen the duchess, the older woman had been very close to friendly, even laughing about some of the events that had seemed so dire the year before.

Joseph had laughed, and said that she will notice that even the most disagreeable people will suddenly be pleasant in front of a wealthy woman with a title. It took Constance a moment to realize that he had been referring to her.

Another waltzing couple passed, and the female smiled at Constance. Harriet Whitestone looked lovely that evening, dancing with the gallant officer. Ever since she had been welcomed into London society as the Duchess of Millington's close friend, she had seldom spent a lonely evening at home with her mending and poetry.

"Joseph," Constance asked, enjoying the feel of his shoulder beneath her palm. "There is something I've been meaning to ask you."

"The answer is no."

"Excuse me?"

"You were going to ask me if I ever took dancing lessons, and the answer is no. I have natural grace."

The dimple appeared below her mouth as she smiled. "You dance beautifully, and you know it. No, I wanted to ask you about the note you sent with my desk."

He frowned, his amber eyes focused on her face. "Do you mean the five-pound note?"

"No. I assumed you had written something personal. After all, you took the trouble to mend my mother's desk."

"My God, Constance, you're blushing!"

"Didn't you write some sort of, well, love note? It vanished. But what did it say?"

"There was no love note. I was making good the bet, do you remember? When I was escorting, or attempting to escort you to Hastings House, we bet five pounds that we would find a place within an hour. I lost the bet, and so I paid you."

"No. There had to be more. You wouldn't have just sent the desk with no note. If I had only known before everything, if I hadn't believed Brown, well, things may have gone more smoothly. Don't you see? Please, Joseph, what did you write?"

An expression crossed his face that made him look like a pirate about to loot a treasure chest. "I do not remember."

"You do! Tell me, Joseph."

"I don't know what you're talking about, woman."

"Don't you try your John Brown act out on me. Just confess, what was in the note?"

"In all honesty, I think I wrapped the fiver in a piece of paper with an old dye formula. What do you think was in the note?"

"I don't know." She looked beyond her husband, imagining what wondrous words he may have penned to her, inspired by his passion. "Perhaps that you love me. That I should not follow you, for you would rather die yourself that have me in any sort of peril. That you would give anything you owned for a few moments in my presence."

"Then that was what I must have said, my love." Slowly he led her from the dance floor. "Shall we go home?"

"Mmm," she sighed, her head against his shoulder.

He collected her wrap and his walking stick. Constance insisted that no self-respecting duke would ever leave his home without a walking stick, so he spent the day leaving it at clubs and Parliament and his own offices.

"Joseph, what was really in that note?"

"Honestly?"

She nodded.

"It was a five-pound note wrapped in a formula for synthetic dye. I jotted it down from a German text-book."

"Why did you send me a formula for dye?"

"I always reuse paper. The formula was no good— seeped like mad. I used it to wrap the five-pound note in. Did you ever get the fiver, by the way?"

"No."

"Blast. No wonder Hastings is so rich, ekes it out five pounds at a time."

"Joseph?"

"Yes?"

"The moment we get into the carriage, will you do me a favor?"

"Of course."

"Will you kiss me?"

He paused on the steps and turned to his wife. "Have I told you that I adore you?"

"And I adore you," she said, barely able to draw breath.

"Home," he said at last. "Let us go home."

The next morning, the gossips had yet another tale about the Duke and Duchess of Millington. They were seen kissing on the steps after the Barrington House ball. It was the one story that everyone, no matter how skeptical, chose to believe.

AUTHOR'S NOTE

Queen Victoria did have a Highland servant by the name of John Brown. He first caught her attention, and that of her husband, Prince Albert, in the early 1850s, when he was a young gillie at Balmoral. Soon he became indispensable on their visits to Scotland, and after Albert's death in 1861, he became indispensable to the grieving queen.

John Brown was both hated and loved. The Prince of Wales could not stand the man who had once boxed his ears and who had won the complete respect of the queen. In other ways, Brown seemed to easily gain everything the prince so bitterly lacked. John Brown was handsome, the Prince of Wales was not. John Brown was consulted in state matters, the prince was never permitted to so much as glance at an official document. John Brown was allowed almost complete access to the queen. The queen frequently avoided the prince, and was often unable to tolerate being in the same room with her eldest son. She always blamed Albert's death on Prince Edward. It was while attempting to straighten out one of the prince's scandalous affairs that Albert caught the fever that eventually killed him. Often, the prince's servants would get into fights with the Highlander and his men, sometimes over trivial matters, other times over more important issues.

There were rumors that Victoria had married John Brown, and "The Empress Brown" pamphlet appeared, published anonymously, purporting to detail the real power on the throne. Their suspected romance also proved to be an excellent and frequent target for the popular humor magazines *Punch* and *Tomahawk,* especially in the late 1860s. One issue of *Punch* featured a mock court circular, reporting the noteworthy news from Balmoral:

> *Mr. John Brown walked on the slopes.*
> *He subsequently partook of a haggis.*
> *In the evening Mr. John Brown was pleased to*
>   *listen to a bagpipe.*
> *Mr. John Brown retired early.*

Although today it seems silly, the John Brown affair created a serious threat to the monarchy, still in a precarious position after the freewheeling Hanoverian kings. Eventually the furor passed, but it took the near-fatal illness of the Prince of Wales, ten years to the day after the death of his father, to rally popular support around the queen and her family once more.

John Brown was a loyal servant, that cannot be denied. But because of his attractive appearance as a youth, and the queen being widowed at such a young age, rumors were bound to circulate. Debate still rages as to whether there was anything more than a deep friendship between the two, although it does seem a bit far-fetched to dub Brown "Rasputin in a kilt," as some historians do.

Whatever existed between the queen and her gillie, it will never be ours to know. She mourned his death as she did her husband's, for the rest of her long life. And when she finally died, one of the new king's first acts was to destroy all busts of Brown, burn his photographs, and have Brown's apartment at Windsor turned into a billiard room. At the time, he explained to those who questioned his actions that Brown had once boxed his ears. Clearly, the hatred ran much deeper than the oft-repeated boyhood story. Although there is absolutely no record of him ever plotting against Brown, it seems that if the prince had ever happened to hear of plans to do Brown any harm, he would likely have made little effort to stop the damage.

Queen Victoria had a great appreciation of male beauty. And from looking at a photograph of a young John Brown, strapping in his kilt, his hair wild and his arms and legs thick with muscles, all one can say is . . . who can blame her?

An All-New Collection of
Heartwarming Holiday Stories

UPON A
MIDNIGHT CLEAR

Jude
Deveraux

Linda
Howard

MARGARET ALLISON

STEF ANN HOLM

MARIAH STEWART

Coming mid-October in Hardcover
From Pocket Books

POCKET
BOOKS

1405